WE CARE
about golf

Thomas E. Warner

Order this book online at www.trafford.com
or email orders@trafford.com

Most Trafford titles are also available at major online book retailers.

Printed in Victoria, BC, Canada.

ISBN: 978-1-4251-2131-0 (sc)
ISBN: 978-1-4269-3418-6 (dj)

*Our mission is to efficiently provide the world's finest, most comprehensive book publishing
service, enabling every author to experience success. To find out how to publish your book, your
way, and have it available worldwide, visit us online at www.trafford.com*

Trafford rev. 05/13/2010

 www.trafford.com

North America & international
toll-free: 1 888 232 4444 (USA & Canada)
phone: 250 383 6864 ♦ fax: 812 355 4082

Dedication

This story is dedicated to the family and founders of the 'Anya Foundation, in Irvine California. For if, it had not been for their inspiration, and encouragement; this story might not have been written.

Acknowledgements

This story is partially a work of fiction; but some of the names and locations are real.

The song titles "Missing You", and "513 Days" mentioned within this story; are copyrighted by Lyon Lazare, and were used with permission.

My special thanks to Tracy Carr at carrgraphics.com for designing my front cover.

I would also like to extend my sincere appreciation to my friends Mark and Larry; for their support and encouragement, during the time of this writing.

Other titles by this Author

"The Saga of Alex and His Friends"

Preface

The Anya Foundation
Mission Statement

To create a world in which all children live in safety and happiness is the wish for all adults. To translate this wish into reality is the duty of all adults. To endeavor towards this goal is within the ability of all adults. To manifest this global wish into local realities is the moving impulse behind the Anya Foundation. Its focus is on ensuring our laws are adequate to maximize the safety of our children in their own homes.

The Foundation's purpose is to educate parents, grandparents, relatives and friends of the importance of child safety. With the Anya Device our goal is to help save at least one child's life per day. Through the Foundation, individuals and businesses can make tax-deductible contributions to ensure the future of all of our children.

Goals

The Anya Foundation was founded to raise the awareness of the importance of child safety. Our goal is to educate families so they can safeguard their children and avoid the loss of a child.

The Anya Foundation conducts and supports awareness programs in the field of home safety as well as child safety devices and monitoring applications. Our contribution to the community includes support, crises counseling and advocacy.

This Author's Commitment

I, Thomas E. Warner, do hereby certify that I am the sole owner and author of, "We Care About Golf", and do hereby make, and confirm the following commitment.

I, Thomas E. Warner, do hereby certify that fifty (50) percent of all net proceeds from the sale of this book will be donated to the 'Anya Foundation' in Irvine California, in support of their missions and goals.

Included among these, are; the research, development, and distribution of the 'Anya Device', the annual 'Anya Foundation' junior golf tournament, and the Anya Foundation's child safety awareness program.

Contents

Chapter 1

Once again, it is time for us to rejoin Alex, and the rest of the United Families of 'We Care'.

The United Families are currently in the gymnasium, where they have gathered together with the rest of the faculty, and the entire student body, for a very important assembly.

Let us join them now and see why this assembly is so important to everyone at 'We Care'.

As we enter the gymnasium, we find Tom standing in front of the assembly calling the meeting to order.

"Good morning everyone, and welcome back to 'We Care'.

We are having this special assembly this morning for the purpose of discussing the possibility of starting a golf team here at 'We Care'. There will be three main speakers this morning. Two of them you already know, and love. The third person's name is Branden, and is currently Steven's new golf instructor."

"Branden, at the age of thirteen, already has a very impressive scoring record at many of the major Jr. golf tournaments. Hopefully, he will be telling us about some of those tournaments, and wins, a little later on during this assembly."

"At this time, and without further ado, I would like to turn this meeting over to the principal of our combined schools." I said.

"Thank you very much for that introduction, Tom. Good morning everyone, and welcome back to 'We Care'. As Tom mentioned earlier, the purpose of this meeting is to discuss the possibility of starting a golf team here at 'We Care'. I have already held a similar meeting as this one, with the student body of my other school. The results of that meeting were outstanding, with twenty boys, and fifteen girls signing up to be on the team, if one is started."

"Mam, how soon will we know if a team is really going to be started?" Billy asked.

"The decision to that question will be announced before the end of this meeting." The principal said.

"Mam, I have already talked to several of the other boys here at 'We Care' about joining the team. Most of us would like to join, but we don't know how to play. Will there be any sort of lessons available, that we can take?" Johnny asked.

"Yes Johnny, lessons will be available, and Steven will be the person in charge of giving them." The principal said.

"Mam, it sounds like there is going to be a lot of boys that are going to need lessons. Will Branden be able to help Steven give the lessons?" Alex asked.

I'm not sure about that Alex. I do know however, that Steven and Branden have been doing a lot of preplanning for a team. It looks like Steven is getting anxious to share that information with us. So, without further ado, I would like to turn this meeting over to him." The principal said.

While Steven was walking to center stage, he shouted out in a loud school spirit filled voice.

"Hey everyone! Who are we?" Steven shouted.

"We're the Fighting Phantoms of We Care!" Everyone shouted, which was followed by a very loud applause from everyone.

When the applause and the excitement had subsided, Steven turned to answer Alex's question.

"Alex, you asked if Branden would be here to help me give the lessons. I sure wish that I could answer that question with a yes, but unfortunately, I cannot. He'll be leaving next week to go back home to California." Steven said, in a sad voice.

Knowing that Steven and Branden had become very close friends, the principal realized how Steven was feeling. She also sensed that he was also on the verge of crying because his friend would soon be leaving. That is when she asked Steven.

"Steven, can you tell the assembly a little about the preplanning that you and Branden have been doing?"

"Yes Mam, I can do that." Steven began. "Branden and I have been over to the golf course several times during the last two weeks. We have explained to Terry how we would like to start a golf team here at 'We Care', and make the 'Putt and Go' our home course." Steven said.

"What did Terry say Steven, when you told him about the team?" I asked.

"He told us that he would be honored to sponsor the team, if we start one." Steven said.

"The idea of having a team sponsor is fantastic Steven. Did Terry say anything about what he would provide the team with, as a sponsor?" I asked.

"Yes he did, Uncle Tom. He said that as a sponsor of the team, he would provide a new set of golf clubs, and a golf club bag for each of the players. Then, in addition to the clubs, he would also provide a team shirt for each of the team members. The shirts would have the 'We Care' logo on them, and the player's name." Steven said.

"Steven, while you, and Branden were talking to Terry, was there anything said about a home course?" Tim asked.

"Yes there was, Uncle Tim. Terry said that as the sponsor of our team, the 'Putt and Go' would be considered as our home course." Steven said.

"That's great Steven. Not only would Terry be providing the golfing equipment for everyone, but he would also be providing the course too." Tim said.

"I've heard some golfers talking about that course in the barber shop. They said that it is not maintained as it should be, and it looks terrible. Steven, you, Branden, and Alex have played the course a few times. What, if anything, did you boys see that makes the course look so terrible?" I asked.

"There were several things that we saw that looked terrible, Uncle Tom. Branden was the first to notice all of them though, because he has played a lot of different courses." Steven said.

"Can you tell us about some of the things that you saw, Steven?" I asked.

"If it's okay with you Uncle Tom, I'll let Branden do that. He'll know how to explain it better." Steven said.

Just as Branden was beginning to explain what they had seen, his cell phone rang. When he looked at his caller ID, he saw that it was his dad calling. He turned and faced Steven, and said.

It is my dad calling from the airport, but he is early. I was not expecting him to call until some time tomorrow afternoon. With him getting here early, it could mean that I'll have to go home now, instead of next week." Branden said sadly.

"I sure hope that isn't the reason why he is calling, Branden. We're all going to miss you when you have to go home to California." Steven said.

"I'm going to miss all of you too." Branden said.

"Boys, we won't know for sure why he is calling until Branden answers his phone. You better not keep your dad waiting Branden; he may need something really important." I said.

"You're right, Uncle Tom." Branden said, as he reached for his cell phone.

"Hi dad, you're calling early. I wasn't expecting you to call until some time tomorrow afternoon." Branden said.

"I had to come back early son, because there is some very important business that you and I have to attend to, here in town." Branden's dad said.

"What sort of business, dad?" Branden asked.

"I can't tell you about it over the phone son, because it would take to long. I'll fill you in on all of the details when we get together." Branden's dad said.

"Okay dad that sounds good to me. Are you going to get a taxi to bring you over here to 'We Care', or would you like for us to come and get you?" Branden asked.

"I would enjoy it more, if you and someone else could come and pick me up." Branden's dad said.

"Hold on for a minute dad, and I'll ask Mr. Warner if we can come and get you." Branden said.

"Uncle Tom, dad needs someone from here to pick him up at the airport, is that possible?" Branden asked.

"It sure is Branden. You and I can do that, while Steven and the principal are finishing up with the assembly." I said.

"Uncle Tom, I'd like to go with you and Branden to pick up his dad. Could we adjourn the meeting until we get back from the airport?" Steven asked.

"That's a great idea Steven. When I was talking to dad, I told him that we are having an assembly, and what it is about. He told me that he would like to be here, for the last part of it." Branden said.

"That sounds like a great idea Branden. I will announce we will restart the assembly in about thirty minutes. I will also announce that we are going to the airport to pick up a special guest." I said.

"Thank you sir. I know that my dad is looking forward to meeting you Uncle Tom, because he has mentioned it many times. If I know my dad as well as I think I do, then 'We Care' is in for a BIG surprise." Branden said smiling.

When Tom, Branden, and Steven arrived at the airport, they found Branden's dad waiting for them in front of the terminal. Once Tom had stopped the car, they all got out to help with the luggage. When Branden and his dad had finished exchanging their own greetings, Branden turned to introduce Tom to his dad.

"Dad, I would like to introduce you to Mr. Warner. He is one of the co-founders of 'We Care', and is the chairman of the board of directors. Uncle Tom, this is my dad, George." Branden said.

"It's an honor to finally get to meet you Mr. Warner. Branden has told me a lot about you, and the work that you have done here at 'We Care'." George said.

"It's an honor to meet you too Sir, but please feel free to call me Tom. Most of the boys at 'We Care' call me, Uncle Tom." I said.

"Now I understand why Branden called you Uncle Tom, when I was talking to him a few minutes ago, on the phone." George said, with a smile.

While Tom, the boys, and Branden's dad were traveling back to 'We Care', their discussion turned to the purpose of the assembly.

"Tom, Branden told me on the phone that the purpose of the assembly is to decide whether or not 'We Care' should start a golf team. Personally, I'm always in favor of a school starting a golf team. The game of golf when played correctly helps to build the player's concentration, determination, and self-esteem. There are hundreds of success stories about young people that have learned to play golf in their late teens, then going on to become world champions. Branden has told me how well Steven has learned the game, and that he may be another one of those success stories." George said.

"Do you really think that I'm that good, Branden?" Steven asked surprised.

"Yes I do Steven. Just in the past two months that I've been giving you lessons, your knowledge and skills of the game have improved tremendously." Branden said.

"Thank you Branden, but I think there are two reasons for that. One, I've always been a fast learner, and secondly, you are an excellent coach." Steven said.

"Steven, you're a very lucky young man, for two reasons. First, you are taking lessons from Branden, and learning his style, which is excellent. Secondly, Branden has just given you a very high comment on your golfing knowledge, and skills. He doesn't give those kinds of comments to anyone, except to the people that he feels will be successful later on in life." George said.

"Thank you both, for those comments, sir." Steven said.

"Uncle Tom, could dad speak at the assembly too?" Branden asked.

"He sure can, Branden. In fact, I had already made plans for that when I told the assembly that we were going to the airport to pick up a special

16

guest. When we get back to 'We Care', and get the assembly started again, I will call you up on stage for your comments. Then when you're finished with what you want to say, you can introduce your dad." I said.

"Thank you, Uncle Tom." Branden said.

"You're welcome, Branden. Steven, call your dad, and ask him to call the assembly back into order. Also tell him that we'll be there in about ten minutes." I said.

"Okay, Uncle Tom." Steven replied, as he began dialing the number.

When Tom and his group had arrived at 'We Care', and had gotten out of the car, they walked directly to the gymnasium. When they entered the gymnasium, two boys in security shirts stopped them. Noticing that Mr. Avery was calling the assembly to order, Tom was curious why he and his group had been stopped. Just as Tom began to ask the two boys what was going on, Steven stepped up along side of him, and said.

"Relax, Uncle Tom. These boys are part of a special guest of honor announcement ceremony." Steven said smiling.

"We have a guest of honor, ceremony? I didn't know anything about it." I said surprised.

"We didn't have one sir, at least not until last night. When Branden told me that his dad was coming to 'We Care', I wanted to have some sort of special reception for him. That is when dad, Jeff, and I got together and came up with this ceremony. It's not a complicated ceremony, but I hope it's a good one." Steven said.

At the exact moment, that Tom started to tell Steven that he was sure the ceremony would be a good one, a young boy interrupted him with this announcement.

"Mr. Avery, sir! Uncle Tom and our guest of honor have entered the room." The young boy announced.

"Thank you son. Would you and the other honor guards, please escort our guests to the stage?" Mr. Avery asked.

"Yes sir!" The boy replied, as he and the other three honor guards took their positions.

George was in the front row, and to the right, which is the highest honored position. Branden was directly behind his dad, in the second highest honored position. Tom was in the position to the left of George, with Steven behind him.

When the group was in position, and ready, the leader of the guard gave the command to proceed.

When the honored guests started walking toward the stage, the entire assembly immediately gave them a standing ovation.

When the honored guests were on the stage and seated, Mr. Avery turned the meeting over to Tom.

"Thank you Mr. Avery, for that wonderful reception. Since it will be lunchtime in a couple of hours, I would like to get this meeting started, without further delay. When we adjourned, the next speaker would have been Branden. So, without further ado, here's our favorite junior golfer, and friend, Branden." I said.

"Thank you, Uncle Tom. I would also like to take this time to thank Mr. Avery, Steven, and everyone else here at 'We Care' for that fantastic reception."

"Now that we have called this assembly back into session, let's get back to the topic at hand. Should we, or shouldn't we, start a golf team here at 'We Care'?"

"Most of you are already aware of how important golf has been to me through out my life. Since the time that I was three years old, my parents have provided me with the best golfing instructors, available anywhere. I wish that my family, and I lived right here in this town, because if we did, then I could teach each of you the skills that I have learned over the years."

"Even though, I will be leaving soon, to go back home in California, I strongly encourage you to start a golf team here at 'We Care'. If you do decide to start a team, I ask that you will please utilize Steven's golfing abilities. I truly believe that with what he has learned from me during our lessons, that he would make an excellent coach, and teacher."

"I would like to take a few minutes now, and talk about the condition of the 'Putt and Go' golf course."

"Last week while I was playing a round of golf at the 'Putt and Go' with Steven and Alex, we saw several sights on the course that were appalling. Most of the sand bunkers looked terrible, because of poor care. The sand along the edges of most of the bunkers had been washed away by rainwater running into the bunkers. There was even rain water still standing in several of the bunkers, that we received last week."

"The tees and greens were in terrible shape also. The tees were covered with hundreds of divots, which were caused by golfers while they were teeing off. We had a very hard time playing each of the greens, because of how rough, and slow, that they were."

"I believe that all of the greens desperately need to be verticuted, aerified, top dressed, and vibratory rolled. I believe that by using these methods of surface preparation that it would greatly improve the playing surface of the greens. Even with the course in as terrible shape as it is though, I still recommend using it as our home course."

"This is just an idea that I thought of after we played the course. We, as a team, could volunteer our services to Terry, to help him with whatever course maintenance that we could do. Since we're not old enough to operate machinery though, it would limit the kind of work that we could do."

"That was a quick run down of what we saw last week on the golf course. Now, at this time, I'd like to bring my portion of this meeting to a close, and introduce our guest of honor."

"Ladies and gentlemen, it is with great honor that I introduce our guest of honor, to you. Millions of people in the golfing world know him as the greatest golf course architect ever known. To me however, he is far more important then any golf course architect could ever be.

Because, our guest of honor, is my dad.
Now, without further ado.
Here is my dad, George.

Chapter 2

"Thank you son, for that very impressive introduction."

"Ladies and gentlemen, as Branden mentioned earlier, golf has always played an important roll in his life."

"Since his mother and I, have played the game most of our lives, we wanted to pass its values onto him. We feel that the game plays a major roll in improving a player's determination, concentration, and self-esteem."

"It's a known fact, that when a new player applies both determination and concentration, that he, or she, will quickly learn the basic skills of the game. Even after a player learns the basic skills of the game, determination and concentration, will continue to play a major roll in the player's game."

"The player will soon discover that this self determination and concentration will also carry over into their everyday lives, and activities. Some of those activities might include their school work, school grades, other sporting activities, and eventually, their careers."

"These two things, when applied in a person's life will also greatly improve their self-esteem. Self-esteem is often referred to as, pride in one's self."

"I'd like to change the subject now, and talk about what Branden mentioned earlier.

First, let me say, that I was not aware of the poor conditions of the 'Putt and Go' that he mentioned. However, I do still agree with him about making it your home course, regardless of its condition.

Over the past several years, Branden has learned many things about the proper care, and maintenance of golf courses. His vast knowledge on this subject has come primarily from me, and by talking to many ground keeping superintendents. I believe that with his vast knowledge, Branden will play an important roll in the improvement of the 'Put and Go'.

"Personally, I've never played the course, but I would like to. Tom, do you think it would be possible to get a 'T' time for shortly after lunch today?" George asked.

"Yes sir, I'm certain that would be possible. Terry has already told Steven that any of us are welcome to come over and play, any time that we want to. He also said that we wouldn't even need to schedule a 'T' time." Tom said.

"That's great Tom, but I think we should still call him and let him know we're coming, and how many of us will be there. That way he'll know how to plan any arrangements that need to be taken care of." George said.

"What sort of arrangements, sir?" Tim asked.

"Branden and I, enjoy eating at the snack bars of the courses that we play. Most of the time we order a nice thick steak for each of us, and the people that we play with. That's why we need to call him, and let him know how many of us will be there." George said.

"I understand what you mean now, sir. All we have to do now is to decide on who will be playing." Tim said.

"That's true Tim, but for this game I'd like to keep it as a business outing. I would like to restrict the size of our group to just Branden and myself, and the members of the United Families. By making it a business outing, it will give us an opportunity to learn more about the course, and its condition." George said.

"That's a good idea, sir. If I may take a moment of your time, I'd like to ask the rest of the board members who will be participating in the outing." I said.

"I'd like to Tom, but I have a lot of work to do in the kitchen, to get ready for dinner." Mary said.

"I won't be able to participate either. I have a lot of paperwork that I have to get ready, for tomorrow. Tomorrow is when we give the boys their annual immunizations." Karen said.

"I'll stay here, and take care of things in the office." Mrs. Avery said.

"That only leaves the men, and the boys. Do any of you; have a conflict with the outing?" I asked.

After a short pause with no answer, Tom continued.

"Mr. Avery, since no one else has a conflict with the outing, could you call Terry for us? Tell him that there will be twelve of us coming." I said.

"I sure can, Tom. Are there any special arrangements that I'll need to tell him about?" Mr. Avery asked.

"Yes there are, Mr. Avery. Here is a piece of paper that I have written them on." George said.

"Dad, what about golf clubs? Branden and Steven are the only ones of us boys, which has any." Billy said concerned.

"That won't be a problem, Billy. Terry has a lot of rental sets that you can choose from." Steven said.

"That's great Steven, but most of the time rental clubs aren't very good. The reason for that is, they're not sized, or fitted to the individual player." Justin said.

"That's true son, but today that shouldn't matter. Our primary goal today, is to have some fun, and check out the course." I said.

After a few minutes had passed, Mr. Avery reentered the gymnasium.

"Here comes Mr. Avery, already. It didn't take him very long, to make that phone call." Alex said.

"You're right about that, Alex. I sure hope that he was able to get a 'T' time for us." Johnny said, in a concerned voice.

"Welcome back, Mr. Avery. Was you able to get a 'T' time for us?" I asked.

"Yes I was, Tom. Terry said that he would see us at one o'clock, this afternoon." Mr. Avery said.

While Mr. Avery was talking to Tom, a kitchen helper entered the gymnasium, and approached the stage.

"Excuse me Mr. Avery. I hate to interrupt, but I thought you would like to know, that lunch will be ready in about fifteen minutes."

"Thank you, Mam. That should give us enough time to finish up with the assembly, and for everyone to wash their hands, before they eat." Mr. Avery said.

"Well everyone, lunch will be ready in about fifteen minutes. Before we dismiss the assembly however, we still need to decide whether, or not, we will be starting a golf team. So at this time, I'd like to turn the meeting back over to Uncle Tom, so he can call for a vote." Mr. Avery said.

"Thank you, Mr. Avery. Well everyone, we are going to do this a little differently, then we usually do. Under normal conditions, the 'United Families make the decisions here at 'We Care'. However, since this meeting is about starting a golf team, it also involves all of you. When I call for a vote, I want everyone, including the 'United Families, to vote at the same time. Are there any questions, before we vote?" I asked.

After a short pause, Tom continued.

"Since there are no questions, I'll call for a vote. All in favor of starting a golf team here at 'We Care' raise your right hand.
Wow! That was very impressive. It looks like everyone voted in favor of the idea. However, I still need to ask the other question, as well. All against the idea of starting a golf team here at 'We Care' raise your right hand.
Congratulations everyone, the vote is unanimous. We will be starting a golf team, here at 'We Care'." I announced.

"That's fantastic, Dad. What will the boys have to do now, that want to join the team?" Alex asked.

"I'm not sure about that, son. Steven, do you and Branden have something planned for that?" I asked.

"Yes we do, Uncle Tom. Starting tomorrow morning after breakfast, we'll be accepting sign up forms from the boys that want to join the team." Steven said.

"Where will you boys be doing that at?" I asked.

"Here in the gymnasium, sir. We'll have some tables set up, here on stage." Steven said.

"That's great, Steven. Is there anything that you and Branden need to know, before we dismiss the assembly?" I asked.

"I can't think of anything, Uncle Tom. What about you, Branden?" Steven asked.

"We'll need to know approximately, how many boys will be signing up. That way we'll know how many forms we'll need to print up." Branden said.

"That's a good idea, Branden. By using a show of hands, how many of you boys will be signing up?" I asked the assembly.

After a short pause, Branden asked.

"I counted ninety hands, Steven. How many did you count?" Branden asked.

"That's what I counted, too." Steven said.

"That's pretty impressive, Tom. Over one-third of the boys are going to sign up." Tim said.

"You're right about it being impressive, Tim. I know one thing for sure; we are definitely going to have a big team.

Mr. Avery, would you dismiss the assembly, please?" I said.

"Well everyone that concludes our assembly for this morning. Be sure to wash your hands before going to the cafeteria to eat. You are now, excused." Mr. Avery said.

While the United Families, Branden, and his dad were walking to the cafeteria, Tom asked.

"George, is it possible for a school to have too many players on their team?" I asked.

"That's possible Tom, but unlikely. The reason for that is, there are several different age brackets for the boys." George said.

"There is something else that we need to remember too, dad." Branden said.

"What would that be, son?" George asked.

"Some of the boys will loose interest in the game, or get frustrated, and quit the team." Branden said.

"That's true son, and that could be as many as 15, to 20 percent of the boys." George said.

"Well, here we are at the restrooms. Lets all meet back here, after we've washed our hands." I said.

After the members of the United Families had reassembled in the hallway, Mary said.

"We're trying something new in the cafeteria today, Tom." Mary said.

"What is that, Mary?" I asked.

"We're using the buffet method, to serve the meals. We feel that it will reduce the amount of time that it takes to feed the boys." Mary said.

"That's a great idea, Mary. Will there be one, or two serving lines?" Karen asked.

"There will be two serving lines, and each of them will have a larger variety of food to choose from." Mary said.

"I'm sure the boys are going to like that, Mary. I know that most boys hate to wait in line to eat." Karen said.

"Boys aren't the only ones that hate to wait in line, Karen. I know a few men around here that hate it, too." Mary said, with a smile.

"Okay hon, stop picking on us men. I know that you women don't like it either. Now come on, let's go eat." Tim said, smiling back at Mary.

"Wow mom! You were right. Having two lines really does speed things up. Most of the boys are already sitting down, and eating." Danny said.

"I'm going to let all of you get your food first. That way I can see what your reactions are, to the different choices of food." Mary said.

"Thank you, mom." Johnny said, as he stepped into the serving line.

When everyone except Mary, and George were in the serving line, Mary asked.

"Are you going to eat, sir?"

"Yes I am Mary, but I'm waiting for someone. When she arrives, then she and I will sit next to Branden, to eat." George said.

"Are you referring to a business associate sir, or your wife?" Mary asked.

"I'm referring to my wife Mary, but please don't tell Branden. He doesn't know that she is coming yet, and we want to surprise him." George said.

"I won't tell him sir. If you'll excuse me for a minute though, I need to make a sitting arrangement change, at the head table." Mary said, with a smile.

"Boys, I have a special request to ask of you. I need all of you on this side of Branden to move down one seat." Mary said.

"Why do you want us to move, mom?" Johnny asked.

"I can't tell you why, son. That's something that all of us, will find out in a few minutes." Mary said.

Several minutes had passed, when Mary approached Branden, and asked.

"Branden, would you happen to know who that lady is, that your dad is talking to?"

"I'm not sure Aunt Mary, because she is too far away. Oh, wait a minute. That is my mom. Hey everyone, my mom is here." Branden said, with excitement.

After getting up from the table, and walking over to where his parents were standing, Branden said.

"Hi mom. This is a pleasant surprise." Branden said, with a smile.

"Hi son. I am happy to hear that we were able to surprise you. Your dad and I were hoping that we could, but weren't for sure." Anya said, with a smile.

26

"I'm definitely surprised mom, but I have a question. Why didn't you and dad arrive on the same flight?" Branden asked.

"I had to take care of some unfinished business, before I came." Anya said.

"Anya, we have a one o'clock tee time, so we better go ahead and eat." George said.

When Branden's parents had gotten their food, and had joined him at the table, Danny said.

"I can't believe that I'm already full."

"Did I hear you right, Danny? Did you say that you're already full?" Mary asked surprised.

"Yes I did mom. I'm so full that I don't think I could eat another bite." Danny said with a groan.

"That's to bad son. If you're that full, then I guess you don't have any room for grandma's cheese cake." Mary said smiling.

"I've heard a lot of the boys, talking about that grandma's cheese cake. They say it's delicious." Branden said.

"It is delicious, Branden. Even though I'm full, I'll still eat a couple of pieces of it." Danny said smiling.

Thirty minutes had passed, and everyone had finished his or her meal, when Branden asked.

"I'm ready for desert. Is anyone else ready?"

"I'm ready." Everyone said, in unison.

"This cheese cake looks delicious, Mary. Do you have it on the menu every day?" George asked.

"No, we don't, sir. We only have it for Thanksgiving, Christmas, and other special meals." Mary said.

"What makes this meal so special, Aunt Mary?" Branden asked.

"It's special because, you and your parents are here today." Mary said, with a smile.

"I have to agree with the boys, Mary. This cheese cake is absolutely fabulous." Anya exclaimed.

"You're right mom. This is definitely, delicious. I wish you had the recipe for it." Branden said, with a smile.

"I do too, son. Mary, would it be possible to get the recipe for it?" Anya asked.

"It sure would be, Mam. I'll write it down some time today, and give it to you at dinner this evening." Mary said.

"Thank you, Mary." Anya said.

"Boys, it's getting close to the time that we need to be leaving. Go ahead and finish your desert first, then go get ready." I said.

"Okay, dad." Alex said.

"Hon., would you like to join us men, in a round of golf this afternoon?" George asked.

"I'd be happy too, hon. it has been a long time since we've played golf together, as a family." Anya said, with a smile.

"We're finished eating now, dad. Do you want us to go ahead and put the golf clubs into the car?" Alex asked.

"That's a great idea, son. If you boys would do that for us, we would really appreciate it." I said.

"Okay dad. I'll let you know when we have them in the car, and we're ready to go." Alex said.

"Hon., did you bring your golf clubs with you?" George asked.

"No, I didn't. I didn't think we would have any time to play, so I left them at home." Anya said.

"Excuse me for interrupting everyone, but we're ready to go." Alex said.

"Thank you, son. Well everyone lets go play some golf." I said with a smile.

When Tom and the rest of the group arrived at the clubhouse, they saw Terry standing outside of the building.
When they approached Terry on the sidewalk, Steven could tell that he was depressed.

"You look depressed today, Terry. Is there something wrong?" Steven asked concerned.

"Yes there is Steven, but I'm afraid to tell you what it is." Terry said.

"You don't have to be afraid, Terry. You already know that you can tell us anything, that's on your mind." Steven said.

"I know that Steven, but what I have to tell you, isn't good news." Terry said with a frown.

"What do you mean, Terry? How bad can it be?" Steven asked concerned.

"It's really bad, Steven. The owner of the golf course has decided to sell it." Terry said sadly.

"Did the owner tell you, why he wants to sell it?" Anya asked.

"Yes he did, Mam. He told me that the course needs too much work done to it, and he couldn't afford it." Terry said.

"Does that mean we can't play golf today?" Johnny asked.

"No, it doesn't mean that. The question I can't answer is how much longer people will be able to play, before they sell it." Terry said.

"Does that mean you won't be able to sponsor our team now?" Danny asked.

"I'm sorry Danny, but that's exactly what it means." Terry said.

"What are we going to do now, Dad? This is going to break the hearts, of everyone at 'We Care'." Alex said, with tears in his eyes.

"I know it is son, but unfortunately there's no way that we can prevent it." I said.

"Anya, may I talk to you in private, please?" George asked.

"You sure can, but let's go inside to talk." Anya said.

"Tom, while we're gone, could you make sure that all of the boys get some clubs? We shouldn't be gone to long." George said.

"Yes sir, I can do that. If you're not back by the time that we're ready, I'll send Branden to let you know that we are."

Chapter 3

Approximately thirty minutes had passed when Branden entered the clubhouse, looking for his parents. Not seeing them in the foyer, or the pro shop, Branden looked else where in the building. After looking in the snack bar, and the banquet room, and not finding them in either of those places, he became confused.

While standing in the doorway of the pro shop, scratching his head in bewilderment, Branden asked himself.

"I wonder where mom, and dad, could be. I have looked everywhere that I could think of, but I could not find them. I know, I'll ask the lady behind the counter, if she has seen them."

"Hi Michelle. I'm looking for my mom and dad, have you seen them?" Branden asked.

"Hi Branden. Yes, I have. They are in Terry's office, talking to him. Would you like for me to contact him on the intercom system, and let him know you're here?" Michelle asked.

"Yes I would Michelle, thank you." Branden said.

"Terry, Branden is here at the counter, looking for his parents." Michelle said.

"Have him come into my office, Michelle. His parents would like to speak to him for a minute. Then if you will please, go out and tell Tom that George and his family will join them in a few minutes." Terry said.

"Terry wants you to come into his office, Branden. He said that your parents would like to speak to you, for a minute." Michelle said.

"Thank you Michelle, but I'm not sure where Terry's office is at." Branden said.

"That's okay. I will take you to it. Then I have to go outside, to tell Tom that you, and your parents, will be a few more minutes." Michelle said.

"Hi son, did you wonder where we disappeared to?" George asked, with a chuckle.

"Yes I did, dad. What's taking you and mom, so long?" Branden asked.

"We've been talking to Terry, about a business deal, son." George said.

"What kind of business deal, dad?" Branden asked.

"Do you remember what we talked about, at our family meeting last week?" Anya asked.

"Yes mom, I remember. We were talking about buying a golf course, if we could find one that was for sale." Branden said.

"That's exactly right, son. Your dad and I have been talking something over, but need to ask you a question first." Anya said.

"What kind of question, mom?" Branden asked.

"We needed to find out, whether or not, you think the 'Putt and Go' would be a good investment for us." Anya said.

"It would be a good course to buy mom, but there are a couple of things, we would need to consider first." Branden said.

"What would those be, son?" George asked.

"Well dad, the first thing is, it would take a lot of money to fix it up. The other problem is we live so far away from it." Branden said.
"If it wasn't for those two things, what would you say?" Anya asked.

"I would say, lets go ahead, and buy it." Branden said.

"I have another question for you, son. While you were on stage at the assembly, you said that you wished we lived here in this town. Did you really mean that?" George asked.

"Yes I did, dad. I really like this area, and I've gained a lot of new friends, at 'We Care'." Branden said.

"That's all we needed to know for now, son. Now, let's go play some golf." George said, with a smile.

After George and Branden had left the room, Anya turned toward Terry, and said.

"I'll call you after we've finished playing nine holes, and let you know what we've decided, Terry."

"Okay Anya, I'll be expecting your call." Terry said.

"We're sorry that we were gone so long, Tom. We started talking to Terry about the golf course, and lost track of time." George said.

"That's okay, George. We were helping the boys with their golf swing, while we were waiting." I said.

"Who is going to tee off first?" Billy asked.

"Ladies are supposed to go first, son." Justin said.

"That's right, dad. I should've remembered that, but I forgot." Billy said.

"That's okay, son. We all forget things, occasionally." Justin said.

"Anya, you tee off first, and then George and Branden will tee off after you." I said.

"Thank you, Tom." Anya said, as she addressed the ball.

After Anya had teed off, Alex asked.

"Branden, what do people mean, when they refer to a golfer addressing the ball?"

"That's when a golfer has taken his or her stance, and has lined up the golf club, to make a stroke." Branden explained.

"It's your turn now, son." George said, after he had teed off.

While Branden was preparing to address the ball, Alex turned toward his dad, and whispered.

"I don't know about you dad, but I think Branden looks like a professional golfer."

"I do too son, but lets not be talking, while he's teeing off." I said.

"That was a great shot, son. It landed right in the center of the fairway, which should give you an excellent approach shot." George said.

"Yes it was dad, thanks. I'm sure glad I had enough height on it, to get over the corner of that lake." Branden said.

When everyone had teed off, the boys began talking about how far they had hit the ball.

"I did a terrible job, hitting that ball. That chunk of dirt flew farther then the ball did." Johnny complained.

"I didn't do much better then you did, Johnny. My ball only went about five feet further then yours did." Billy said.

"That may be true Billy, but at least you made it to the fairway." Johnny said, with a frown.

"Well boys, I can tell you what part of your problem is. You're not teeing your ball, high enough." Justin said.

"Why would that make a difference, dad?" Billy asked.

"Most of the time, when a golfer tees the ball to low, they will end up making a deep divot." Justin explained.

"Is that the reason why there are so many holes, here in the tee box?" Billy asked.

"Yes it is, Billy. The golfers that made them, should've filled them with sand, but didn't." Branden said.

"Where do the golfers get the sand from?" Billy asked.

"There is a small box on every golf cart, which is supposed to have sand in it. The sand in those boxes is supposed to be used, to fill the divots." Branden said.

"Should we go ahead and fill the divots that we made?" Alex asked.

"Normally you would Alex, but not today. While we were talking to Terry, he told us that he is having a divot party, this weekend. He also said that all of us are invited." George said smiling.

"We're invited to a party? That is fantastic. I love parties." Billy said, with excitement.

"Well boys, we better get moving, if we expect to get eighteen holes played today." Anya said.

"The other boys have caught up with you now, son. Go ahead, and make your approach shot." George said.

"Okay, dad. When my ball lands on the green, watch how fast it stops rolling. These greens are so slow, that when your ball lands, it won't roll more then a foot." Branden said.

"You were right son, that green is slow. Are they all that bad?" George asked.

"Most of them are dad, but some of them, are even worse." Branden said.

"If they're all this bad son, maybe we should only play four or five holes. What do you think?" George asked.

"That's a good idea, dad. Lets ask everyone else, what they think, when we get on the green." Branden said.

"Hey Billy! Everyone else is already on the green. Are you having trouble, getting out of that sand-trap?" Steven asked.

"Yes I am, Steven. Could you come over here, and help me, please?" Billy asked.

"Sure Billy, I'll be right there." Steven said.

"I can't figure out what I'm doing wrong, Steven. I've hit the ball three times, but I can't get any loft on it." Billy said, sadly.

"There are three things you have to do. First, you have to keep the face of your club almost flat, until you have hit the ball. Secondly, you have to enter the sand about two inches before you get to the ball. You only want to go down about an eighth of an inch into the sand though. Then, and most importantly, you have to follow through completely, with your swing." Steven said.

"That doesn't sound too difficult, Steven. Let me try that, and see if I can do it." Billy said.

"Okay Billy. Good luck with your shot." Steven said.

"That was a great shot, Billy. Your ball stopped about a foot from the hole." George said, with a smile.

"Son, you're farther away from the pin then anyone else, so you putt first." Anya said.

"Thank you, mom. It looks like I'm going to have to putt it pretty hard, so I can get it to the hole." Branden said.

"That's true son, but I'm sure you can do it." George said.

"Thanks for the vote of confidence, dad." Branden said smiling, as he stepped up to the ball.

"It looks like you may have hit it too hard, Branden. I think it's going to roll pass the hole, on the right hand side." Steven said.

"You may be right, Steven. I didn't mean to hit it, as hard as I did." Branden said.

"Dad, did you see that ball change directions?" Alex asked.

"Yes I did, son. It must have changed directions by at least ten degrees." I said.

"I wonder what happened, that caused it to do that?" Alex asked.

"It hit a ball mark, Alex. That's exactly why people should repair them, when their ball makes one." Anya said.

"Wow! Did you see that, dad? It hit another ball mark, and now it's heading toward the hole." Alex exclaimed.

"Branden, I think it's going to go into the hole." Billy shouted with excitement.

"I can't believe, what just happened. That ball stopped right on the very edge of the hole, with half of it hanging over the edge." Johnny gasped.

"I've been playing golf over ten years, and I've never seen a ball do that." Justin said.

"What do the rules say about something like this, George?" I asked.

"The rules say that the player has ten seconds to decide if the ball is at rest, once they have walked to the ball." George said.

While the group was moving closer to the pin to watch Branden make his next putt, the wind began to blow.

When Andy noticed a small funnel shaped cloud heading toward them, he became hysterical and asked.

"Dad, is that a tornado?"

"No son, it's not a tornado. Most people refer to them as dust-devils." Justin said.

"They're not dangerous, but I need for everyone to kneel down, and cover your eyes, until it passes." I said.

"Dad, if they're not dangerous, then why do we need to cover our eyes?" Alex asked confused.

"For safety reasons, son. Even though they are not dangerous, they are still whirlwinds, and may have spinning dust, dirt, or sand in them. If any of that spinning debris would happen to hit a person in the eye, it could cause eye damage." I said.

"Hey dad, it looks like we got lucky. That dust-devil has changed directions." Danny said.

"Yes it does, son. Now Branden can go ahead, and finish his putt." Tim said.

"That's true dad, but where is his ball at? I don't see it now." Johnny said.

"The wind may have blown it into the hole, so check there first." Anya said.

"That's exactly what happened, Anya. I saw it fall into the hole, when that second gust of wind, hit us." Mr. Avery said.

"Since the wind blew it in, does that count as a stroke?" Billy asked.

"No it doesn't, Billy. Branden only has to count the strokes that he made." Mr. Avery said.

"Then that means, Branden scored a three on this hole." Andy said.

"Yes it does, son. Since this is a par four hole, and he scored a three on it, that's referred to as one under par, or a birdie." Justin said.

"Congratulations, son. You scored lower then any of us, on this hole." Anya said with a smile.

"Thanks mom, but the wind helped me a lot, too." Branden said.

"May I have everyone's attention, please? Due to the poor conditions of the greens, Branden and I would like to ask all of you a question. What would you think of the idea of only playing four or five holes, instead of eighteen?" George asked.

"That sounds like a good idea to me George, but what holes would we play?" I asked.

"I suggest we play every other hole, with the ninth one being our last." George said.

"That sounds good to me hon. but what about the business deal that we discussed earlier?" Anya asked.

"I think that by playing four or five holes, and evaluating the ones we don't play, we'll save some valuable time in making our decision." George explained.

"That's a good idea, dad. Now if you and mom, and everyone else are ready, lets move on to the next hole, and look it over." Branden said.

Chapter 4

"This tee box is in worse condition then the last one was. Not only are there hundreds of divot marks, but there is also a severe case of grass fungus." Branden said.

"You've told us how the divots would have to be repaired, Branden. What would have to be done, to get rid of the fungus?" Billy asked, concerned.

"The first thing that would have to be done is to decide what type of fungus it is. Once that is accomplished, then the correct chemical would be applied to get rid of it." Branden said.

"Would it be better to apply the chemical before, or after the tee box is aerified?" Alex asked.

"I'm not sure Alex, but I would say, before it is. I believe that if it's sprayed before its aerified, then it will prevent the fungus from spreading." Branden said.

"I've been writing down some notes about the condition of this tee box, son. I have also included what you've said about the fungus, and the application of the chemical." George said.

"Is there anything else that we need to discuss about this tee box, before we leave?" I asked.

"I don't believe that there is, Tom. I think we've covered everything." George said.

"Branden, do you remember those weeds that we saw, along the edge of the creek?" Alex asked.

"Yes I do, Alex. I also remember the comment that you made about them. You said, 'those weeds make the course look terrible'." Branden said.

"Where are those weeds at, son?" Anya asked.

"They're along the edge of the creek, between here and the green. When we get to the bridge, we'll point them out to you." Branden said.

While admiring the layout of the course, the group proceeded down the path toward the bridge.
When they had arrived, and had stopped on the bridge, everyone instantly noticed the obnoxious looking weeds.

"You were right, boys. Those weeds do make the course look terrible." Anya said, with a frown.

"That's not all they do, Mam. Sometimes, they'll even interfere with a golfer's game." Steven said.

"How would they do that, Steven?" Johnny asked.

"If a golfer's ball lands in front of them Johnny, it's almost impossible, to hit it through the weeds." Steven explained.

"Dad, would it be possible to manicure the edge of that creek, like they do at the course in Tustin?" Branden asked.

"Yes it would be, son. That wouldn't be hard to do, and it would improve the looks of the course, tremendously." George said.

"I've heard you mention that golf course before, Branden. What's so special about it?" Andy asked.

"It's a big golf course that's located near our home, Andy. They take such good care of it, that it's in excellent condition." Branden said.

"Has Branden ever told you boys that he plays in a tournament there?" Anya asked.

"No, he hasn't, Mam. Is it a big tournament, with a lot of participants?" Johnny asked.
"Yes it is, Johnny. There is always over two-hundred participants, which are divided into four age brackets." Anya said.

"I don't mean to interrupt anyone, but lets go ahead and move on up to the green. We still need to take a few minutes, and evaluate it." George said.

After arriving at the green, and walking out onto it, Branden said.

"Dad, this green looks as bad as the first one did, if not worse."

"It sure does, son. I can't believe that the current owner allowed the greens, to get in such terrible shape." George said, in a disappointed voice.

"Branden, have you noticed the bunkers, yet? It looks like they have a foot of water standing in them." Steven said.

"Yes I have, Steven. The reason the water is standing in them, is because of poor drainage." Branden said.

"What would be the best way to fix that problem, son?" George asked.

"Well dad, since the existing sand is saturated with debris, I'd recommend removing it first. Then once the sand has been removed, the drain can be repaired." Branden said.

"Branden, once the drain has been repaired, what would have to be done next?" Danny asked.

"The next thing that would need to be done is to install a new bunker liner. Once that is completed, the bunker would then be refilled, with new sand." Branden explained.
"What is a bunker liner, and what does it do?" Alex asked.

"It's a thin, fiber like material that water can pass through but nothing else. The main purpose of it is to keep debris out of the drain." Branden further explained.

"I like that suggestion, son. It sounds to me, like that would be the best way to do it." George said.

The group had been discussing how to repair the bunkers for several minutes, when Anya suggested that they move on, to the next hole.
When the group arrived at the next tee box, the boys were shocked at what they

41

saw. Shocked, because of the massive stretch of water that was between the tee box, and the green.

"How am I ever going to hit the ball over that water? I'm not strong enough to hit it that far." Andy said.

"I know how you feel, Andy. I'm not strong enough to hit it that far either." Johnny said.

"Boys, may I make a suggestion that might help you?" Anya asked.

"You sure can, Mam. We'll take all the help that we can get." Andy said.

"I think you'll be able to make it over the water, if you aim for the closest end of the fairway." Anya suggested.

"That sounds like a good idea, Mam. Thank you for that suggestion." Johnny said.

"Alex, we're going to let you and the other boys go first. Then Branden and I will tee off before the adults." Steven said.

"Thank you, Steven. Before I tee off however, I have a question." Alex said.

"What's your question, Alex?" Steven asked.

"What club should I use on this hole?" Alex asked.

"I suggest that you use your five wood, Alex. I've seen you use it in other cases like this, and you've done a great job." Steven suggested.

"That's what I'd suggest too, Alex. When you use the five wood, you're able to get the height, and distance, that you need." Branden said.

"What club are you going to use, son?" Anya asked.

"I'm going to use my seven iron, mom. I have better luck using it, in situations like this." Branden said.

"Alex, when you tee off, don't forget to use the two most important rules of golf." Steven said, with a smile.

"What rules are you referring to, Steven?" Alex asked.

"Proper form, and follow through." Everyone said, in unison.

"Wow! That tee off felt great." Alex exclaimed.

"It was a great tee off, Alex. Not only did you follow the two main rules of golf, but you also landed on the green." George said, with a smile.

"Boys, I'm very proud of each and every one of you. All of you made it across the lake on your first try." Justin said.

"Thank you, dad. I consider myself very lucky that I even made it." Billy said.

"That shot was more then luck, Billy. In addition to following the two rules of golf, you also applied a lot of power, to your swing." I said.

"Thank you, grandpa. I knew that if I didn't hit it hard enough, I wouldn't make it over the water." Billy said, with a smile.

"Now that we've all teed off, lets go ahead and move on up to the green." Anya said.

Not everyone's ball had landed on the green, when they teed off. Johnny's ball had landed in the sand trap, while Andy's had landed approximately five feet in front of it.

"Johnny, do you remember what Steven told Billy about getting out of a sand-trap?" Branden asked.

"Yes I do, Branden. I'm going to try my best to hit the ball, exactly that same way." Johnny said.

"Johnny, you go ahead and hit your ball first. Then when you're finished, Andy will take his turn." Tim said.

"Okay dad. Wish me luck everyone." Johnny said.

Johnny had done an excellent job of hitting his ball out of the sand trap. After it had landed, it continued rolling until it came to a stop, just six feet from the hole. After putting the ball twice, Johnny finally made it into the hole.

When everyone had finished playing the hole, the scores were tallied. Excluding Branden, the boys had all scored equally on the hole. Branden however, had scored a one under par, once again.

Arriving at the fourth tee box, George asked.

"Should we evaluate this tee box son, or go on to the green?"

"I'm getting thirsty dad, so we need to stop anyway. Then after we get a drink, we can go ahead and evaluate the tee box." Branden said.

"That's a good idea, Branden. I'm starting to get thirsty too." Steven said.

"Branden, now that you and I have gotten a drink, lets walk over to the tee box." Steven said.

"This tee box needs a lot of repair too, doesn't it son." I said to Alex.

"Yes it does, dad. I have to agree with what George said earlier about the current owners, and the lack of maintenance to this golf course." Alex said.

"I do too, son. I do too." I said.

"Has anyone else noticed that boy sitting up there on that hill, other then myself?" Alex asked the group.

"I saw him when we first got here son, but he was standing up then. I just assumed that he was looking for a golf ball." I said.

"Dad, that boy could be sitting in a dangerous spot. If a golfer on that fairway would happen to hit his ball wrong, he might get hit." Branden said.

"That's true, son. Why don't you take Steven and Alex with you, and go up there and talk to him? Be polite to him, but tell him that he could be sitting in a dangerous spot." George said.

"Okay dad. We'll be back in a couple of minutes." Branden said.

"I don't know why, but that boy looks familiar from the back." Alex said, as they got closer to the boy.

"Excuse us, but may we talk to you for a minute?" Branden asked the boy.

"Are you talking to me?" The startled boy asked, turning around quickly.

"Yes, we were talking to you. We wanted to tell you that . . ." "Aaron? Is that really you, Aaron?" Alex asked, in a surprised voice.

"Yes, that's my name. How did you . . . Alex! Oh Alex, I am so happy to see you. I haven't seen you for over a year. How have you been?" Aaron asked with excitement.

"I've been doing fantastic, Aaron. You may not know this yet, but my life has changed tremendously, since I saw you last." Alex said.

"Alex, I don't mean to interrupt, but how long have you known each other?" Steven asked.

"We've known each other since kindergarten, Steven. Aaron is my best friend, and I'm his." Alex said, with a smile.

"Boys, what is going on up there? Are you having any sort of problem?" I asked.

"No dad, everything is fine. Come up here though, because I want all of you to meet my best friend, Aaron." Alex said.

"Okay son, we're on our way." I said.

When everyone had arrived at the top of the hill, and the introductions had been made, Alex asked.

"Why have you been sitting up here, Aaron?"

"I usually come here to watch the golfers play, Alex. Today however, I've been watching that little funnel cloud, over there." Aaron said.

"Dad, do you think that little cloud could be Jimmy?" Danny asked hopefully.

"It could be son, but I wouldn't want to say for sure." Tim said.

"Have you ever seen that funnel cloud before, Aaron?" Danny asked.

"No, I haven't, Danny. Today is the first time that I've seen it." Aaron said.

45

"Have you been watching it very long?" Billy asked.

"Yes I have, Billy. I've been watching it for the last two hours. I've seen it hovering above the number three and four tee boxes, and also the greens." Aaron said.

"Other then here, are those the only places that you've seen it?" Johnny asked.

"Yes it is, Johnny." Aaron said.

"Boys, I don't mean to interrupt your reunion, but we really should be going." Anya said.

"You're right, mom. After all, Terry did say that he would be expecting a call from us." Branden said.

"I wish we didn't have to go so soon. I haven't seen Aaron in a long time, and I'd like to spend some time with him." Alex said, with tears in his eyes.

"I have an idea, boys." George said, with a smile.

"What sort of idea, sir?" Alex asked.

"It's an idea that I think will make both of you boys, very happy. If Aaron wants to, and if it's okay with his parents, he's more then welcome to come along with us." George said.

"That's a great idea, dad. That will give Alex and Aaron a chance to catch up, with what has been happening in each of their lives." Branden said.

"That sounds like a great idea to me too. I'm going to call my dad, right now." Aaron said, as he dialed the number.

"Hi dad. This is your son, Aaron. You're not going to believe this, but Alex is here with me." Aaron said, with excitement.

"Alex who, son?"

"Alex Hamilton, dad. Don't you remember him? He was, and still is, my best friend." Aaron said.

"That use to be my last name Aaron, but it isn't now. Now my last name is Warner." Alex said, proudly.

"That's not the only reason that I called you dad. Alex and his family, want me to spend the afternoon, and evening with them. Can I dad? Please." Aaron asked, hopefully.

"You sure can, son. I know exactly how it feels to lose track of a good friend, and then to find that person a year later." Aaron's dad said.

"Thank you, dad. I really do appreciate you letting me spend time with them. They're getting ready to leave now dad, so I have to go. I will talk to you later. Bye for now." Aaron said.

While riding along with the group, and taking part in the evaluation, Aaron was having a fantastic time. Updating each other on their life's events during the passed year, Alex and Aaron had once again become best of friends.

Aaron was overwhelmed and excited, at what Alex had told him about his life. Alex however was saddened at what Aaron had told him about his.

Being extremely depressed at what Aaron had told him, Alex knew in his heart that he must do something, to help his friend.

Prior to evaluating the eighth green, Alex asked Branden and Steven for a special favor.

"Branden, could you and Steven do me a big favor?"

"We sure can Alex. What can we do for you?" Branden asked.

"I need to talk to the adults alone, without Aaron around. Could you have him to go with you, and check out the next tee box? By the time you get finished checking it out, we'll be there." Alex said.

"That's not a problem, Alex. We will be more then happy to do that for you. We'll see you at the next tee box." Steven said.

"Thank you, Steven. I really do appreciate your help." Alex said.

"Son, you don't look very happy. Is there something wrong?" I asked.

"Yes there is, dad. May I speak to you, and the other adults, in private please?" Alex asked.

"This really must be important, dad. I've never heard my brother sound any more serious, then he does right now." Justin said.

"It is important, bro. It's about Aaron, and his family." Alex said.

"What about them, son? Are they having some sort of problem?" I asked.

"Yes they are dad, but it's financial. Aaron told me a few minutes ago, that his dad is unemployed, and that there is no family income. They do not have any money to pay their bills, or even to buy food. Aaron also told me, that their electricity has been shut off, and that they're three months behind on their rent." Alex said, with a frown.

"I'm sorry to hear that, Alex. How long has your friend's dad been unemployed?" Anya asked.

"Ever since the warehouses closed, Mam. That has been almost two years ago now." Alex said.

"Do you have any idea, what kind of work he did, while he was working there?" George asked.

"I'm not exactly sure, sir. I do know however, that he was the Vice President in charge of operations." Alex said.

"That's fantastic, bro. With a position like that, it only means one thing. He knows exactly how to get things done, and done correctly." Justin said.

"It's also for that reason Alex, that if we decide to buy the course, that we will be offering him, a job." Anya said, with a smile.

"Thank you very much, Mam. What about the other problems, they have right now?" Alex asked.

"You don't have to worry about those problems either, Alex. I just got off the phone with my associates at CPS. They have assured me that they will have everything taken care of, by the time Aaron goes home this evening." Tim said.

"Thank you everyone, thank you very much. I love each and every one of you, very much." Alex said, with tears of happiness.

"You're welcome, Alex. We love you too." Tim said, with a smile.

"Now that we've finished evaluating this hole, lets move on to the next one, and rejoin the other boys." Anya said.

Chapter 5

"How are you boys doing, with the evaluation?" George asked, as they arrived at the ninth tee box.

"We've already completed it, dad. We finished up with it, about ten minutes ago." Branden said.

"What did you decide, son? Is it in any better shape, then the other ones were?" George asked.

"No, it isn't dad. I'd say it looks about the same." Branden said.

"What were you doing, while you were waiting for us son?" Anya asked.

"We've been standing here, and looking the area over, mom. We've been looking at the fairway, the lake, and watching three funnel clouds." Branden said.

"Where are those clouds at now, Branden?" Alex asked.

"They're hovering above the number nine green, Alex." Branden said.

"Let's go ahead and tee off, everyone. I'm sure they'll be gone, by the time we get there." I said.

"This hole looks like it is going to be a challenging one, dad." Justin said.

"You're right about that, son. This fairway is so narrow, that there isn't going to be much room for mistakes." I said.

"Well boys, which one of you wants to, tee off first?" Anya asked.

"Aaron hasn't played any yet, mom. Steven and I have talked him into it, so we'll let him go first." Branden said.

"I didn't know that you knew how to play golf, Aaron. How long have you been playing?" Alex asked.

"I've been playing for almost a year now, Alex. I had started taking lessons, before you disappeared." Aaron said, as he stepped up to address his ball.

While the group was teeing off, each of the boys got an excellent hit, with plenty of lift on their ball.
With each of the balls landing along the right side of the fairway, they were now in perfect alignment with the green.
With part of the lake in front of them, Johnny said.

"That water in front of us, reminds me of the number three hole."

"I know what you mean Johnny, it does me too." Billy said.

"Don't let the water intimidate you, boys. Just remember how you played number three, and you'll do fine." Anya said, with a smile.

"Those funnel clouds are leaving, dad. Now we can take our next shot." Branden said.

"Everyone has taken their turn now son, with the exception of you. Go ahead and take your shot, and good luck." I said.

"That sure wasn't, the right way to do it. I've never, landed in the water on this hole, before now." Justin said, frustrated.

"What do you have to do now dad, since you landed in the water?" Andy asked.

"I have to drop, and use another ball, son. When I drop it, it will count as my second stroke. Then when I hit it, it'll count as my third stroke." Justin explained.
"Why do you have to count it as two strokes, when you only hit it once?" Billy asked, confused.

"That's another one of the rules of golf, son. The extra stroke is called a penalty stroke." Justin said, as he dropped the other ball.

51

"I know you can make it over the lake, son. Just be sure to relax, and concentrate on your swing." I said.

"That was a great shot, dad. From here, it looks like it landed close to the pin." Billy said.

"Now that we're all across the lake, lets move on up to the green." Tim said.

"Billy was right about your ball, son. It did stop close to the pin." I said, with a smile.

"It sure did dad, and I'm glad it did. Now I can still make par, on this hole." Justin said.

When everyone had finished putting his or her ball into the hole, Danny said.

"Look over there, everyone! Those funnel clouds are above the number nine tee box now."

"Those things are really starting to confuse me. I can't help from wondering, what they're up to." George said.

"Dad, you may think I'm crazy, but I have a feeling that they're trying to tell us something." Branden said.

"No son, I don't think you're crazy. I would never think any thing like that, about you." George said.

"I've been thinking the same thing, Branden. Dad, would it be possible for us to go back over to that side of the lake? I want to get closer to them, and see what they're doing." Alex said.

"Do you think that would be a safe idea, Alex? After all, they are funnel clouds." Anya said.

"I'm sure it . . ." Alex started.

"Look everyone! One of the little clouds is writing a message to Danny." Andy shouted.

"Danny, tell your friends that it's okay. We will not harm any of you." The cloud wrote.

"Well Alex, I guess that answers my question." Anya said, with a smile.

"Okay everyone lets move to the other side of the lake, so we can watch them." George said, smiling also.

When the group arrived on the other side of the lake, they stopped in the middle of the fairway to watch.

With the group now in position, the three funnel clouds touched down, and began spinning furiously, covering every inch of the tee box. The sight of flying sand, dirt, and grass particles were breath taking to behold.

Not knowing exactly what was happening, Andy asked the question that was on everyone's mind.

"What are they doing, dad? Are they destroying the tee box?"

"I'm not sure what they're doing, son. I can't see the clouds, because of all the dust, and dirt that they've stirred up." Justin said.

"How long has it been now dad, since they started?" Billy asked.

"It has been about ten minutes now son, but I think they're beginning to slow down." Justin said.

"Now it's starting to rain on the tee box, dad. That should settle the dust, so we can see what's happening." Billy said.

"It is settling the dust, son. I'm beginning to see the grass, now." Justin said.

"Look how much greener the grass is now. It sure didn't look like that when we teed off." Branden said.

"If we decide to buy the golf course George, those funnel clouds would be nice to have around." Anya said, with a smile.

"I know exactly what you mean, Anya. With their help, we could turn this course into a five star country club, in just a few days." George said.

"That may be true dad, but I think we've scared them away." Branden said.

"I don't think they're leaving Branden, because they have stopped. Now it seems like they're waiting for us to approve the work, that they've done." Danny said.

"You may be right about that, son. Let's go ahead and check the tee box out again, and see what it looks like now." Tim said.

"This tee box looks great now, dad. This grass has a beautiful

deep rich green color and it feels like velvet." Branden said.

"That's true son, and there isn't a single divot mark, either." George said, with a smile.

"Well George, what do you and Branden think?" Should we buy it?" Anya asked.

"I'm not sure yet, Anya. Shouldn't we figure out what the repair costs would be first, before we decide?" George asked.

"I guess you're right about that dad. I wish we didn't have to wait that long though." Branden said, in a disappointed voice.

"Look everyone! Those clouds are starting to write something again." Andy shouted.

"If you buy it — we'll fix it"
"Because"
"We Care — About Golf"

"I wasn't expecting, anything like that to happen." George said, surprised.

"I wasn't either George, but now that it has, what do we do?" Anya asked.

"With an offer like that, there's only one thing we can do. We buy the course." George said, with a smile.

"Do you want me to call Terry now, and tell him what we've decided?" Anya asked.

"That's a good idea, Anya. Also, while you're talking to him, tell him that we'll be ready for dinner in a few minutes." George said.

"Boys, now that we've finished our game, I'd like to tell you something." George said.

"What do you want to tell us, sir?" Johnny asked.

"For never playing golf before in your lives, each of you did a great job today." George said, with a smile.

"Thank you sir. We have a lot more to learn though, before we're good enough to play in any sort of competition." Billy said.

"That's true Billy, but that shouldn't take to long. With what I saw today, you boys are going to be fast learners." George said, with a smile.

"Dad, there is something else we don't want to forget about." Branden said.

"What is that, son?" George asked.

"There are a lot of golf courses that hold tournaments for beginners." Branden said.

"That's true son. That is something that I had forgotten about. If the 'Putt and Go' doesn't have something like that, we'll change it." George said.

"I hate to interrupt, but is anyone other than me, getting hungry?" Tim asked.

"I am dad. I am starving. I didn't realize that playing golf could cause a person to work up such an appetite." Danny said.

"We're hungry, too." The rest of the boys said, in unison.

On the way to the clubhouse, Anya overheard Alex, and Aaron talking.

"Do you remember when my dad use to work here, Alex?" Aaron asked.

"Yes I do, Aaron. If I remember right, he was the superintendent in charge of taking care of the golf course." Alex said.

"Actually, he was only the assistant superintendent. I think, he should've been the main superintendent though, because he was smarter then the guy they had." Aaron said.

"You're probably just saying that Aaron, because he is your dad." Danny said.

"That isn't the only reason that I said it, Danny. I said it, because it is the truth. My dad has a Master's degree in turf management, and in chemical application. The person that was my dad's boss, had no formal education, and knew absolutely nothing about taking care of a golf course. You can even ask Terry, about that." Aaron said.

"How long has it been now Aaron, since your dad worked here?" Mr. Avery asked.

"It has been five years now, Mr. Avery. When he left here, he started working at the warehouses." Aaron said.

"Now I understand why the course started looking so bad, about that time." Mr. Avery said.

"Do they still have the same superintendent now, as they did back then?" Anya asked.

"Yes they do, Mam. His name is Richard." Aaron said.

"I've met that guy, and I didn't like his attitude. He gave me the impression that he doesn't care about anything, or anybody, except himself." Branden said.

"You're not the only person that feels that way about him, Branden. I have talked to many people that use to be members here, and they all feel the same way. They also told me that he is the reason, why this course doesn't have any members anymore." Mr. Avery said.

"Mr. Avery, what did the course look like, when Aaron's dad was in charge here?" George asked.

"The entire course looked fantastic, George. It looked exactly like the ninth tee box does now." Mr. Avery said.

"I don't know about you George, but I think we'll be needing a new superintendent." Anya said, with a smile.

"I think we will too, Anya. Aaron, could you call your dad please, and ask him to meet us here at the clubhouse? Be sure to tell him not to eat anything though, before he comes." George said, with a smile.

"Okay sir, I'll call him right now." Aaron said, as he began dialing the number.

Chapter 6

"Here comes my dad now, Alex. He just turned into the driveway." Aaron said.

"When he gets inside Aaron, could you introduce him to all of us?" Anya asked.

"I'd be honored to, Mam. I'll go and meet him at the front door, then escort him here." Aaron said.

"I haven't seen your dad in a long time Aaron, so I'll go with you." Alex said.

"While you boys are doing that, we'll finish getting things ready at the table." Michelle said.

"Hi dad. This is my friend, Alex. Alex, this is my dad, Michael." Aaron said.

"Hi Alex, it's good to see you again." Michael said, with a smile.

"Thank you, sir. It's good to see you again, too." Alex said.

"How has your day been, dad?" Aaron asked.

"Well son, this morning was just like all other mornings have been lately. This afternoon however, was completely different and full of surprises." Michael said.

"What do you mean, dad? What sort of surprises?" Aaron asked, as they walked into the banquet room.

"Well to start with, a pickup truck full of food was delivered to our house. Then about thirty minutes later, our electricity was turned back on. During the next hour, while I was still putting the food away, the doorbell rang. When I saw that it was the landlord at the door, I was afraid to answer it, but did anyway." Michael said.

"Oh dad, please don't tell me that he was there to evict us." Aaron said, in a trembling voice.

"That's what I was afraid of too son, but that wasn't the case. The only thing he wanted was to give me a rent receipt. Someone, not only paid the back rent that we owed, but also three months in advance." Michael said.

"That's fantastic dad, but I'm confused. Who would've done all of that, for us?" Aaron asked.

"I'm not sure, son. All I know is what each of them told me when I asked them, that same question." Michael said.

"What did they tell you, dad?" Aaron asked.

"The only thing that they would tell me was, 'that it was complimentary from your friends at We Care'." Michael said.

"Alex, I don't know if you had anything to do with this or not, but if you did, thank you very much." Aaron said, with a smile.

"Aaron, if you and your dad will follow me, I'll show you where you'll be sitting." Michelle said.

"Will they be sitting close to Branden, and his parents?" Alex asked.

"Yes they will be, Alex. They'll be sitting on the opposite side of the table from them, so they can discuss business." Michelle said.

"Aaron, now that you and your dad know where you'll be sitting, Anya would like for you to introduce him, to everyone." Steven said.

With the formal introductions now completed, everyone began sitting down for a delicious meal.

During the meal, Aaron's dad had once again mentioned the surprises of that afternoon, when Aaron said.

"Dad, I know those surprises seem big to you right now, but you haven't seen anything yet." Aaron said, with a smile.

"What do you mean by that, son?" Michael asked.

"What Aaron is referring to Michael, is the future of this golf course, and your possible employment with it." Anya said.

"Michael, this golf course is currently for sale, and we've decided to buy it. When the sale is completed, we will need a qualified grounds Superintendent, to take care of it." George said.

"What about Richard, sir? Have you considered him for the position?" Michael asked.

"We've already seen how he takes care of it, or should I say, doesn't take care of it." George said, with a frown.

"I've already told them about your degrees, dad. They have also seen how the course would look, if you were the Superintendent." Aaron said.

"Michael, your experience, and qualifications as a highly qualified grounds Superintendent, has preceded you. That is why; we would like to hire you as the new grounds Superintendent." George said.

"The course is in terrible shape, sir. I would need a fairly large budget, to get it back in shape." Michael said.

"We want the course to be taken care of properly, Michael. How does an unlimited budget, sound to you?" George asked, with a smile.

"That sounds fantastic, sir. The first year of operation will be a very expensive one. We will have the expense of all new equipment, along with the other major expenses on the course itself." Michael said.

"George, Michael hasn't asked you this question yet, so I will. Will you be keeping Richard on, as an assistant?" Terry asked.

"No, we won't, Terry. Richard's career here at the 'Putt and Go' will be terminated, when the sale is final." George said.

"I'm glad to hear that, sir. Richard and I could never get along, when I worked here before." Michael said.

"What do you think, Michael? Would you like to be our new Superintendent?" Anya asked.

"Yes I would, Mam. I would enjoy that very much." Michael said.

"Now that we have our new Superintendent, is there anything else we need to discuss?" George asked.

"Should we start working on the membership problem?" Michelle asked.

"Yes we should, Michelle. We are going to have a membership, and activity committee after the sale is finalized. Would you be interested in becoming the chairperson of that committee?" Anya asked.

"Yes I would be, Anya. I would be honored, to accept the position." Michelle said.

"Thank you, Michelle. Is there anything further that we need to discuss?" George asked.

"Dad, what about the tournament for beginners?" Branden asked.

"I'm glad you reminded me about that, son. Terry, could you start the process to do that for us, please?" George asked.

"It would be my pleasure, George. Would you like for the tournament to be an annual one, or a one time thing?" Terry asked.

"We want it to be an annual event, Terry." Anya said.

"That sounds good to me, Mam. I'll start the process, first thing in the morning." Terry said.

"Speaking of tournaments, Branden. Didn't you tell me earlier that you have one next month?" Steven asked.

"Yes I did, Steven. The official starting date of the new season is the first. Then on the eighth, I'll be playing in the first tournament of the season." Branden said.

"Where will that tournament be held at, Branden?" Billy asked.

"Since it's the first tournament of the season Billy, it'll be held in Los Angeles, California." Branden said.

"Is that the only tournament, you're signed up for, Branden?"

"No, it isn't, Johnny. I am also signed up for two other tournaments. Two of the three tournaments, will be held next month. The third one however, will be held on the first weekend in May." Branden said.

"Where will those two tournaments be held?" Alex asked.

"One of them will be at the course on Catalina Island on April 22nd. The other one will be held on the first weekend in May, at the course in Tustin." Branden said.

"Branden, does that tournament in Tustin, have a name?" Johnny asked.

"Yes it does, Johnny. It's called the 'Anya Foundation Junior Championship Golf Tournament'." Branden said.

"Is that the same one you mentioned earlier today, Branden?" Alex asked.

"Yes it is, Alex. Out of all the tournaments, that I play in during the year that one is my favorite. Not only is it my favorite, but it is also very special to me, and my family." Branden said.

"Why is that particular tournament, so special to you, and your family?" Billy asked.

"That's a long story, Billy. I would tell you, but it would take too long. If you would like to learn more about it though, you can go to its online web page." Branden said.

"I'd like to learn more about it, Branden. What is the URL address of the web page?" Alex asked.

"The URL address is. http://anyafoundation.com

"Thank you, Branden. I'll check that web page out, when I get home this evening." Alex said.

"Terry, this meal has been delicious, but we should be going." I said.

"You're right Tom. We do need to be going. I'd like to make a couple of announcements to everyone at 'We Care', while they're still eating." George said.

"Dad, do you think we'll get back to 'We Care', in time for desert?" Branden asked, with a smile.

"I hope so, son. I'd like to have another piece of that delicious grandma's cheesecake that we had for lunch today." George said.

"George, I agree with you and Branden about the cheesecake, but I'd like to make a toast before we go." Anya said.

"That's a wonderful idea, Anya. With what we have already accomplished here today, the future of the 'Putt and Go' looks very promising." George said.

"Here's to the promising future of the 'Putt and Go', and its new and wonderful staff." Anya said, as she raised her glass in a toast.

"Now that we're finished here, I'd like to invite all of you over to 'We Care', for desert." I said.

"Terry, could you do us a favor, and call the current owners for us, please. If you can, set up a meeting with them for tomorrow afternoon. We'd like to finalize this sale as soon as possible." George said.

"I'll go and do that right now, George. Then when I come over to 'We Care', I'll let you know what they said." Terry said.

"Okay Terry, we'll see you when you get there." George said.

Chapter 7

When the group entered the cafeteria at 'We Care', they were greeted by Mary. Being curious about how the afternoon had gone for the boys, she asked.

"Did you boys have fun this afternoon?"

"We sure did, mom. We had a lot of fun." Johnny said.

"I'm glad to hear that you had fun. Did you learn anything new?" Mary asked.

"Yes we did, mom. We learned a lot of new things today. One of the things that we learned was that playing golf can really work up an appetite." Danny said.

"You boys shouldn't be hungry now, you just ate." Tim said.

"The only thing that we're hungry for dad, is some desert." Johnny said, with a smile.

"Mom, is there any cheese cake left over from lunch?" Danny asked.

"No there isn't, son. There wasn't any of it left, not even a crumb." Mary said.

"That's a shame, Mary. We were all hoping to have a piece of it, for desert." Anya said.

"Mom, didn't you say at lunch that we always have it on special occasions?" Danny asked.

"Yes I did son, and that's why we made more of it." Mary said.

"Danny, why are you just standing there? Come on; let's go eat some cheese cake." Alex said, with a smile.

"Boys, sit down after you get your desert. It's almost time for announcements." Mary said.

"Where should I sit at, Mam?" I've never been here before." Aaron said.

"He's a friend of mine, Aunt Mary. Would it be okay, if he sits with us?" Alex asked.

"Yes, it's okay Alex. Since he is a friend of yours, he can sit at the head table, whenever he visits us." Mary said.

"That maybe quite often, Mary. We just hired his dad, as the new grounds Superintendent of the 'Putt and Go'. We'll be making the official announcement, in a few minutes." George said.

"May I have everyone's attention, please? Several things happened this afternoon that has greatly affected our golfing program. It is for those reasons that our announcements will be primarily about golf. Steven, we'll start with your announcement." Mr. Avery said.

"Thank you, dad. Well everyone, I guess it is up to me, to tell you the bad news. Terry informed us today that the golf course is for sale, and therefore can no longer sponsor our team." Steven said.

"What are we going to do now, Steven? I was really looking forward, to being on the team." Jeff said.

"We're still going to have a team, because that problem is going to be eliminated. Branden's parents have the solution to our problem, and have already started working on it. I'll let George tell you about that though." Steven said, with a smile.

During the next thirty minutes, and amongst the several standing ovations, George explained in detail the events of that afternoon. When he was nearing the end of his speech, George said.

"Ladies and gentlemen, it gives me great pleasure to introduce to you our new grounds keeping Superintendent, Michael. Michael, would you like to say a few words to the group?" George asked.

"Yes I would George, thank you. First, I would like to say thank you, to you and your family, for giving me this opportunity. I'm aware of the terrible shape that the course is currently in, and have made it my top priority to right that wrong."

"My next priority is to assist Terry and Michelle in organizing an annual tournament for young golfers."

"In regards to the tournament, I'd like to see it become the best in the nation, second only to the 'Anya Foundation Junior Championship Golf Tournament'."

"Now I'd like to introduce my son, to all of you. Aaron, would you stand up please?" Michael asked.

"Thank you for the introduction, dad. May I say a few words, also?" Aaron asked.

"Yes you may, son." Michael said.

"First, I'd like to thank everyone here at 'We Care', for the big surprises that my dad and I received at home, this afternoon."

"When I woke up this morning, I was expecting it to be just another boring, and depressing day. That all changed however, when I discovered that my best friend Alex was still alive and well."

"There's one thing that George intentionally, left out of his speech. He left it out, because he wanted me to surprise my dad with it."

"Dad, do you remember what you told me, about how long it would take to get the golf course, back into shape?" Aaron asked.

"Yes son, I remember. I said that it would take at least a year." Michael said.

"Personally, I don't think it will take that long, dad. With what we witnessed today, I would guess maybe a few days, at the most." Aaron said.

"What do you mean by that, son?" Michael asked.

"Excuse me, Michael. I don't mean to interrupt you and Aaron, but here comes Mr. Avery." I said.

"What did you find out, Mr. Avery? Were you able to get a meeting set up with the sellers?" Anya asked.

"Yes I was, Mam. They said they would be happy to meet with you and your family, tomorrow afternoon at one o'clock." Mr. Avery said.

"That's fantastic, Mr. Avery. George, now all we have to do is to find a lawyer in this area that is knowledgeable in real estate matters." Anya said.

"That's true, Anya. The problem is though; I don't know any lawyers, from around here. Tom, do you know of any?" George asked.

"Yes I do, George. You're sitting next to one." I said, with a smile.

"Justin, I didn't know you were a lawyer. Do you know anything about real estate?" George asked.

"Yes I do, George. Most of my cases over the past five years have been real estate cases. That amounts to over three hundred cases." Justin said.

"Dad, I've seen Uncle Justin's certificates. His office wall has at least thirty of them, on it." Branden said.

"Justin, would it be possible to hire you, as our legal representative?" George asked.

"Yes it would be, George. I'd be honored to represent you, and your family." Justin said, with a smile.

"Now that we have that taken care of, let's enjoy this delicious cheese cake." Anya said.

"That reminds me of something, Anya. I still have to give you the recipe for it. I have it written down on a recipe card, but it is in my office. I'll go and get it, and come right back." Mary said.

After a few minutes of being in her office, Mary returned to the table.

"Here's the recipe for the cheese cake, Anya. If you have any questions while you're making it, feel free to call me."

Grandma Wells's
Cheesecake Recipe

Part 1
30 (1/3 sections) graham crackers
1 tablespoon of powdered sugar
One stick of butter or oleo

Part 2
1 small box of lemon jello
1 cup of boiling water

Part 3
One large package of cream cheese
1 cup of sugar
1 teaspoon of vanilla extract

Part 4
1 small can of (chilled) mil-not

Mix step 2, and set aside to cool
Mix cream cheese, sugar, and vanilla extract and set aside.
Roll graham crackers until extra fine. Blend powdered sugar, and melted oleo into the graham cracker crumbs. Press the crumb mixture evenly into a 9"X12" pan.
Beat mil-not until stiff, then add steps 2 and 3, and blend together. Pour the mil-not mixture over the crumbs, and then place in refrigerator for several hours to cool. (9-12 servings)

"Mary, is there really a grandma Wells?" Anya asked.

"There use to be Anya, but she's gone now. She was Tom's grandmother, on his mother's side of the family." Mary explained.

"The recipe was handed down from my grandmother, to my mother. Then my mother handed it down to me, after I got married. Now, since I consider everyone here at 'We Care' as part of my family, I have chosen to share it with them, as well." I said.

"Does that mean you consider my parents and me, a part of the 'We Care' family?" Branden asked.

"Yes it does, Branden. In fact, all of us here at 'We Care' already consider you and your parents, a part of the United Families." I said.

"Thank you, Tom. Speaking on behalf of my family, we consider it an honor to be part of the United Families." George said, with a smile.

"Son, before Mr. Avery arrived, we were discussing how long it would take to fix the course. You said, 'no more then a few days, at the most'. What did you mean by that?' Michael asked.

"We're going to have some help fixing it, dad. While we were playing the ninth hole, the clouds started fixing the tee box. Even in as bad of shape as it was, it only took them fifteen minutes to fix it." Aaron said.

"What are you talking about, son? How could a cloud do anything like that?" Michael asked, confused.

"Mr. Avery! Come quick, you have to see this. I think we're being invaded by funnel clouds." Jeff shouted, from near the window.

Chapter 8

That evening after arriving home, Alex excused himself to go to his room.

"Are you going to bed already, son?" I asked, confused.

"No, I'm not going to bed yet, dad. I want to look at that web page that Branden told us about today." Alex said.

"I had forgotten about that, son. Do us a favor, and let us know when you have found it. We want to look at it, too." I said.

"Okay dad, I'll do that." Alex said.

"Dad, George said earlier that with the help of the clouds, the course could have a five star rating within a few days. Do you think that's really possible?" Justin asked.

"Yes I do, son. Just remember, how long it took for them to clean up the warehouses, and decontaminate the soil." I said.

"Dad, if you're ready, I've found that web page." Alex said.

"Okay son, we'll be right there." I said.

"Alex, I love that piano music. Whoever is playing it is very, very good." Karen said, smiling.

"Yes he is Aunt Karen, and he is only twelve years old. He also has a couple of sisters, and they're playing on some of the other pages, of the web sight." Alex said.

"How did you know how old he is, and that he has sisters, bro.?" Justin asked, confused.

"Branden told us those things today, while we were playing golf." Alex said.

"I agree with you son, he is good. Let's go ahead and look the web sight over now, and see what all it says." I said.

After several minutes of looking over, and reading the web page, Karen said.

"That web page has a very important message to all adults, and especially to parents."

"Yes it does, Karen. I know I am only one person, but I am going to figure out a way that I can support their mission, financially. Even if it isn't very much, I still want to help." I said.

"That's great dad, but what do you have in mind?" Alex asked.

"I'm not sure yet, son. I'll sleep on it, and let everyone know in the morning." I said.

"I'm glad that Branden told us about this web page. I've really learned a lot, by reading it." Danny said.

"I have too, Danny. I can also understand now, why the tournament is so special to him, and his family." Billy said.

"Well everyone, I think I'll go to bed now. It's starting to get late, and I'm tired." I said.

"I'm tired too, dad. Playing golf today, really took the strength out of me." Alex said.

"Good night everyone." I said.

"Good night, dad. We'll see you in the morning." Justin said.

While sleeping that night, a dream came to Tom that would unquestionably, change the future of his book.

Being fully awakened by the reality of the dream, Tom consciously made his decision about how he would help the foundation.

Unable to get back to sleep, Tom went to the kitchen and fixed his morning coffee.

Being awakened by the sound, and smell of the fresh brewing coffee, Andy crept to the kitchen to investigate. Seeing his grandpa in an extremely happy state of mind was very confusing to Andy. Not knowing exactly what else to do, Andy rushed quietly to his parent's bedroom, to get help.

"Mom! Dad! Wake-up, I think there's something wrong with grandpa." Andy shouted, in a scared voice.

"What do you mean, 'there's something wrong with grandpa', son?" Justin asked.

"I don't know how to describe it, dad. All I know is that I've never seen him act that way before." Andy said.

"Okay son, we'll be right there. While we're getting dressed, I want you to run and wake the other boys up. After you do that, I want all of you to meet us in the kitchen." Justin said.

"Okay, dad." Andy said, as he ran out of the room.

"Dad, what's wrong?" Alex exclaimed, as he and the family, rushed into the kitchen.

"There's nothing wrong, son. What made you think, there was?" I asked.

"Andy told us that there was, dad. He was scared, when he woke us up. He was afraid that there was something wrong with his grandpa." Alex said.

"Come here Andy, and stand next to grandpa." I said with a smile.

"Okay grandpa, but I hope you're not mad at me." Andy said.

"No Andy, grandpa isn't mad at you. I just want to explain to you and the family, why I got up so early this morning." I said.

"I hope it isn't anything serious, dad." Justin said.

"It isn't, son. I just wanted to tell all of you that I have figured out a way to help the 'Anya Foundation'." I said.

"How are you going to do it, dad?" Alex asked.

"I'm going to donate fifty percent of all the royalties that I earn, from the book that I'm currently writing." I said, with a smile.

"Are you referring to the book entitled, 'We Care About Golf'?" Karen asked.

"Yes I am, Karen." I said.

"Fifty percent, dad? Isn't that going to be a lot of money?" Alex asked.

"I hope so son, but I don't care about the money. The goal of the 'Anya Foundation' is to educate the public about child safety in the home. Since I'm a parent, and a strong supporter of child safety education, that's why I've decided to do it." I said.

"Grandpa, is that fresh baked biscuits that I smell?" Billy asked.

"It sure is, Billy. I wanted to surprise all of you this morning, by fixing biscuits and gravy." I said.

"That's fantastic, dad. We haven't had biscuits and gravy, in a long time. Will Uncle Tim and his family, be here for breakfast, too?" Alex asked.

"Yes they will be, son. I called them a few minutes ago, and they'll be here shortly." I said.

"Good morning, everyone. When we came out of our house, we could smell the delicious aromas of biscuits and gravy cooking. Were they coming from here?" Tim asked, with a smile.

"Good morning, Tim. To answer your question about the aromas, yes they were." I said.

"If everyone will sit down, I'll start serving breakfast." Karen said.

When the United Families were close to being finished with their delicious breakfast, the phone rang.

"Good morning, you've reached the Warner's residence, Justin speaking."

"Good morning Justin. This is George. Anya and I were wondering if we could meet with you and your dad, before breakfast this morning."

"We would be more then happy to, George. May I ask what this is in regards to?" Justin asked.

"It's in regards to the purchase of the course, Justin. Terry was telling us about a home that is also part of the course. We'd like to go over there this morning, and take a look at it." George said.

"We can meet you at 'We Care' in ten minutes, George. If that's okay with you." Justin said.

"That's fine with us, Justin. We'll see you there, in about ten minutes." George said.

When the United Families arrived at the 'We Care' facilities, Branden and his parents were already there.

"Good morning, George. How are you and your family this morning?" I asked.

"We're doing fantastic, Tom. Especially after what Terry told us last night, about the house." George said.

"Actually George, Terry couldn't think of the right words, to describe it. That's why he excused himself, and left the room for a few minutes." Anya said.

"Why did he leave the room?" Justin asked.

"He went to his office, and brought back this pamphlet. It's the description of the house." Anya said, as she handed it to Justin.

The home is located, and centered on ten acres of timberland. Many of the trees on this land are, oak, black cherry, and black walnut. Several pieces of fine furniture located in the home have been artistically designed, and crafted from some of those trees.

It is a beautiful two-story brick home, with an upper rear deck, that overlooks the magnificent courtyard.

As you enter through the twelve-foot, black wrought iron, entrance gate, you are greeted by the grandeur of the home.

The entrance driveway is made of asphalt, and has a six-inch concrete base. In the center of the driveway's circle, is a beautifully lighted fountain.

The first main room you come to, upon entering the house, is the living room. Here you will see a beautiful grandfather clock made from solid black walnut. In the center of the room, accenting it with a touch of royalty is an eloquent crystal chandelier.

In addition to the clock, and chandelier, is a magnificent double-faced fireplace. This fireplace provides warmth and comfort, to both the living room and family room.

The grandfather clock which stands six feet tall, along with the crystal chandelier, will without a doubt, become a conversation topic between you and your quests.

Moving from the living room, into the family room, we see yet another beautiful sight.

The first thing we notice is the deep luxurious carpet. The carpet is so luxurious, that it seems to cry out an unspoken invitation, to the weary family member to lie down on it, for a nap.

The room's existing furniture includes a ten feet long, trophy case made from black cherry.

The patio doors in the room, lead out onto a wrap around patio, which overlooks the beautiful courtyard.

The beautiful winding staircase, reaches from the luxurious family room, to the upper floor.

The next room we come to is the recreation room.

For those of you that enjoy playing a good game of billiards, there is a professional size table.

If you'd like to practice your putting instead, there is a nine hole putting green outside of the recreation room. This putting green is located next to the patio, which allows the spectators to relax while watching.

The downstairs bathroom is located in the recreation room.

Leaving the recreation room, we enter into the dinning room. Here we see the high quality, artistically designed oak dinning table, and chairs.

The room is lighted by an eloquent crystal chandelier, which is controlled by a variable dimmer switch. The ability to regulate the brightness of the light, gives the family the opportunity to have a romantic dinner, if they desire.

The next room is the kitchen. This fully modern kitchen is equipped with a center island, and built in appliances. With the abundance of space in this room, meal preparation is greatly simplified.

Upstairs, there are five bedrooms, two baths, and a den.

The master bedroom has its own bath, while the other bedrooms share a bath.

The den is furnished with solid black cherry furniture, and bookshelves. Also in the den, is a safe for the family's valuables.

In addition to the beautiful courtyard and fountain, there is also a three-car garage.

"If this description is correct, then that home is absolutely beautiful." Justin said.

"That's what we were thinking too, Justin. Let's go on over there, and take a look at it." Anya said, with a smile.

Chapter 9

When the families turned into the driveway, they were greeted by the view of the magnificent home.

With landscaping, that had been professionally laid out, and meticulously manicured; the home looked fabulous.

Once inside of the home, George and his family were immediately awestruck by the home's interior beauty.

The viewing of the home had taken over an hour to complete, due to the many questions that had been asked.

When the family had finally finished viewing the home, Branden asked.

"Dad, this house is beautiful. When the sale is final, can we give it a name?"

"That's a great idea, son. Do you have any ideas, what we could call it?" George asked.

"Yes I do dad, but I'd like for it to be a family decision." Branden said.

"What do you think we should call it, son?" Anya asked.

"I was thinking that 'Havencrest Estates' would be a good name. The word haven refers to a sheltered safe place, or refuge. The word crest refers to the top of a hill or ridge. Since the house sits on the top of a ridge, 'Havencrest' would be one idea." Branden said.

"I love that name, son. What do you think of it, George?" Anya asked.

"I think it's a fantastic name. We could call our home 'Havencrest Estates', and the golf course 'Havencrest Country Club'." George said, with a smile.

"I like those names, dad. With the names being similar, it will let people know that the two are connected, in some way." Branden said.

"Now that we've seen the house, and decided on a name for it, let's go and eat some breakfast." Anya said.

"That's a great idea, mom. I'm really starting to get hungry." Branden said.

"Terry, now that we're on our way back to 'We Care', there's something that I've been meaning to ask you." Were you able to get a meeting scheduled with the sellers?" Anya asked.

"Yes I was, Anya. They said that they will meet with you and George at two o'clock today, in the banquet room." Terry said.

"Dad, would it be possible to get the news media involved, so the public will know about the signing?" Branden asked.

"That would be a good idea son, but I don't know anyone, at either one of the stations." George said.

"George, I'm good friends with the managers at both of the stations. If you would like for me to, I could make those arrangements for you." I said.

"If you'd do that for us Tom, we'd appreciate it." George said.

"I know someone else that would like to be there too." Justin said.

"Who are you referring to, Justin?" Anya asked.

"Everyone knows her as Judge Riley, Anya. If for any reason, we would have to go to court about the sale, then she'll be the presiding judge." Justin said.

"That's a great idea, son. I know she really helped us a lot, while we were getting 'We Care' organized." I said.
That is a great idea, Justin. Could you give her a call when we get back to 'We Care', and invite her to the meeting?" Anya asked.

"It would be my pleasure, Anya. Dad and I will make our phone calls while you and your family are eating breakfast." Justin said.

After getting out of the car in front of 'We Care', Branden said.

"I can smell breakfast all the way out here. It sure smells good."

"It sure does, Branden. I can even smell the cinnamon rolls baking." Alex said, with a smile.

"Son, if you and the other boys are still hungry; you can go get something to eat, if you want to. We'll join you in a few minutes." I said.

"I'm not really hungry dad, but I always have room for one of those delicious cinnamon rolls, topped with icing." Alex said, with a smile.

"I know what you mean Alex, I like them too. Just do us a favor, and save us a couple." Justin said.

"We'll try to bro., but we can't promise that we'll be able to." Alex said.

While everyone else went to the cafeteria to get something to eat, Tom and Justin went to the office to make their calls. When their calls were completed, they rejoined the rest of the United Families, at the head-table.

"Tom, it sure didn't take you and Justin very long to make your calls. I hope you don't have any bad news for us." George said.

"No George it's not bad news, it's all good. The managers at both stations have agreed to have their reporters at the signing. They also informed me, that they will be interrupting their regular scheduled broadcast, for a live coverage of the events." I said.

"That's fantastic, Tom. That is even more coverage, then I had expected. What did you find out, Justin?" George asked.

"My conversation with Judge Riley was very interesting, George. Along with agreeing to attend the signing, she will also be bringing some important documents." Justin said.

"Did the judge say what type of documents that she was referring to?" Anya asked.

"Yes she did, Anya. She is going to bring the completed title, deed, and abstract searches, for both the house, and golf course." Justin said.

"I've always thought those searches took thirty days to complete." Tim said.

"Normally they do Tim, but not when Judge Riley gets involved. She agreed to clear her schedule for today, and work on expediting the paperwork for George's family." Justin said.

"Why would she do something like that for us, Justin? She doesn't even know us." George said, confused.

"That's just how Judge Riley is, George. Whenever something comes up that pertains to the 'United Families', Judge Riley will do anything she can to help them." Justin said.

"Judge Riley sounds like a wonderful person, Justin. I'm looking forward to meeting her, this afternoon." Anya said.

While the United Families were eating their breakfast, Mr. Avery stood up to make the morning announcements.
"Good morning, everyone."
"This morning's announcements are very important, so I'll need everyone's up-most attention."
"As I'm sure most of you already know, Branden's parents will be buying the 'Putt and Go', this afternoon. They have invited all of us here at 'We Care' to attend the event, and we have accepted their invitation.

When Mr. Avery announced that everyone at 'We Care' was invited to the signing events, the entire cafeteria erupted in a window rattling jubilation.
It had taken Mr. Avery almost ten minutes to regain control of the situation, and calm the assembly down, when he said.

"Thank you everyone, for that show of appreciation. I would like to turn the announcements over to Steven at this time. He'll be telling you about this afternoon's activities, and what will be expected from each of you."

"Thank you for that introduction, dad."
"Good morning, everyone. I would like to talk to you about this afternoon's activities, and how we will be playing a roll in it.
First, I have been informed that due to the afternoon's activities, lunch will be served at eleven, instead of twelve. This change was made to allow us enough time to change our clothes, and get organized, before we leave for the golf course." Steven said.

"Steven, since this is going to be an important event for us, can we wear our school uniforms?" Jeff asked, hopefully.

"That's a great idea, Jeff. I really enjoy seeing all of you boys on your uniforms. The light blue slacks, and dark blue blazers, are a very prestigious combination." Karen said, with a smile.

"I agree with Karen, Steven. The uniforms, would definitely, add an extra touch of class this afternoon, to the activities. They would also look nice on the boys during the live T.V. broadcast that will be there too." Justin said.

"Then that's settled. We will be wearing our school uniforms, and doing it with pride." Steven said, proudly.

"This afternoon, once everyone has finished eating lunch, and changed into their uniform, we'll re-assemble outside of the cafeteria, by the memorial fountain. Then, once we are organized into several smaller groups, we will walk from there over to the 'Putt and Go'.

By the time we get there, Branden and his parents will be meeting with the sellers, in the banquet room. However, since it is a business meeting, only those authorized to be in the banquet room, will be allowed to enter it. Even though we won't be able to enter the banquet room, we'll still be able to see what's happening, through the windows." Steven said.

"What windows are you talking about, Steven? I'm sure Branden's parents won't want us hovering around the door, like a flock of vultures." Aaron said.

"I'm sorry, Aaron. I should have been more precise about the windows that I was referring to. The ones that I was referring to are the ones facing the patio, outside of the banquet room." Steven said.

"How will we find out when the sale is final, Steven?" Aaron asked.

"Branden will let us know. When the sale is final, and they own the course, he will come outside and make the official announcement." Steven said.

"Steven, did I hear Uncle Justin right, earlier? Is the T.V. station going to be there and broadcasting live?" Jeff asked.

"Yes, you heard him right, Jeff. That is why; all of us must be on our best behavior this afternoon. After all, we will be representing 'We Care' and Branden's family too." Steven said.

"Dad, that's everything I need to cover. Do any of you have anything, you'd like to add?" Steven asked.

"No, son. That should be everything that we need to cover at this time. If the boys are finished eating, they may be dismissed. Remind them however, that we'll see them at eleven, for lunch." Mr. Avery said.

"Okay everyone, that's all of the announcements for this morning. Before I dismiss you though, I would like to suggest that you stop by our in house cleaners and pickup your uniforms. By picking it up between now and lunch, it will save valuable time after lunch. You are now dismissed. Oh, by the way, don't forget that lunch is at eleven." Steven said, as an after thought.

The members of the in house cleaning staff knew that Steven's dismissal applied to them also. Having the authority to use the side door of the cafeteria, the staff members were waiting at the counter, when the boys began arriving.

Within five minutes, approximately one hundred boys were waiting in line, to get their uniforms.

Alex, Johnny, and the other boys of the 'United Families' had remained in the cafeteria to finish their breakfast. When they finally left the cafeteria, they were stunned at the sight of the long waiting line in front of the cleaners.

"Wow Steven! I'm sure glad I don't have a uniform to pick up. It's going to take an hour, or longer, to go through that line." Branden said.

"Oh, I'm sorry Branden. I must have forgotten to tell you, but you do have one." Steven said, with a sly grin.

"Steven, why are you boys standing way back here, at the end of the line?" Mrs. Avery asked, as she approached the boys.

"Oh, hi mom. We're waiting our turn to get our uniforms." Steven said.

"You boys should've already known this, but none of you have to wait in line. That is one of the benefits, of being a staff member. Follow me, and we'll go inside the cleaners, and get your uniforms." Mrs. Avery said.

The time between breakfast and lunch had passed quickly. When the last boy had picked up his uniform, and had turned to leave the cleaners, the lunch bell rang.

When everyone had filled their plates, and had sat down to eat, Steven stood up to make the noon announcements.

"May I have your attention, please? There are a couple of things I need to tell you, while you're eating."

"When you have finished eating, you're dismissed from the table, and may go change into your uniforms.

Then, after you have changed into your uniforms, we will need for all of you to gather together outside, near the memorial fountain.

Once everyone is gathered together by the fountain, we will break off into smaller groups. Each of those groups will consist of fifty boys each." Steven said.

"Why do we need to form groups of fifty, Steven? Wouldn't it be easier, if we just walked over there in single file?" Jeff asked.

"That's one way that we could have done it Jeff, but we decided against it. We feel that by using the group method, that it would provide the answer to two very important questions." Steven said.

"What questions are those, Steven?" Jeff asked.

"What is the quickest and easiest way, to move a group of people from one point to another? We also want to maintain a sense of organization, and prestige, among the groups while in formation." Steven explained.

"Thank you, Steven. Now I understand why the military uses that method. It's the best method." Jeff said.

"Okay boys, I'll let you finish eating now. We'll see all of you outside, when you're finished." Steven said.

Due to the boy's love for great tasting food, most meals in the past, had taken at least forty-five minutes to complete. Today however, that record was shattered when the last boy stood up, and left the table, after only twenty minutes.

Outside, and approximately forty-five minutes later, the groups had all been established, which included a leader for each group. The assigned leaders were, Steven, Alex, Johnny, Danny, and Billy.

Finally, after some last minute instructions, it was now time to start their walk over to the 'Putt and Go'.

While Steven and the leaders were escorting the boys to the golf course, Andy noticed a breath taking, but scary sight.

"Steven! Look at all of those funnel clouds over there in the sky. There must be over one hundred of them." Andy said.

"There are over a hundred of them, Andy. I spotted them a couple of minutes ago, and counted them. Unless I miscounted, there are one hundred sixty seven of them." Jeff said.

"I wonder if those clouds are friends with the ones we saw on the ninth tee box yesterday." Andy asked.

"I'm sure they are Andy. There are more of them today, because this time they'll be repairing the entire golf course." Alex said.

"It looks like they're heading for the clubhouse. Let's hurry up, and get over there. I don't want to miss any of the action." Aaron said, with excitement.

Chapter 10

As the boys from 'We Care' were approaching the 'Putt and Go', Branden saw them and made a comment to his parents.

"Hey mom, and dad. Here comes Steven, and the rest of the boys. Look how great their uniforms look, with the sunlight hitting them. It's like the uniforms are actually radiating the sunrays back off of them." Branden said.

"That's true, son. Have you noticed anything else about the uniforms, as the boys are walking up and down those small ridges?" George asked.

"No I haven't, dad. What exactly, are you referring to?" Branden asked.

"Look closely at the overall view of them. What does it remind you of?" George asked.

"Oh, now I see what you're talking about, dad. With the boys walking up and down those little hills, and wearing that shade of blue, they look like small ocean waves. When they get here, can I go outside and talk to Alex and Steven, for a little while?" Branden asked.

"Yes son that will be fine with us. The sellers will not be here for almost another hour, so you will not be missing anything. Justin however, will be arriving in about fifteen minutes with Judge Riley." George said.

"I should be back, before they get here. It looked to me like the boys were looking at something in the sky, a couple of minutes ago. I want to find out what it was, if anything." Branden said.

"Okay, son. Just be sure to come back inside, and let us know what you find out." Anya said.

"Hi Steven. Hi Alex." Branden said, greeting the boys.

"Hi Branden. Why are you outside? We thought you'd be inside with your parents, when we got here." Steven said.

"I was inside, until we saw you boys coming across the yard. That's when I came outside, to find out what most of the boys were looking at in the sky." Branden said.

"We were looking at all of those funnel clouds, over there. They must be getting ready to repair the golf course." Steven said.

"I think you're right about that, Steven. With that many clouds doing the repairing, it shouldn't take very long." Branden said, with a smile.

"Here comes our dads', Alex. That man with them must be from the T.V. station." Steven said.

"I better get back inside, Steven. I told my parents that I wouldn't be out here very long." Branden said.

"Okay, Branden. We'll see you when you come back out, to make the announcement." Steven said.

By the time that Branden had gotten back inside, the sellers had arrived, and were ready to start the meeting.

He was hoping to be able to tell his parents and Uncle Justin about the clouds, but was unable to.

"I can't tell them about the clouds now, so I'll wait until the meeting is over." Branden thought to himself.

Branden had been expecting the meeting to last for at least four hours. He knew that four hours was the customary length of time, for a business meeting. He received a pleasant surprise however, when it came to a successful conclusion after only two hours.
With an excited look of anticipation on his face, Branden awaited his dad's signal.

"Son, you may make the announcement now." George said, with a smile.

Expecting to make his announcement when he stepped outside, Branden was greeted by some unexpected confusion.

"Steven! Steven! Look at the clouds! What do you think they're doing?" Shouted Andy.

Apparently, the funnel clouds had sensed Branden's forth-coming announcement. Because suddenly, they had began swooping, swirling, dodging, and dipping with excitement.
The movements of the clouds were fascinating to watch. So fascinating in fact, that Branden excused himself and ran back inside to tell his parents.

"Mom. Dad. I know you're not going to believe this, but there are over one hundred funnel clouds in the sky, and they're dancing." Branden said, with excitement.

"Did you say dancing, son?" Anya asked.

"Yes I did, mom. That's what it looks like to me, at least." Branden said.

"I'd like to see that, George. Since we're almost finished here, let's all take a short break, and go see what Branden is talking about." Anya suggested.

"I'd like to see it too, Anya. Justin, you and Judge Riley are more then welcome to join us, if you'd like." George said.

"The sight of a dancing cloud isn't a sight we can see everyday, George. We'll be right behind you." Justin said, with a smile.

When George, and the rest of the group, stepped outside of the building, they were amazed at the sight of the dancing clouds.
While they continued watching the clouds, Tom, Mr. Avery, and the T.V. broadcasting crew joined them.

"That's quite an impressive sight, isn't it George?" I asked.

"Yes it is, Tom. I've never seen anything like it before, in my life." George said.

"George, Tom and I have been showing the T.V. crew around a little bit. They have been getting some excellent footage of the clouds, their antics, and then broadcasting them live to the public." Mr. Avery said.

"They have also taken some footage of the present conditions of the tee boxes, fairway, and green on number one." I said.

"Mr. Avery is right, George. We have been getting some excellent footage of the clouds. Our viewers however, are getting anxious to see what the clouds are going to do. Do you have any idea, when they will start performing their miraculous repair job?" The reporter asked.

"If I was to make a guess, I would say that they are waiting for Branden's official announcement. With all of the confusion going on right now, he hasn't had a chance to make it yet. If you'll excuse me please, I'll get things calmed down, so he can." George said.

After George had calmed the crowd down, and had introduced Branden, Branden began his announcement.

"Good afternoon, everyone. On behalf of my parents and myself, I'd like to welcome each of you to this afternoon's events."
"I especially want to welcome our guests of honor, the funnel clouds. They will be doing some major repair on the course, in a few minutes. We do ask however, that you do not approach any of the clouds, while they are touching the ground."
"Now, without further ado, it gives me great pleasure to announce that my parents have purchased the 'Putt and Go'." Branden said, with a smile.

With Branden's announcement now completed, there arose such jubilation among the crowd, that it was heard for miles around.
In addition, as prearranged and agreed upon, the entire group of funnel clouds swooped gracefully to the ground, at the conclusion of Branden's announcement. When they were on the ground and ready, each one of them, began spinning furiously.
With over one hundred funnel clouds on the ground, it seemed as if they were everywhere you looked. That is because they were.
The funnel cloud's flamboyant repair project was providing a spectacular show for the crowd. So spectacular in fact, that one of the younger boys in the crowd was overheard to say.

"This is the greatest show, I've ever seen. It's even better then my favorite cartoon show."

Among the crowd of boys were Danny, and Billy from the 'United Families'. Curious about something, Billy turned to Danny, and asked.

"Danny, do you think they'll fix the entire course, like they did the tee boxes on number nine?" Billy asked.

"Yes I do, Billy. My friend Jimmy is one of those clouds, and he has already said that they will be fixing it, the same way." Danny said.

The clouds had been working for about twenty minutes, when Branden made the following announcement to the crowd.

"May I have everyone's attention, please? It appears, as if the clouds have started watering their repaired areas. Watering of the repaired areas is the final step of their repairing process. It should not be long now, before they are finished. When they have finished, my dad will make the announcement." Branden said.

Approximately ten more minutes had passed, when George stepped up to the microphone.

"May I have your attention, please? At this time, I am proud to announce that the clouds have finished their repair work. On behalf of my family, and myself, I'd like to extend our heartfelt appreciation to each and every one of the clouds."

"In a few minutes, my family and I, along with the entire staff from 'We Care', will be making an inspection tour of the course. I have also invited the T.V. crew to ride along with us, so they can show you the live results of the clouds repair work"

"For those of you remaining here while we're gone, there will be refreshments served here on the patio. Thank you for your attention."

As George and the rest of the inspection team were boarding their golf carts, a familiar voice rang out.

"Hey George, you're not leaving without us, are you?"

"Oh, hi Lee. I wasn't aware that you and your evaluation team were here. When did you arrive?" George asked.

"We've been here since the beginning of your event, George. We heard that you and your family were buying this course, and wanted to check it out. We wanted to see if it is worthy of a five star rating." Lee said, with a smile.

"Thanks a lot for coming, Lee. We appreciate your interest in our course." Anya said.

After the formal introductions had been made, George and the inspection team, set out across the course, to inspect it.

During the inspection, each member of the inspection team was closely scrutinizing the new condition of the course. They were amazed at how beautiful it was now, compared to its previous condition.

The sand in the bunkers, which had been lusterless and dingy, now sparkled anew with color, and beauty.

The previous, radically destroyed condition of the tee boxes, fairways, and greens, now flaunted a deep rich, and luxurious carpet of divotless green grass.

The inspection had taken approximately forty-five minutes to complete. While the team was traveling back to the clubhouse, Anya said.

"I think the course looks fantastic now, George. What do you think?"

"I think it does too, Anya. When do you and Branden, think we should open it to the public?" George asked.

"I think we should open it, as soon as possible." Branden said, with a smile.

"I agree with you, son. Would tomorrow be soon enough?" Anya asked.

"Yes it would be, mom. In fact, it would be great." Branden said, with excitement.

"Then that decision is settled. We open the course to the public, tomorrow." George said.

"What time are you going to open it to the public, George?" Lee asked.

We will begin our Grand Opening celebration at ten o'clock. Then at one o'clock, my family and I will be the first people to tee off, followed by the 'United Families'." George said.

"When we get back to the patio, we'll make the official announcement about the Grand Opening." Anya said.

"George, if it's okay with you, I'd like to make an announcement too, after you have finished with yours." Lee said, with a smile.

"Yes Lee, that would be fine with us." George said.

Once the team had arrived back at the patio, George stepped up to the microphone to make his announcement. After telling the crowd and the T.V. audience about the Grand Opening ceremonies, he said.

"Several people have already asked my family and me, if the course will continue to be known as the 'Putt and Go'. I am proud to say, that it will not be. The new name that my family and I have chosen is, 'The Havencrest Country Club'. That concludes my portion of the announcements, but a friend of mine would like to say a few words to you also." George said.

"Thank you, George. As most of you may already know, George is a world renowned golf course designer."
"My team and I have had the privilege many times of visiting, and evaluating the courses that he has designed. Many of those courses have been awarded the five star mark of excellence. This award is given to golf courses based on the excellent conditions of the course, and its beauty. However, there is also an honorary, six stars mark of excellence award, which is given when the course exceeds a five star ranking. In all the history of the game of golf, there have only been three such awards given. That is, until today."
"George, it is with great honor that we present this honorary, six star mark of excellence to you, your family, and 'The Havencrest Country Club. Congratulations." Lee said, with a smile.

"Well, this is quite a surprise, Lee. On behalf of my family and myself, I'd like to say thank you, to you and your team." George said.

"Ladies and gentlemen, that concludes our events for today. We would be honored to see all of you here tomorrow, at the Grand Opening of the new 'Havencrest Country Club'. Until tomorrow, good night." George said.

Chapter 11

The night prior to the grand opening ceremonies proved to be a very busy time for Terry, Michael, and several of their friends. They had spent most of the night constructing a raised platform in front of the clubhouse, for the ceremonies. The platform had been built so elaborately, that it would have met even the most rigid requirements, of any king, or monarch.

In addition to the many various ribbons, banners, and flags that the platform was adorned with, there was also a full public address system.

Included in the adornment of the platform, were five potted flowers. These potted flowers however, would, without a doubt, bring confusion to people's minds.

Centered, and spaced evenly along the front edge of the platform, were five large potted dandelion plants, in full bloom. Confused, about why anyone would want potted dandelion plants at a grand opening ceremony, Michael asked.

"Terry, why does George want these dandelion plants on the platform?"

"I wondered the same thing at first Michael, so I asked him. The only thing that he would tell me was, 'They are in memory of a loved one'." Terry said.

"Well Terry, now that the potted flowers are in place, is there anything else we need to do?" Michael asked.

"No, there isn't, Michael. That is everything for tonight, so I will see you in the morning. Thank you everyone, for your help tonight." Terry said, as he headed for his car, and home.

The weather the following morning was beautiful. The sun was shinning bright, with light and variable winds. With only a few puffy white clouds drifting lazily across the sky, it was an excellent day for a game of golf, and the grand opening ceremonies.

Having the desire to get a spot close to the ceremony's platform, people began arriving as early as eight thirty.

Within an hour however, several hundred people had shown up for the ceremonies. Amongst the crowd, were the boys and staff from 'We Care', many of the people from the local community, and the T.V. crew.

When ten o'clock finally arrived, George and his family, stepped up to the podium, to begin the ceremonies. With Anya to his right, and Branden to his left, George stepped up to the microphone.

"Good morning everyone, and welcome to the grand opening ceremonies, of the new, 'Havencrest Country Club'."

"My family and I, along with our staff, feel that you'll be surprised at what you'll learn here today."

"First, and foremost, our goal here at the 'Havencrest Country Club', is to make it the best played, and most famous, golf course in the nation."

"We feel that it's because of the previous high prices, and poor maintenance, that has caused this course to lose many of its valuable customers. I am proud to announce that those problems have been eliminated. Starting today, the prices for open play have been reduced by five percent, while the price for an annual membership, has been reduced by fifteen percent." George said, followed by a roar of applause from the crowd.

When the applause had subsided, George continued.

"In addition to the price decreases, we will be offering a variety of events, and competitions. These will include both children, and adult divisions."

"One specific area that we will be concentrating on is the children's division. Branden will be in charge of this division, and will be working closely with his mother and I. Together we will strive to make the 'Havencrest Country Club's' children's division, the best in the nation. In addition to being in charge of that division, Branden, along with his friend Steven, will also be offering golfing lessons to children, who have the desire to learn the game."

"At this time, I'd like to turn the microphone over to Branden, who will tell you more of his ideas, for the children's division." George said.

"Thank you dad, for that introduction."

Ladies and gentlemen of all ages, today is the beginning, of some new and exciting times, here at the 'Havencrest Country Club'.

As a young adult and golfer, I have visited many different golf courses in my life. I am sorry to say however, that many of those courses lacked sufficient, if any, children's divisions.

We all know, even as children, that if children are not kept busy with some sort of activity, that they will soon become bored and uncontrollable. That is why; I have decided to make it my own personal goal, to assure that boredom does not become a problem, here at this course. I believe that by providing a variety of weekly activities for the children, that goal is achievable. In addition to the weekly activities, we will also be hosting several tournaments, throughout the season.

In a couple of weeks, we will be hosting our first major event, here at the 'Havencrest Country Club'. This event will be an open play tournament, for anyone under the age of eighteen. The planning stage for that tournament will begin tomorrow morning at nine o'clock. Anyone interested in participating in the tournament, is encouraged to sign up as soon as possible, starting tomorrow afternoon.

The next major event, that we will be hosting, will be held on the second weekend in May. Currently, we do not have a name for that event, but will announce it as soon as we do. We do know however, that it will be a fund raising event, with all of the proceeds going to the 'Anya Foundation', in Irvine California.

We also know that it will be an annual event, here at the 'Havencrest Country Club'.

Noticing that Alex had raised his hand, Branden asked.

"Alex, do you have a question?"

"Yes I do, Branden. You have told us before, that you will be playing in a tournament in California, the first weekend in May. Will you be back in time, to play in the tournament that you just mentioned?" Alex asked.

"Yes Alex, we'll be back in plenty of time. My parents and I, always fly whenever we are traveling. We should be back, no later then Wednesday evening." Branden said.

After answering Alex's question, Branden continued.

"Ladies and gentlemen, that concludes my portion of the opening ceremonies. I am looking forward, to working with all of you, in the coming days. At this time, I'd like to turn the microphone, back over to my dad." Branden said with a smile, and a wave.

While George was getting up out of his chair to walk to the podium, the funnel clouds suddenly appeared above the crowd. Knowing that the clouds were harmless, the crowd remained calm. When George had stepped up to the microphone, he said.

"Ladies and gentlemen, it appears that our cloud friends have joined us, for the ribbon cutting ceremonies. Let's give them a round of applause, for the work they have done, here on the course." George said.

The crowd complied with George's request, with enthusiasm and exuberance. Their ear splitting cheers and applause were so loud, that they rattled the clubhouse windows.

In an attempt to regain the crowd's attention, but failing, George continued to wait a little longer. Finally, after waiting for about ten minutes, the crowd once again became quiet. After stepping up to the ribbon with the family, Anya said.

"Ladies and gentlemen, once we have cut the ribbon, we would like for you to join us on the patio, for the reception. During the reception, you will have the opportunity to meet the staff and their families, and to ask any questions that you may have." Anya said.

As George's family prepared to cut the ribbon, the high school band began to softly play, one of Branden's own personal compositions. Once the ribbon had been cut, George said.

"Ladies and gentlemen, I'm proud to announce that the 'Havencrest Country Club', is now open to the public. We're looking forward to seeing all of you on the patio, in a few minutes."

Gathering as a group on the patio, the staff members took a few minutes to greet each other, and their family members.

"Good morning, Michelle. Who is that pretty little girl, standing behind you?" Anya asked.

"That's my ten year old daughter, Reilly. She's a little shy sometimes, when it comes to meeting new people." Michelle said, with a smile.

"That's okay, Reilly. I use to be the same way, until I started playing golf. Do you play golf?" Branden asked, as he held out his hand in friendship.

While shaking hands with Branden, Reilly said.

"I'd like to play, but I don't know how."

"Steven and I would be happy to teach you, if it's okay with your mom." Branden said.

"She would like that, Branden. When will you begin giving lessons?" Michelle asked.

"We hope to get started, a week from today. With you being part of the staff though, we could start giving Reilly lessons, tomorrow afternoon." Branden said.

"Thank you, Branden. Let us know what time you want to get started, and we'll be here." Michelle said.

"Okay Michelle, we'll let you know. Well George, we still have to get something to eat, and then mingle with the crowd." Anya said.

The next two hours had passed quickly, when Steven stepped up to the microphone, to make a special announcement. After introducing himself to the crowd by name, and as a friend of Branden's, he said.

"Ladies and gentlemen, in approximately thirty minutes, we will begin a very special segment of these ceremonies. This segment will be a very solemn and quiet portion of the ceremonies. During that time, Branden will be playing several of his own piano compositions."
"To show our respect to the family, we ask that you remain as quiet as possible, during that time." Steven said.

Not having any idea, what Steven was referring to, George and Anya turned toward Branden, and asked.

"What's this all about, son?" George asked.

"It's an extension of the potted plant idea, dad. Steven, and I were talking last night, and he suggested the idea to me. He suggested that I play several of my piano songs, as a tribute to our loved one." Branden said, with a smile.

"That's a great idea, son. Are there any other surprises, we should know about?" George asked.

"I'm not sure yet, dad. Steven did say however, that he was going to ask his dad to talk to a friend of his at the air force base, about something." Branden said.

"I wonder what that was about." Anya asked.

"I'm not sure, mom. The only thing I remember was, it had something to do with a fly over." Branden said.

"I'm sure whatever Mr. Avery, and Steven has in mind, that it will be in good taste." George said.

"I'm positive it will be, dad. Neither Steven, nor his dad, would do anything that would bring disrespect to our family."

"I don't mean to rush off mom and dad, but it's time for me to get ready." Branden said.

"Okay, son. We'll see you after your recital." Anya said.

After putting on his dark blue blazer, and picking up his song- book, Branden headed off toward his piano.

The piano, which was a luxurious, and beautiful black ebony, sat in the middle of the highly decorated outdoor stage.

Among the decorations, and placed every ten feet around the stage, were many national flags. These flags had been placed on height adjustable masts, with a boy from 'We Care' stationed at each one.

When the time came to begin the special portion of the ceremonies, Steven stepped up to the microphone, and said.

"Ladies and gentlemen, it is now time for us to begin the solemn segment of these ceremonies."

"At this time it gives me great honor, to introduce our friend Branden, at the piano. Branden began playing the piano at the early age of three, and by the time he was eleven, he had already written, and composed, his very first piano music. Since then, he has written, composed many new songs, and played in several concerts around the world. Personally, I consider his music to be the best, I've ever heard."

"Prior to Branden's last song for this afternoon, there will be a special announcement by General Smith, from the local air force base. Now without further ado, and for your listening enjoyment, here's Branden."

As Branden began playing his first selection of the afternoon, the boys from 'We Care' began lowering the national flags, to half-mast. His professional playing abilities, combined with his wonderful music, were awe inspiring to the crowd.

For the next twenty minutes, Branden had no problem of holding a captivated audience. With mouths a gaped, the audience had been spell bound, by Branden's music.

While Branden was turning the pages to his final selection, General Smith stepped up to the microphone.

"Ladies and gentlemen, my name is General Smith, and I'm the commanding officer at the local air force base."

"I have been asked, and given the honor, of announcing the title of Branden's next selection. Before I do that though, I'd like to say a few words."

"When Mr. Avery called me yesterday, and explained the purpose of this special segment, I was touched deeply. It was at that time, I offered the services of the air force flying team, stationed at our base."

"It is with great respect to George and his family, that I have authorized that flying team to make a fly over, here at the 'Havencrest Country Club'. When the team flies over our location, they will be flying in the missing person formation."

"At this time, I'm proud to turn the stage back over to Branden, who will be playing his own composition entitled, *"Missing You"." The General said.

When the General had finished speaking, and before Branden had started playing, the roar of approaching jets could be heard in the distant sky.

Shortly after Branden started playing, his music had once again, captivated most of his audience. The only person that he had not captivated however, was a little boy named Andy. Andy admired the sight of a flying jet, so he was to busy watching the sky, to be captivated.

When Branden was nearing the end of his selection, Andy noticed the vapor trails of the fast approaching jets. While tugging on his dad's shirt-sleeve to get his attention, Andy was jumping up and down, and pointing toward the rapidly approaching jets.

The arrival of the jets and the ending of Branden's song had worked out perfectly. For when the last note of the song was softly sounding, the jets were making their final approach.

With all eyes turned toward the sky, the crowd watched solemnly as the jet formation, passed overhead. When the jets were out of sight, Branden once again joined his parents at the podium. Stepping up to the microphone, George said.

"Ladies and gentlemen, that was a very impressive segment of the ceremonies. On behalf of myself, and my family, I would like to thank those of you that helped to arrange it. I'd also like to thank all of you, for giving my son your undivided attention, while he was playing." George said.

"George, I think most of us, if not all of us, really enjoyed your son's music. Will there ever be a time; we'll hear him play again?" The General asked.

"That's a decision that we'll have to leave up to him, sir. So unfortunately, I can't answer your question, at this time." George said.

Turning, and whispering to his mom, Branden said.

"Mom, I'd be happy to play for the people again. Maybe we could have a miniature concert after the tournament, the second weekend in May." Branden said.

"That's a great idea, son. Let's get your dad's attention, and tell him your idea." Anya said, with a smile.

After getting George's attention, George excused himself from the microphone, to speak to his family. When the conversation with his family had ended, George returned to the microphone, with a smile on his face.

"Ladies and gentlemen, Branden would like to personally answer General Smith's question. So at this time, I'd like to turn the microphone over to him." George said.

Approaching the microphone, Branden was astonished at the standing ovation that he received. Assuming that the applause would end shortly, Branden waited, and waited.

Turning toward his parents, with a confused look on his face, he asked.

"What should I do, mom? They won't stop applauding."

"That's their way of showing you, they enjoyed your music, son. Be polite to them, and take a bow. Then step up to the microphone, and thank them. Doing it that way, will normally regain your audience's attention, and they'll let you speak." Anya said, with a smile.

"Okay mom, I'll try that." Branden said.

"Anya, I think our son has a fan club." George said, with a smile.

"I believe you're right, George. We'll know for sure, after he finishes his announcement." Anya said.

When the audience's applause had finally subsided, Branden stepped back up to the microphone, to make the announcement. The crowd with an enthusiastic applause received his announcement of an upcoming concert.

Knowing now, how to show his appreciation to the crowd, Branden took his final bow, waved to the crowd, and stepped away from the podium.

While Branden was walking away from the podium, George was walking toward it. After stepping up to the microphone, George said.

"Ladies and gentlemen, it is now time to bring our opening ceremonies to a close. For those of you that play, we invite you to sign up for a tee time, and a wonderful afternoon of golf. Until we meet again, Happy Golfing.

Chapter 12

While George and his family were preparing for their afternoon game of golf, Branden noticed several more camera crews walking on to the patio. Wondering why there were so many of them now, Branden asked.

"Dad, have you noticed all of the camera crews that have shown up? There are about a dozen of them now." Branden said.

"No, I haven't son. I knew that they were going to be here though, because Lee told me about it yesterday." George said.

"I wonder why there are so many of them?" Branden asked.

"Because it's our grand opening son, and also because we were awarded the six star mark of excellence." George said.

Branden was getting ready to ask his dad another question, when Lee walked up to them.

"Hi, Branden. Are you going to beat your mom and dad, in a game of golf this afternoon?" Lee asked, with a smile.

"I'm going to try my best, sir. I think I can though, because I'm feeling lucky today." Branden said.

"I have no doubt that he'll beat us Lee, but don't let him fool you though. It's not luck that he has but skill, and lots of it." Anya said proudly.

"George, I don't mean to change the subject, but the camera crews are ready to get into position, and set up. Is that okay with you?" Lee asked.

"Yes, that's fine with us Lee. Tell them that we'll be ready to tee off, in about thirty minutes." George said.

As Lee was walking out to the patio, he noticed that one of the camera crews had already taken its position on a nearby hilltop.

"That's a good position." Lee thought to himself. "Not only will they be able to film things happening around the clubhouse, but people teeing off at the first tee as well."

While watching Lee, and the camera crews through the windows, Branden noticed the same initials on most of the cameras. Confused, he turned toward his parents, and asked.

"Dad, I've noticed that most of the cameras have the letters 'NSN' on them. What do those letters stand for?"

"They stand for the broadcasting networks name, son. The 'NSN' stands for the 'National Sports Network' and it's the largest sports network in the country." George said.

"Wow! That is great, dad. Does that mean we'll be on national television this afternoon?" Branden asked, with excitement.

"Yes it does, son. Today is the day, the entire nation will finally find out, how well you can play golf." George said.

"George, are you two finished talking about your national debut? If you are, then we need to get our clubs loaded up, and ready to go." Anya said, with a smile.

While George's family was loading their clubs into their cart, they were approached by a 'NSN' camera crew.

"Excuse me, sir. May I have a word with you?"

"Yes you may, sir. How can I help you?" George asked.

"My name is Jason, and I'm the supervisor of the 'NSN' camera crews. My camera crew and I were wondering if we could accompany you and your family, during your game." Jason said.

"What do you think, Anya? Would you and Branden, like to have our own camera crew this afternoon?" George asked.

"I would, dad. I think it would be great." Branden said.

"I think it would be a good idea, George. Not only would it be good advertising for us, but the people would also see that we can actually play the game." Anya said.

"Well sir, there's your answer. My family and I would be delighted, if you would join us. If you need to set up your camera, we'll be ready to tee off in about five minutes." George said.

"Thank you, sir. We won't need to set up though, because our camera is portable." Jason said.

"Son, it's almost time for us to tee off. We're going to let you go first, so go ahead and get ready." Anya said.

Even though he was nervous, and excited at the same time, Branden still had the composure of a professional golfer. Once he was ready, and knowing that he was about to make his national debut, Branden stepped on to the tee box with pride.

With sincerity and determination in his every step, Branden walked up and placed his ball on the tee. Then, with millions of eyes watching him on national T.V., Branden stepped up and addressed the ball. With the poise of a veteran world champion, Branden took aim and teed off. With his exceptionally long drive, Branden had not only started the game, but had set a new course record as well.

Four and a half hours had passed, and Branden and his parents had really enjoyed their game together. It was now time however, to make their final approach to the eighteenth hole.

Branden knew that he had been having an exceptionally good game. What lay ahead however, was going to be just one of the three biggest surprises, Branden had ever received.

"Son, you're about one hundred twenty five yards away from the green. What club are you going to use?" George asked.

"I'm going to use my seven iron, dad. I'm usually pretty good with it, from this distance." Branden said.

"That's a good choice, son. That's the one I would've chosen too." George said, with a smile.

It is a known fact that all golfers will occasionally make hits that are less then perfect. Branden would soon discover that his next shot would be one of those times.

After he had addressed the ball and began his swing, a small flock of honking geese, flew over him. Being distracted by the noise, caused him to hit the ball improperly. The improper hit which at first looked to be disastrous would soon turn in to a miracle.

Branden's hit was low, but extremely fast. Whizzing along just inches above the ground, the ball dropped even lower, as it approached the lake's edge. Maintaining its speed as it dropped on to the water's surface, the ball skipped and danced across the water.

Hitting a rock on the opposite shoreline, the ball bounced approximately twenty feet, straight up in to the air. As Branden continued to watch the flight of his ball, he was shocked when he saw a goose grab it in mid-air.

"Dad, did you see that? That goose grabbed my ball in mid-air. Now what am I going to do?" Branden asked.

"Keep watching the goose, son. It may decide to drop it." George said.

Thinking that George was talking to it, the goose dropped the ball several feet closer to the green. Landing on yet another rock, the ball once again bounced into the air. This time however, it bounced in a forward direction, and with a slight backspin.

With a look of ultimate surprise on his face, Branden watched as the ball landed behind the hole, and back-spun in to it.

"Dad, the ball finally went in to the hole. Do I count that as a single stroke?" Branden asked, confused.

"Yes you do, son. The reason that you do, is because the ball never came to a stop, before it entered the hole." George said.

Even with his big surprise on the eighteenth hole, Branden had still played an exceptionally good game. When his parents had finished their game also, all of them tallied up their scores.

When the scores had been tallied, they not only surprised Branden, but his parents as well.

"Mom, I can't believe my own eyes. If I figured up my score right, then this has been the best game, I have ever had. Could you do me a favor, and double check my figures?" Branden asked.

"Yes son, I can do that for you. I have a feeling that you're right though, because you're a straight "A" student in math." Anya said.

"What total did you come up with, son?" George asked.

"I came up with a score of sixty-seven, dad." Branden said.

"That's what I counted too, George. Congratulations, son." Anya said, as she gave Branden a hug.

"Anya, we need to go ahead and move off of the green. Tom and his group are coming up behind us. We don't want to hold them up, any longer then we have to." George said.

"That's a good idea, dad. Besides that, I'm starting to get hungry." Branden said, with a smile.

"I am too, son. Let's go get something to eat." George said.

While Branden and his parents were approaching the clubhouse, Aaron came running out from inside to meet them.

"Excuse me, sir. Terry sent me out to give you a message, and he said that it was urgent." Aaron said, gasping for breath.

"Slow down, Aaron. If you catch your breath first, it'll be easier to tell us." Anya said, in a concerned voice.

"I would Mam, but this is important. Terry wanted me to tell you that 'NSN' will be broadcasting our grand opening ceremonies, in a few minutes. They also said something about the national debut, of a very talented young golfer. I think they were referring to you Branden." Aaron said, with a smile.

"I have a feeling that Aaron is right, son. I bet they were referring to you. Let's hurry up, so we don't miss any of the broadcast." Anya said.

"Dad, could you call Uncle Tom please, and tell him about the broadcast?

I'm sure they would like to see it too." Branden said.

"That won't be necessary son, because here they come now." George said.

As they entered the clubhouse, Terry greeted Branden and his parents, with an update about the broadcast.

"Hi, Terry. Has the broadcast started yet?" Branden asked.

"No it hasn't, Branden. They made an announcement a few minutes ago though, saying that they are waiting for a phone call from their on sight supervisor. I'm not sure who they were referring to though." Terry said.

"I'm the person that they were referring to, Terry." Jason said.

"Since you're the supervisor Jason, how long will it be before you make the call?" Branden asked.

"There's still one thing I would like to do yet, before I make it." Jason said.

"What would that be?" Branden asked.

"I'd like to interview you, and your parents for the broadcast. The questions that I would be asking you would be primarily about the game that you just finished, and your hobbies."
"The questions that I would ask your parents, would be more in depth, and would pertain to the golf course. Would that be permissible with you, and your wife sir?" Jason asked.

"Yes, sir. That would be fine with us." George said.

"Thank you, sir. I'd like to start with you Branden, if I may." Jason said.

"That's fine with me, sir. I may be a little nervous at first though, because I've never been interviewed before." Branden said.

"That's okay Branden, I'm sure you'll do fine. My first question is; what sort of hobbies do you have?" Jason asked.

"I have three hobbies, sir. I enjoy playing the piano, golfing, and researching my family's genealogy." Branden said.

"Out of those three, which one do you enjoy the most?" Jason asked.

"That's a tough question, sir. I would have to say that it would be between playing the piano, and playing golf. To pick one over the other one though, would be a very difficult decision for me." Branden said.

"Here at the 'NSN', it's our goal to help young athletes, and young musicians, to make their national debut."
In a few minutes, we are going be broadcasting the grand opening ceremonies, to the entire nation. During that time, our national T.V. audience will be seeing you for the first time, while you're playing golf, and the piano."
"It's my understanding that you have already written, and composed several of your own piano selections. Is that correct?" Jason asked.

"Yes, that's correct sir. All of the piano selections that I played this afternoon were written and composed, by me." Branden said, with a smile.

"I enjoyed your music very much, Branden. Were those the only songs that you've written?" Jason asked.

"No they're not, sir. I've written over fifty songs, all together." Branden said.

"That's fantastic, Branden. I'm sure that when our broadcast is over with this evening, our network is going to be flooded with calls about your piano performance." Jason said, with a smile.

"Why would so many people call your network about me, sir?" Branden asked, confused.

"To find out if your music is available to the public." Jason said.

"It's already available to the public, sir. Both of my CD's are available online, at the 'Anya foundation's' website. They'll also be available here, at 'The Havencrest Country Club." Branden said.

"After today you'll probably be selling a lot of CD's, Branden. What do you plan on doing with all of the money, you'll be earning?" Jason asked.

"I'll be donating it to the 'Anya Foundation', sir." Branden said.

"Why would you want to do that? If you sell several thousand of them, there's going to be a lot of money involved." Jason said.

"I don't want the money for myself, sir. In addition to my own personal reasons, I want to support the foundation's mission and goals." Branden said.

"We're almost out of time for the interview Branden, but I have one more question. How can our audience find out more about the 'Anya Foundation", and purchasing your CD's?" Jason asked.

"By visiting the foundation's website sir, at http://anyafoundation.com. On behalf of my parents and myself, we believe that they'll be glad they did." Branden said.

After turning toward the camera, Jason said.

"There you have it Ladies and Gentlemen. This very talented and ambitious young man has unselfishly given of himself, to support a very worthy cause. On behalf of Branden's family and myself, I encourage each and every one of you to visit the foundation's website, and get involved."
I'm Jason, and this has been 'NSN's' coverage of the new 'Havencrest Country Club's', grand opening ceremonies. Until next time, thank you for watching, and good night.

"Now that you've concluded your interview sir, how long will it be before the broadcast?" Branden asked.

"It should be about fifteen minutes. I have to use the restroom first, and get something to drink before I make the call. When they receive my call, they'll immediately interrupt their normal programming, for this special report." Jason said.

"That's very kind of you, Jason. When did you decide to make it a special report?" Anya asked.

"I made that decision, while Branden was playing the piano, Mam. His music was so beautiful that tears actually came to my eyes. This may sound silly, but I thought I could even feel his inner pain, while he was playing." Jason said.

I am sure you could feel a small portion of it, sir. Branden has a unique ability, of putting his feelings into his music." Anya said.

"It's like I've said before, mom. I let my feelings travel through my fingertips, to the keyboard. It's the only way I know how to play, when I'm remembering our loved one." Branden said.

"Son, we better let Jason go for now. He still has a couple of things he has to do, before he makes his phone call." George said.

"Okay, dad. We will talk to you later, Jason. Thank you for everything that you've done for us, today." Branden said, as he shook hands with Jason.

"You're welcome, Branden. It was my pleasure, but I'll be looking forward to seeing you and your parents again someday soon." Jason said, before he walked away.

"George, do you think Terry would video tape the special report for us, while we're eating?" Anya asked.

"I'm one step ahead of you, Mam. I already have the VCR set up, and ready to go." Terry said, as he walked up to them.

"Thank you, Terry. I wanted to make sure that we had a copy of it, for Branden. It's not everyday that a young golfer makes his debut, on a national sports network." Anya said.

While deciding on a table to eat at, George and his family were joined by the other members of the 'United Families.'

After ordering their food, the group had begun talking amongst themselves, when they heard the following announcement on the TV.

"Ladies and gentlemen, we interrupt our normally scheduled programming, to bring you the following special report."

During the next three hours, George and his family were very pleased at 'NSN's' excellent coverage, of the grand opening ceremonies. Branden however, was even more pleased. He had discovered that his special segment of the ceremonies had not been interrupted by any commercial breaks.

"I'm glad they didn't have any commercials during the special segment, mom. They always seem to interfere with a person's thought pattern. At least, I think they do." Branden said.

"I agree with you, son. I don't like commercials either, especially when I'm watching something I enjoy." Anya said.

Three and a half hours had passed, and the boys of the 'United Families' had learned a lot, by watching Branden on TV. Finally, when the special report had ended, and gone off the air, George turned to Tom and asked.

"Tom, I know it's already too late for dinner at 'We Care'. Would it be possible to call a special assembly, when we get there? I'd like for the rest of the boys, to see the tape too." George said.

"Yes George, we can do that. If you and your family are ready to go, I'll call Mr. Avery and have him get the boys assembled." I said.

"We'll be ready in a few minutes, Tom. I need to talk to Terry, first though." George said.

"That will work out perfect, George. It usually takes about fifteen minutes, for all of the boys to get to the cafeteria. I'll go ahead and call Mr. Avery, and let him know that we'll be there in about fifteen minutes." I said.

"Okay, Tom. I'll go talk to Terry now, and get the video tape while I'm there." George said, as he headed for Terry's office.

"'We Care', Mr. Avery speaking. How may I help you?"

"Hi Mr. Avery, this is Tom. I need you to get all of the boys together, for an assembly. George and his family have a video tape; they would like to share with them." I said.

"Okay, Tom. Getting the boys together for an assembly, will not be a problem. They're already in the cafeteria." Mr. Avery said.

"What's going on, Mr. Avery? Why are they in the cafeteria?" I asked.

"It's a surprise for Branden, Tom. Steven does not want me to tell anyone about it, so I better not. All I can say about it, is you'll find out more, when you get here." Mr. Avery said.

"What about Alex, and the rest of the boys of the 'United Families', Mr. Avery? I'm sure they would like to help too." I said.

"I'm sure they would Tom, and we could sure use it. If you can talk to them without Branden overhearing, tell them I need their help with something." Mr. Avery said.

"That won't be a problem either, Mr. Avery. Branden went into Terry's office with his parents. I'll let you go for now, so I can talk to the boys. We'll see you in a few minutes." I said.

"Okay, Tom." Mr. Avery said, as he ended the call.

After telling the boys that Mr. Avery needed their help, and why he needed it, the boys took off running back to 'We Care'. Tom however, had to drive his car back.

Upon entering the cafeteria's hallway like foyer, the boys were astounded at what they saw.

The foyer had been beautifully decorated with an abundant selection of pendants and pictures, of many of the greatest golfers known to humanity.

Amongst the pictures was Branden's favorite golfer, and the sole winner of the coveted 'Grand Slam Award', Mr. Bobby Jones. Surrounding the picture of Mr. Jones was a double strand of twinkling Christmas lights. These lights had been intentionally added, in order to draw the attention of the viewer, to the display.

While standing and admiring the beautiful decorations, which had been placed there, Alex saw his dad drive into the parking lot. Then, after quickly telling the other boys that he would be right back, Alex ran out to the car, to meet his dad.

"Dad, come quick! You're not going to believe how nice Steven has the foyer decorated. It looks fantastic." Alex said, with excitement.

"Okay son, but we're going to have to hurry. Branden and his parents will be here shortly." I said, as we hurried toward the door.

While Alex was outside greeting his dad, the other boys went on into the cafeteria. Noticing that the boys had entered the room without Alex, Steven went over to them, and asked.

"Where is Alex at, Johnny? Didn't he come with you?"

"Yes he did, Steven. He went out to the parking lot to meet his dad, and should be in here shortly." Johnny said.

Before any of the boys could say another word, Tom and Alex came through the door.

"Hi, Uncle Tom. How do you and Alex, like the decorations?" Steven asked.

"I love them, Steven. I'm sure Branden will too." I said.

"I do too, Steven. I especially like that big poster; you have hanging in front of the room." Alex said.

"That was Andy's idea, Alex. He specifically wanted it to say,

'Congratulations on your national debut, Branden. From all of us, here at 'We Care'." Steven said, with a smile.

"Steven, I don't mean to interrupt your conversation, but they're here. They just now, pulled into the parking lot." Jeff said.

"Wow that was close. I'm glad we were able to finish the decorating, before they arrived." Steven said, with a sigh of relief.

"Take your places, everyone. Branden and his parents are coming up the sidewalk." Mr. Avery announced.

"I'll meet them outside, dad. I want Branden to have his eyes closed, when he comes into the building. I'll take Andy with me, so he can hold the door open for us." Steven said, with a smile.

"Okay, son. If you want to, ask his parents to close their eyes too. That way it'll be a surprise to them also." Mr. Avery said.

"Okay, dad. I'll ask them, but I'm not sure if they will." Steven said, as he left the cafeteria.

"Johnny, do you think Branden will like his surprise?" Danny asked.

"Yes I do, Danny. We'll know for sure, in a couple of minutes." Johnny said.

After greeting Branden, and his parents outside of the building, Steven said.

"Branden, the boys and I have a surprise for you, but you have to close your eyes first."

"I like surprises Steven, but do I really have to close my eyes?" Branden asked.

"We would like for you to, because it adds to the suspense." Steven said, with a smile.

"Go ahead son, and close your eyes. We'll even close ours too." Anya said.

"Okay, mom. I have them closed now Steven, if you're ready." Branden said.

"Andy, if you'll please hold the door open for us, I'll lead them in." Steven said.

"Okay, Steven." Andy said, as he opened the door.

Chapter 13

While walking slowly, and feeling their way cautiously through the door-way, Branden and his parents were getting anxious to open their eyes once again.

Steven knew that once Branden opened his eyes, he would be overjoyed with the decorations. That is when he said.

"Branden, in honor and recognition of this special day, the other boys and I, have a little surprise for you."

"Since you and your parents have arrived here, all of us have become very close friends. That is the reason, for the surprise. Now, you may open your eyes."

When Branden and his parents opened their eyes, they too were astounded at what they saw.

"Steven, this is absolutely fantastic. Thank you." Branden gasped.

"Don't thank me yet Branden, because this isn't all of your surprise. What about you, Mam? How do you like it?" Steven asked.

"Branden was right Steven, it is fantastic. How long did it take you boys, to do all of this?" Anya asked.

"It took us three days to get everything ready Mam, but only two hours to do the actual decorating." Steven said.

"That's amazing, Steven. Can you boys to help me decorate our new home, once we've moved in?" Anya asked, with a smile.

"We'd be happy to, Mam. Just let us know when you're ready." Steven said.

"Look dad, they even remembered my favorite player." Branden said.

"I noticed that son, and they even put lights around his picture." George said.

"This all looks great Steven, but there's one thing I haven't figured out yet. What goes in that large area, where those lights are? All I can see there is a plaque that has 'Our Favorite Player' inscribed on it." Branden said.

"I can't tell you right now, Branden. You'll have to wait a little longer, to find out." Steven said, with a sly grin.

"Okay Steven, I'll wait. I hope it's someone special though." Branden said.

"There's no doubt about that, Branden. It's definitely someone special.' Steven said, with a smile.

"Steven, they're ready for us in the cafeteria now." Andy said.

"Thank you, Andy. Well everyone, shall we proceed on into the cafeteria? Branden, I'll let you and your parents go in first." Steven said.

"Thank you, Steven. That's very kind of you." Anya said.

"You're welcome Mam, but its part of the surprise." Steven whispered.

As Branden was approaching the set of double doors, they began to open as if by magic. Stepping through the doorway with an expression of confusion on his face, Branden was welcomed with a thunderous....

"SURPRISE!" Shouted everyone in the room.

Branden was preparing to thank everyone for his or her welcome, when he was abruptly interrupted.

"Mr. Avery, sir! Our friend Branden and his parents have entered the room." The senior honor guard announced.

"Thank you, son. Would you and the other honor guards please escort them to the head table?" Mr. Avery asked.

"It would be our pleasure, sir." The boy replied.

While Branden and his parents were being placed in their honorary positions, two other boys were rolling out the red carpet.

"Look, mom. They're even rolling out a red carpet for us." Branden said.

"It's not for all of us son, it's only for you. Since you're the guest of honor at this party, then the red carpet is meant for you also." Anya said, with a smile.

"What have I done to deserve all of this, mom? I haven't done anything special that I know of." Branden said, confused.

"I know you may feel that way son, but it isn't true. I'm sure if you would ask any of the boys in this room that same question, their answers would surprise you." Anya said, with a smile.

Before Branden could respond to his mom's comment, Justin started playing the school's theme song on the piano. The music was the honor guards cue to begin escorting Branden, and his parents to their positions at the head table.

When they arrived at the head table Branden's parents sat down, but he decided to remain standing. It was his desire to thank everyone for his or her fabulous welcome, but he soon realized he would have to wait a few minutes to do it. Even with the window rattling applause that had erupted, Branden had said 'thank you' several times, but with no success.

"Mom, I thought you told me that if I would say thank you to the crowd, they would stop applauding and let me talk. Since they're not doing that, what do I do now?" Branden asked.

"That works most of the time son, but not always. Since this is one of the times that it isn't working, the only thing you can do is wait." Anya said.

After the boys had given Branden a standing ovation for over five minutes, the room once again became quiet. With his eyes filled with 'tears of joy', Branden said.

"Thank you everyone, for that wonderful reception. I'm not sure what I've done, to deserve it though. Steven, can you answer that question for me?" Branden asked.

"I could answer it Branden, but you already know what my answer would be. What you may not realize however, is how the other boys would answer it. That's why we're going to let several of them, give you their answers." Steven said.

For the next thirty minutes, Branden listened intently to the boys while they shared their deepest feelings, and praises for him. They had thanked him for being like a brother to them, and for respecting them regardless of what they were, before they came to 'We Care'.

The boy's discussions were beginning to draw to a close, when the kitchen personnel began passing out their ultimate desert. The desert, which was 'grandma's cheesecake, was welcomed by everyone in the cafeteria. With the individual serving sizes being three times larger then usual, the boys were ecstatic.

Before anyone could take his or her first bite though, Tom stepped up to the microphone, and said.

Hold on everyone, don't start eating yet. In recognition of this special occasion, and because it's Branden's favorite desert, we are going to use it to make a special toast in a few minutes. Before we do that though, Steven has a special presentation he'd like to make."

"Branden, several months ago, you and your dad gave me a large picture frame as a gift. Inside of that frame, there were three pictures of you. In one of those pictures, you were preparing to make your final approach shot, to the eighteenth green. In one of the other pictures, you were standing in the center of the little arched bridge, on the same fairway. I remember you telling me that those pictures were taken at the golf course, in St. Andrews Scotland."

"During my research on the game of golf, I remember seeing several pictures of famous golfers, standing on that same bridge. Those players have all gone on to win the major championship tournaments. All of us here at 'We Care', believe that you'll do the same."

"Also in the picture frame, you included one of your monogrammed golf balls, and a golfing glove that you had worn in some of your tournaments. I must admit that I felt especially honored, when I discovered you had autographed the ball, and glove."

"I want you and your parents to know, I have cherished that picture frame more then all of my other possessions combined. I would never relinquish my possession of it, unless by doing so, it would bring extreme honor to you. It is for that reason, and that reason only that I now dedicate it to be placed on our 'Wall of Fame'. It will be placed in the area that you saw earlier next to 'Bobby Jones', and under the plaque that read, 'Our Favorite Player'." Steven said, with a smile.

"I'm awe struck, Steven. Nothing this wonderful has ever happened to me before. So I'd like to thank all of you for this wonderful party, and for being such wonderful friends." Branden said, with sincerity.

"You're welcome, Branden. It has always been our pleasure to be your friend, and it always will be. I'm not sure if you are aware of this, but you have a fan club of three hundred and one members." Steven said.

"Three hundred and one members, Steven? How can that be when there are only three hundred people at 'We Care', including my family?" Branden asked, confused.

"You're right about the three hundred people, Branden. The other person however, is the writer of this story. Along with all of us here at 'We Care', he too hopes to see you playing professional golf someday. We're also hoping that you'll be the next winner, of the cherished 'Grand Slam Award'." Steven said.

"Thank you, everyone. I really appreciate everything you've done for me today, and your support regarding my future."
"Winning the 'Grand Slam Award' would be fantastic, but to do so I'd have to start out small. By that I mean, I would have to compete in tournaments such as the national championship for juniors." Branden said.

"When will the next national championship for juniors be held, Branden?" Andy asked.

"The regional playoffs start in two weeks, Andy. Then two weeks after that, the semi nationals will be held. Which is followed a week later, by the national championship game." Branden explained.

"What adult championship is the junior championship equal to, Branden?" Johnny asked.

"I'm not sure about that Johnny, but I believe it's the 'U.S. Open'. Dad, do you know?" Branden asked.

"Yes I do son, and you were right." George said.

"Branden, I'd like to see you put your application in, and compete in those playoffs. Personally, I think you could win." I said, with a smile.

"I wish it was that easy Uncle Tom, but it isn't. The only way a person can compete in the playoffs, is by receiving a personal invitation from the national director of junior golf. To get one of those is next to impossible." Branden said, with a frown.

"Don't give up hope yet, Branden. Stranger things have been known to happen around here, then a phone call. Who knows, you may receive that invitation when you least expect it." Mary said.

"I hope you're right, Aunt Mary. I know if I do receive one, I will try my best to win. I'd want everyone here at 'We Care', to be proud of me." Branden said.

"Even if you did lose Branden, we'd still be proud of you. Don't forget, we're your friends and that isn't going to change, no matter what." Steven said, with sincerity.

During the celebration, Tom noticed that there were three phones setting on the head table. Two of those phones were in front of George and Anya, while the third one was in front of Branden. He had also noticed that the one in front of Branden was red. Curious about why they were there, Tom turned to Mr. Avery, and asked.

"Mr. Avery, why are there three phones on the table?"

"They're another part of Branden's surprise, Tom. Since I didn't want to spoil it for him by telling you out loud, I wrote down the details instead." Mr. Avery whispered, as he handed me a piece of paper.

After reading the note, and looking at the clock, Tom stood up and said.

"Well everyone, it's starting to get late and tomorrow is going to be a busy day, for one of us. Before we dismiss for the evening though, Steven would like to make a toast." I said.

"Thank you, Uncle Tom. Before I make my toast, I'd like for everyone to cut off a bite of cheese-cake, and hold it up…"

After a short pause, Steven continued.

"Branden, this toast is to you, and for being such a wonderful friend to all of us. May your future be bright, and include the invitation that you so sincerely desire." Steven said.

Branden was preparing to thank Steven for the toast, when the telephone on the table rang. With everyone temporarily startled by the sound, the phone rang for the second time.

"George, could you answer that, please? It's an important phone call for you, from someone in California." Mr. Avery said, with a smile.

"I wonder who it could be, George. I'm sure I had everything taken care of, before I left." Anya said.

"I don't know who it is Anya, but we're about to find out." George said, as he reached for the phone….

Chapter 14

"This is George, how may I help you?"

"Good evening, George. My name is Mr. Fairway, and I am the national director of junior golf. It is my understanding that you and your wife recently purchased the 'putt and go' golf course. Is that correct?" Mr. Fairway asked.

"Yes it is sir, but we've changed the name of it. It is now called, 'The Havencrest Country Club'. Is there some sort of problem?" George asked, confused.

"No sir, there isn't a problem. I just needed to verify that I was talking to the right person. George, this call is in regards to your son, Branden. I really need to talk to you and your wife at the same time. Is that possible?" Mr. Fairway asked.

"Yes it is, sir. She is sitting right next to me, with an extension phone in front of her. If you'll hold for a second, I'll ask her to join us." George said.

"Good evening, Mr. Fairway. This is Branden's mother, how may we help you?" Anya asked.

"I'm glad you could join us, Mam. George, are you still with us?" Mr. Fairway asked.

"Yes sir, I'm still here." George said.

"I'm sure both of you are wondering why I've called you, and how it involves Branden." Mr. Fairway said.

"You're right sir, we are curious about that." Anya said.

"Are either of you aware that the western division junior championship playoffs, will be held in two weeks?" Mr. Fairway asked.

"We are now, sir. Branden informed us of that fact, just a few minutes ago. He didn't say where the playoffs would be held though." George said.

"He wouldn't have known that, George. That information was just released to the public today." Mr. Fairway said.

"Where will the tournament be held, sir?" Anya asked.

"It will be held on Catalina Island, Mam." Mr. Fairway said.

"How can that be possible, sir? Catalina Island is scheduled to have its own tournament, in two weeks." Anya said.

"You're right about that, Mam. That's why the location of the playoffs, wasn't announced until today." Mr. Fairway said.

"What are you referring to, sir? Are you saying that the two have something in common?" Anya asked, confused.

"Yes I am, Mam. This year the tournament on Catalina Island will actually be the western division's playoffs." Mr. Fairway said.

"George, if that's the case, then Branden won't be able to play in Island's tournament this year. He isn't going to like that." Anya said, with a frown.

"He might be able to, Mam. It'll depend on how you and George answer the next few questions."
"When I was talking to Mr. Avery this afternoon, he told me about Branden's surprise party. I'm hoping that the result of this phone call can be added to that list of surprises." Mr. Fairway said.

"Are you saying that you have a surprise for Branden too, Mr. Fairway?" Anya asked.

"Yes I am, Mam. Before I can tell you the details though, I need to find out something first. Is Branden sitting within hearing distance from you?" Mr. Fairway asked.

"Yes he is, sir. He is sitting about four feet from us, and looking straight at us." George said.

"I need to ask you the next few questions without him being close enough, to overhear the conversation. Would it be possible to get him, and a few of the other boys to leave the room for a few minutes?" Mr. Fairway asked.

"That won't be a problem, sir. He will always do what we ask him to, without asking us why." Anya said.

"Son, there's a gentleman on the phone that would like to ask your mother, and I a few questions. However, he would like for you to be out of the room when he does. Could you please step out of the room for a few minutes, until we're finished?" George asked.

"I sure can, dad. I'll be in the kitchen, getting another piece of that delicious cheesecake. The first piece didn't last very long." Branden said, with a smile.

Thank you, son. We'll let you know when we're finished, and you can come back in." Anya said.

"Okay Mr. Fairway, Branden is out of the room now. What's this all about?" George asked.

"It's about an invitation that I would like to offer Branden, and your permission to let him do so." Mr. Fairway said.

"Before we can give him our permission sir, we need to know what the invitation is to." George said.

"I would like to give him my personal invitation, to participate in the western division playoffs." Mr. Fairway said.

"That's fantastic, sir. I know for a fact that he'll be thrilled, to receive your invitation." Anya said.

"Thank you Mam, I'm glad to hear that. Now all I need to know, is will you and your husband, give him permission to participate?" Mr. Fairway asked.

"Yes by all means, Mr. Fairway. Is there anything else George and I have to do, so he can play?" Anya asked.

122

"Yes there is, Mam. You have to agree to be his sponsor, and pay all applicable fees for him." Mr. Fairway said.

"We'll be happy to be his sponsor, sir." Anya said.

"Yes, we'll sponsor him sir. The financial aspect of it isn't a problem either." George said.

"That should cover all of the questions I have. Do either of you, have any for me?" Mr. Fairway asked.

"Yes sir, I have a few." Anya said.

"Okay, Mam. I'll try to answer them for you, if you don't make them to difficult." Mr. Fairway said, with a little chuckle.

"How many participants, will there be in the tournament?" Anya asked.

"There will be one hundred and twenty-eight participants, Mam." Mr. Fairway said.

"How were they selected?" George asked.

"By using a very lengthy and detailed search method. That search has been ongoing, for the last two months." Mr. Fairway said.

"Was Branden one of the last boys chosen, Mr. Fairway?" Anya asked.

"Actually Mam, Branden's name didn't even come up during our search."

"Then how did you find out about him?" Anya asked.

"From my close friend Jason, Mam. He works for 'NSN', and he called me this afternoon to inform me about Branden's TV debut. He also told me that he couldn't believe how talented Branden is, and that I should watch the TV special."

"I've known Jason long enough Mam, to know that he has an excellent eye for talent. That's when I told him, I would be sure to watch it."

"By the time the TV special was over with, I too realized how talented your son really is. That's when I decided to call you, and invite Branden to enter the playoffs.

"Personally Mam, I feel Branden has the talent, and the ability to win the national championship." Mr. Fairway said.

"Thank you, sir. Everyone here at 'We Care', share those same feelings." Anya said.

"I have one last question, sir. Will we need to fill out an entry form for Branden?" George asked.

"Yes you will, George. I can fax it to you, if you'll give me your fax number." Mr. Fairway said.

"I'd like that, sir. Let me ask Mr. Avery what the number is. I'll be right back, so please don't hang up." George said.

"While George is getting the number Mam, could you send one of the boys after Branden?" Mr. Fairway asked.

"Yes sir, I can do that… Steven, could you go out and get Branden for us, please?" Anya asked.

"It would be my pleasure, Mam." Steven said.

After a short pause, George returned to the phone, and said.

"I have the fax number now, Mr. Fairway. It's 1-800-4we-care."

"Thank you, George. I will go ahead, and have my secretary fax the form out to you. You should receive it, in a few minutes." Mr. Fairway said.

"Branden is back in the room now, sir. Would you like to speak to him?" Anya asked.

"Yes I would, Mam. I won't tell him about the surprise though, until after you have received the entry form." Mr. Fairway said.

"Son, the gentleman that we have been speaking to, would like to speak to you now." George said.

"Okay, dad. Do you have any idea, what he wants to talk to me about?" Branden asked.

"Yes I do son, but it's a secret right now. By the time you're finished talking with him, you'll know what it is too." George said, with a smile.

"Hello sir, this is Branden. How may I help you?" Branden asked.

"Hi Branden, this is Mr. Fairway. How are you this evening?"

"Other then being extremely tired sir, I'm okay." Branden said.

"I can understand why you're tired, Branden. You've had an extremely busy day. I also understand that the boys there at 'We Care', gave you a surprise party this evening. What did you think of that?" Mr. Fairway asked.

"It's been great, sir. I've learned a lot of new things that I didn't realize, before the party. I've learned how much the boys here like me, and consider me their brother."
When I found that out it surprised me sir, but that wasn't the biggest surprise. The biggest surprise came when my friend Steven, dedicated his cherished picture of me to the 'Wall of Fame'. I couldn't believe this happened either sir, but they hung the picture under a plaque that read, 'Our Favorite Player'. In addition to that, it's hanging right next to my favorite golfer's picture." Branden said.

"Who would that be, Branden?" Mr. Fairway asked.

"'Bobby Jones", sir."

"Can you tell me a few things that you like about 'Mr. Jones'?" Mr. Fairway asked.

"Yes I can, sir. I like how honest he was, and his mechanics and swing, while he was playing golf. He was so honest; he even called a foul on himself during one of his major tournaments. He's also my inspiration to try and win the 'Grand Slam Award', when I grow up." Branden said.

"That's going to be a few years yet, Branden. Have you heard the latest news, about junior golf?" Mr. Fairway asked.

"I don't know if I have or not, sir. What are you referring to?" Branden asked.

"I'm referring to the 'Grand Slam Award for juniors', Branden. It's something new, we've started this year." Mr. Fairway said.

Missing the key word 'we've' in Mr. Fairway's comment, Branden said.

"That's fantastic, sir. When does that start?"

"It starts in two weeks Branden, on Catalina Island."

"That's usually the weekend for the Island's tournament, sir. Have they decided to cancel it, for some reason?"

"There will still be a tournament held there, but not the usual one. This year it'll be the western division playoffs, for the national championship." Mr. Fairway said.

"I was going to play in the Island's tournament this year sir, but now I can't." Branden said, with disappointment.

"Why can't you play?" Mr. Fairway asked.

"Because, I haven't received a personal invitation from the national director of junior golf, sir. Without one of those, I can't participate." Branden said.

"George, are you and your wife still with us?" Mr. Fairway asked.

"Yes sir, we're both here." George replied.

"Have you received the fax yet?" Mr. Fairway asked.

"Yes we have sir, and it's already filled out." Anya said.

"What are you talking about, mom? What do you have filled out?" Branden asked.

"Go ahead and show him the form, George. Then once he's done reading it, I'll give him some unexpected news." Mr. Fairway said.

After reading the form, Branden said.

"What's going on here, mom? This is an entry form for the playoffs."

"You'll have to ask Mr. Fairway, son. He'll be able to answer that question for you." Anya said, with a smile.

"Mr. Fairway, I'm totally confused. What's going on here?"

"Branden, you've had a very busy and unusual day. You've made your national debut as a wonderful piano player, and a very talented young golfer."
"You were also interviewed by both a national sporting scout, and the national director of junior golf." Mr. Fairway said.

"I still don't understand what you mean, sir. I'm positive that I would remember speaking to a national sporting scout, and especially the national director." Branden said.

"I'm sure you would Branden, providing you knew what their official titles were. Do you remember speaking with Jason from 'NSN'?" Mr. Fairway asked.

"Yes I do, sir. He's a great guy, and very polite." Branden said.

"What you don't know about Jason is that he works for me. He's also the national sporting scout, I was referring to." Mr. Fairway said.

"That's fantastic sir, but what's your title?" Branden asked.

"I'll let you figure that out for yourself, Branden. Do you still have the entry form in front of you?" Mr. Fairway asked.

"Yes I do, sir." Branden replied.

"Look at the title, and the name under it, in the upper right hand corner. What does it say?" Mr. Fairway asked.

"The title line says, National Director of Junior Golf. The name under it is Mr. Robert Fairway." Branden said.

Temporarily shocked by the last name, Branden asked.

"Mr. Fairway, just out of curiosity, what's your first name?"

"It's Robert, Branden. That's my name on your entry form."

"Do you mean I'm actually talking to the 'National Director of Junior Golf'?" Branden asked.

"Yes you are, Branden." Mr. Fairway said.

Mr. Fairway's affirmative answer caused Branden to turn a ghostly white, and drop his phone's receiver.

"Branden? Branden, are you okay?" Mr. Fairway asked, concerned.

"He'll be okay in a moment, sir. I believe your response surprised him. It's not everyday he gets a phone call, from someone as important as you are." Anya said.

"I'm okay now, Mr. Fairway. I am sorry for dropping the receiver though. Are you okay?" Branden asked.

"Yes, I'm okay. Thank you for asking though."

"I'm glad to hear that, sir. Sir, I would like to thank you for calling me, but I have a question. Why did you call me?" Branden asked.

"I've called you, because I want to give you one of the biggest surprises, you've received today." Mr. Fairway said.

"What sort of surprise, sir?" Branden asked.

"My personal invitation to you, to participate in this year's national play-offs. Those playoffs begin in two weeks, on Catalina Island." Mr. Fairway said.

"Thank you very much, sir. I really appreciate your invitation, because you've made my biggest wish come true." Branden said.

"You're welcome, Branden. I need to speak to your parents again, but before I do, do you have any questions?"

"Yes I do, sir. Are the participants allowed to have their own galleries?" Branden asked.

"Yes they are, Branden. Each participant can have as many supporters as they want. Do you think you'll have a gallery?"

"Yes I do, sir. I have a feeling; it'll have at least three hundred people in it." Branden said.

"That's great, Branden. The more fans you have watching you, the better you will do. I better let you go for now, so I can speak to your parents. I'll see you in two weeks." Mr. Fairway said.

"Okay, sir. Good night and thank you again for the invitation." Branden said.

"George, be sure to get Branden's entry form back to me, no later then this weekend." Mr. Fairway said.

"It's on its way right now, sir. Mr. Avery just went to his office, to fax it to you." George said.

"Thank you, George. I'm looking forward to meeting you and your family in two weeks."

"Thank you, sir. We are looking forward to meeting you too. Until we meet on Catalina Island sir, good night." George said.

After both of his parents had hung up their phones, Branden shouted with excitement.

"Hey everyone, I'm going to the national playoffs!"

"On behalf of everyone here Branden, I'd like to congratulate you, and wish you the very best of luck." I said.

"I wish we could go with you Branden, because I'd like to see you play. Since we can't though, I hope the game will be on TV." Andy said.

"I don't think it'll be on TV Andy, but the other idea may be a possibility." Branden said.

"I was thinking the same thing, son. We'll discuss that possibility tomorrow, at our morning meeting." George said.

"Thank you, dad. I was hoping you'd say that." Branden said, with a smile.

'Boys, this has been a wonderful party for Branden, but I have some disappointing news. It's getting late, and since Branden is going to be very busy tomorrow, we better bring the party to a close." Mr. Avery said.

"Dad, before we say good night to the boys, may I make another toast to Branden?" Steven asked.

"Yes you may, son." Mr. Avery said.

Steven's toast was a very meaningful and heartfelt toast. Consisting of praises, and well wishes of the highest degree, his toast had made Branden feel honored to be a member, of the 'United Families' of 'We Care'. When the toast had been made, and the jubilation had subsided, Branden stood up and said.

"Thank you Steven, for that wonderful toast. I would also like to thank everyone for this fabulous party, and the many surprises that you have given me today. Since its bedtime now, I will wish each one of you a good night, and sweet dreams.

Chapter 15

After a long and restless nights sleep, Branden and his parents arrived early for breakfast. Branden however, was not the only one who didn't sleep very well. Because when Steven walked into the cafeteria, he too was yawning really big, and rubbing his eyes.

When Steven walked up to Branden to wish him a good morning, Branden said.

"Good morning, Steven. It looks like you may have tossed and turned all night too, like I did. I don't know why, but I just couldn't get to sleep. I guess it was because I was so excited about going to the playoffs." Branden said, before yawning once again.

"I have a feeling that was part of my problem too, Branden. The other part was the dreams I had." Steven said.

"Did you say dreams, Steven? How many did you have?" Branden asked.

"I had two different ones, Branden. One of them made me really happy, and I hope it comes true. The other one however, made me extremely sad." Steven said.

"I'd be interested in hearing about them Steven; providing you want to talk about them." Branden said.

"We'd like to hear about them too, son." Mr. Avery said.

"I'd be happy to tell all of you about them, but I need something to drink first." Steven said.

"I agree with you, Steven. I need my morning cup of coffee, so I can finish waking up." I said, with a smile.

"Let's all get our drinks, and meet back at the head table." Mr. Avery said.

After the members of the 'United Families had sat down at their table, Andy asked.

"I'm interested in hearing about your dreams, Steven. Are you about ready to tell us about them?" Andy asked, impatiently.

'Yes I am, Andy. Which dream do you want to hear about first; the good one, or the bad one?" Steven asked.

"Start with the bad one, Steven. Then by the time you've finished with the good one, breakfast will be ready." Mary said.

"Let me start by saying that both dreams were about Branden, and the playoffs."
"The first thing I saw was all of us standing in the parking lot saying our good byes, to him and his parents. They were getting into their car to go to the airport, and then on to the playoffs."
"The next part was really sad, because as we watched them leave the parking lot, we all began crying. I think Andy was taking their leaving the hardest though, because he started running after them."
"I had started talking to Alex and Johnny about that time, when suddenly I heard Billy yelling; 'Andy, come back here! You can't go with Branden!' When I looked back toward the parking lot, Andy was nearing the sidewalk. The thought of him getting hit by a car really scared me, so I took off running after him."
"When I was finally able to get close enough to him, I could hear how hard he was actually crying. His crying however was more like a wailing, then a cry. He was even yelling something, with hopes that Branden would hear him." Steven said.

"What was I yelling, Steven?" Andy asked.

"Between your wails Andy, it sounded like you were saying, 'Branden! Branden! Please come back Branden, I want to go with you!'" Steven said, with tear-filled eyes.

"Did you finally catch up to him, son?" Mrs. Avery asked.

"Yes I did mom, but it took me a long time to get him calmed down." Steven said.

"I can understand why he would feel like that, Steven. Andy and I have become very close friends also. I even consider him as my little brother." Branden said.

"What happened next in your dream, Steven?" Anya asked.

"The rest of the dream was mostly a blur Mam, except for the ending. I hate to say it, but that part of my dream was even sadder and more disappointing then I mentioned earlier." Steven said.

"Why was it so sad, Steven?" Branden asked.

"Because you lost the tournament, Branden. You finished the tournament in last place, with a score of twenty-five strokes over par." Steven said.

"That must have been a horrifying dream, Steven. Was there anything else that went wrong in it?" Karen asked.

"Yes there was, Aunt Karen. Mr. Fairway talked to Branden and his parents after the tournament, and told them how disappointed he was in Branden's performance. He also told them that Branden could never compete in another playoff game again, unless his fan club came with him." Steven said.

"That wasn't a dream Steven, it was a nightmare." Alex said, in disbelief.

"Son, did you wake up crying by any chance, after you had that dream?" Mrs. Avery asked.

"Yes I did mom, but I had been crying before I woke up. When I woke up, I discovered that my pillowcase was soaked with tears." Steven said.

"That was a terrible dream, Steven. I hope I didn't do anything wrong, to cause you to have it." Branden said.

"No, you haven't done anything wrong, Branden. It was just a weird dream that I had, and I don't know why." Steven said.

"Let's move on to your good dream, son. I think between all of us this morning, we've already shed enough tears for a week." Mr. Avery said.

"I started having that dream this morning dad, shortly before I woke up. Unfortunately, though, there isn't much I can remember about it, except for a couple of things. The rest of it was nothing but a blur." Steven said.

"That's okay, Steven. Tell us about the two things, you can remember." Tim said.

"Okay, Uncle Tim. The main thing that I can remember was the large group of boys, and the color of their uniforms. I thought it was strange at first, but their uniforms looked exactly like ours."

Then, as my dream continued and became more vivid, I finally recognized a couple of the boys. Andy, those two boys were you, and Branden." Steven said.

"Could you tell where we were at, Steven?" Andy asked.

"Yes I could, Andy. Branden was competing in the playoffs, on Catalina Island. You and the other boys were in his gallery, and were cheering for him." Steven said.

"Was I wearing my uniform too, Steven?" Branden asked.

"Yes you were, Branden. The sight of all of us in our uniforms was awesome. Even some of the spectators, thought they looked nice." Steven said.

"What about the score, Steven? Could you tell how I was doing?" Branden asked.

"Yes I could, Branden. You were tied for first place, with the defending champion." Steven said.

While Steven was answering Branden's question, a kitchen helper walked up to Mary, and said.

"Mary, I don't mean to interrupt your conversations, but breakfast is ready."

After Mary had thanked the helper for her information, George turned to Branden, and said.

"Son, we'll be having our morning meeting after breakfast is over. Do you want to attend the meeting, or start practicing for the tournament?" George asked.

"If I go to the meeting dad, will we be deciding on whether or not, the boys will be going to the tournament?" Branden asked.

"Yes we will, son. In fact, I'm sure that will be the main topic this morning." George said.

"That's fantastic, dad. Then I'll attend the meeting first, and go practice after it's over." Branden said.

While the members of the 'United Families' were enjoying their breakfast, the adults were discussing Steven's dreams. The boys however, were having their usual morning chat session.

Mrs. Avery was a cautious person, and skeptical of the idea of everyone leaving 'We Care' to attend the tournament.

"It'll leave the school unprotected and vulnerable while we're gone. I'm afraid someone will break in to the building and destroy it." She said, concerned.

"I'm sure we can prevent that possibility, hon. I'll call General Smith after breakfast, and invite him to our meeting. I'm sure he'll have a solution to your security concerns." Mr. Avery said.

"That's a good idea, Mr. Avery. I'll call and invite Judge Riley and the police captain too." Justin said.

When breakfast was finally over, the 'United Families' went to the conference room for their morning meeting. With everyone present and accounted for, Tom began the meeting.

The first things on the agenda were the financial report, and any old business. With those two items quickly taken care of, it was now time to discuss their possible trip to Catalina Island.

By this time, Judge Riley and the police captain, had quietly entered the room and sat down. Tom was getting ready to ask Mr. Avery if General Smith was coming, when he too walked into the room.

The trip's lengthy discussion consisted of Tim's interpretation of Steven's dreams, security of 'We Care', and transportation to and from the tournament.

With Branden's best interest in mind, and Tim's persuasive interpretation of Steven's dreams, the board members immediately approved the trip to the tournament. The matters of security, and transportation were quickly resolved also.

General Smith would see to it that first class flying arrangements, along with top rated security for 'We Care', would be provided. The city's police department would assist the air force with security, when and if needed.

When the morning business was completed, Tom asked for any last minute comments or questions. Hearing neither, he proceeded to adjourn the meeting.

"This is fantastic, Branden. We're all going with you to the tournament." Andy said, with excitement.

"You're right Andy, it is fantastic. I just hope Steven's second dream, is the one that's right." Branden said.

"I'm sure it is son, but you'll still need to practice. Remember what your instructor said, 'if you want to become a professional golfer, then you must practice, practice, and practice some more'." Anya said.

"You're right mom, he did say that. Since the meeting is over with now, I'm going to the golf course and get started. Steven, are you going with me?" Branden asked.

"I'd like to Branden, but wouldn't I be a hindrance to you?" Steven asked.

"No Steven, you wouldn't be a hindrance. In fact, you would be a big help to me. You know how to play golf well enough; you'd be a challenge for me." Branden said, with a smile.

"Dad, before Branden and I leave for the golf course, when will we be telling the boys about the trip?" Steven asked.

"We'll tell them this evening son, after they've finished eating their dinner." Mr. Avery said.

"Okay dad that sounds good to me. We're going to take off now, so we can be back in time for lunch." Steven said.

"Okay, son. We'll see both of you when you get back." Mr. Avery said.

Steven and Branden's game did not last the usual four and a half hours, of an average game. With their combined speeds and accuracy from tee to cup, they had reduced their playing time by forty-five minutes.

With their clubs now put away, and knowing that lunch would be served in fifteen minutes, they wasted no time in returning to 'We Care'.

Seeing the boys as they entered the room, Branden's parents walked up to them, and asked.

"Welcome back, boys. How did your game go?" Anya asked.

"It went fantastic mom, but it was a tough one." Branden said.

"What do you mean by, 'it was a tough one?" George asked.

"Steven and I both ended up with the same exact score, dad. In fact, we actually tied on every hole." Branden said.

"Did either of you have to take any mulligan's, or penalties?" Anya asked.

"No we didn't, mom. Both of us always got good hits off of the tee, and kept them in the fairway." Branden said.

"That's fantastic, boys. I bet you've worked up an appetite though, haven't you?" Mary asked.

"We sure have Aunt Mary; we're starving." Steven said, with a smile.

"I doubt if you're starving Steven, but I can definitely hear your stomach growling. All of you go ahead and fill your plates, while I tell the rest of the staff." Mary said.

During the meal everyone at the head table, were discussing Steven and Branden's game. Confused about why the boys tied, Andy asked.

"Steven, I'm glad that you and Branden tied, but I have a question. Why didn't Branden win? I thought he knew how to play golf better then you."

"I can answer that question for you, Andy. It's true that I use to be better then Steven, but not any longer. Since I've taught him everything I know about golf, he's just as good as I am now." Branden said.

"That's great, Branden. Now I understand what you meant when you said, 'Steven would be a challenge for you'." Andy said.

The rest of lunch, and the afternoon had passed quickly. During the afternoon however, the boys had heard that Mr. Avery would be making one of his 'Special Announcements' at dinner. Anxious to find out more about it, they began arriving earlier then usual in the cafeteria. Unfortunately though, no one would give the boys any clues about the secret announcement.

"We're sorry boys, but we can't tell you anything about the announcement. The only thing we can say about it is that you're really going to enjoy it." Justin said.

The boys were still talking to the staff members, when Mary made the following announcement.

"Dinner is now served, everyone. Boys, be sure to let the staff members go through the line first." Mary said.

While going through the serving line to make their selections, the boys could not help but notice the extraordinary selections of fine foods. Knowing that something very special was about to happen, they joyously filled their plates and sat down to enjoy their meal.

During the meal, the air of suspense and silence filled the room, as if compared to a heavy morning fog.

The sound of silence had become deafening, when Steven said.

"Dad, something must be wrong with the boys. No one is saying anything."

"They're okay, son. They're just thinking about the announcement that I am going to make. We'll give them a few more minutes to think about it, and then I'll make it." Mr. Avery said, with a smile.

Nearing the end of the meal, Mr. Avery stood up to make the evening's announcements.

"May I have everyone's attention, please? I have a very important announcement to make this evening."

"As you remember, last night Branden received his personal invitation to participate in this year's national playoffs. Since then, many of you have voiced your desires to go to the playoffs too, and cheer for him.

I am happy to announce that this morning's staff meeting was dedicated entirely to that possibility. With General Smith, and Judge Riley in attendance at the meeting, the board members overwhelmingly approved the trip."

"We will be leaving next Wednesday, from General Smith's air force base. The General will provide bus transportation for us, from here to the base. There, we will board a specially converted military aircraft, which will take us to California. Once we're over California, we'll be landing at the International Airport near Irvine."

"In Irvine, once we've claimed our luggage, we'll once again get on some buses for the next segment of our trip."

"The beginning of that segment will consist of a special surprise, and our evening meal, which will be provided by George and his family. Then, Wednesday night we will be staying in a motel, which is located near Branden's California home. Thursday will be a very busy day for us, so bedtime will be at nine o'clock."

"Thursday morning the staff will wake all of you up at 6:00AM. That should give you plenty of time to take your morning showers, before breakfast at seven. Breakfast by the way, will be served in the motel's dinning room, between the hours of seven and eight. Then, at approximately eight-thirty, we'll board our buses for a wonderful day of sight seeing, and entertainment."

"I'm sure that day will prove to be a lot of fun for all of us, but an exhausting one as well. So with that in mind, we will return to the motel at approximately seven o'clock, for our evening meal and a good night's sleep. Branden and his parents will join us for that meal also."

"Friday will be a busy day also. Since Branden has to start his practice round at one o'clock in the afternoon, we will leave the motel at eight that morning. Boys, since that portion of our trip is so closely timed, it is imperative that you be on the buses no later then seven-forty-five, for roll call. We must leave the motel no later then eight, so we can make our connection with the ferry, which will take us to Catalina Island."

"Special motel arrangements have been made to accommodate us for Friday, and Saturday night's, there on the island. Then, once the award ceremonies are over with on Sunday afternoon, we'll begin our trip back here, to 'we Care'."

"Since that was the only announcement I had for you this evening, you may now finish your meal." Mr. Avery said, with a smile.

Awestruck for only a moment, the boys responded to Mr. Avery's announcement with an earsplitting applause. When their applause had subsided after approximately five minutes, Jeff stood up and said.

"Mr. Avery, on behalf of the boys and myself, I'd like to thank the staff for their decision. We realize that with so many of us going, organization and discipline might become a problem. If it would be of any assistance to the staff, I'd like to make a suggestion."

"What sort of suggestion, Jeff?" Steven asked.

"I suggest we use the group method, Steven. Like the one we used, when we took the boys to the golf course." Jeff said.

"I like that idea, Jeff. My parents and I, were watching all of you that day, and were really impressed by how organized all of you looked." Branden said.

"I agree with you son; and they were well disciplined too. I think it would be a good idea to use that method, but we'll need a chain of command also." George said.

"What is a chain of command, sir?" Alex asked.

"In our situation Alex, the chain of command would be as follows. The boys in each of the groups would report to the leader of that group. Then the leader of that group would report to Steven. Then Steven would report to Mr. Avery. How does that idea sound, to the rest of the staff?" George asked.

"That's a great idea, George." The staff members said, in unison.

"The boys may need a little practice with the group idea, dad. Should I start working with them, and help them to understand it better?" Steven asked.

"That would be a good idea, son. When do you want to do that?" Mr. Avery asked.

"I'll start doing it tomorrow afternoon, dad. Branden has to practice in the morning, and he wants me to be his competition." Steven said.

"Son, there's something else you'll need to do, before tomorrow afternoon. Since you'll no longer be a leader of an individual group, you'll need to appoint a replacement leader, for the group that you had." Mr. Avery said.

"That won't be a problem, dad. Since Jeff is already my assistant, I choose him. Jeff, would you like to be my replacement leader?" Steven asked.

"Yes I would Steven; I'd be delighted to take the position." Jeff said.

"Thank you, Jeff. Boys, I would like for all of you to meet me outside tomorrow afternoon, by the memorial fountain. Group leaders, I'd like to meet with all of you this evening, after we have finished eating." Steven said.

The week prior to departure from 'We Care' had been hectic, but very satisfying. With his diligent and persistent leadership, Steven had successfully organized, and trained each of the different groups.

One of the techniques that he had incorporated into his training, was the use of hand signals to give commands. He knew that hand signals would be quieter then vocal commands, and would gain respect for the group from the public.

The week had also been very prosperous for Branden. Because of his daily practice rounds with Steven, Branden had successfully reduced his score by several strokes. Knowing that Steven had played an important roll in the reduction, Branden thanked him for being his competitor during practice. When Branden had finished speaking, General Smith stood up, and said.

"Good morning, everyone. I'm not sure if my announcements will be as interesting as Steven and Branden's were, but I hope so."

"As all of you may know, the military never goes on any sort of maneuver, without first giving it a code name. Since your trip is a special military maneuver, it has been given the code name, 'Operation We Care'. We'll commence 'Operation We Care', after you have been dismissed from breakfast this morning, and have boarded the buses."

"Once our aircraft is airborne, we will be joined by a military escort of F4's. That escort will remain with us, until we're approximately one hundred miles away from this location."

"During our flight to California, we'll be treated with a hot meal, and a couple of movies to enjoy."

"For now, I'll refrain from telling you anymore about the trip, and turn the meeting over to Mr. Avery." The General said.

"Thank you, sir. Boys, do any of you have any questions, before I dismiss you?" Mr. Avery asked.

"I have a question, Mr. Avery. Will the General be going with us on the trip?" Jeff asked.

"Yes, he'll be going with us Jeff. He's going with us because of military reasons, and also to watch Branden play in the playoffs." Mr. Avery said.

"I have a question for Grandpa, Mr. Avery. Grandpa, I know you'll be going on the trip with us, so you can watch Branden play in the tournament. What I don't know however, is will you be writing more about our adventures, while we're gone?" Billy asked.

"Yes I will be, Billy. Writing about our adventures here at 'We Care', is something I really enjoy doing. I'm going to do something different with the story though, while we're away on our trip." I said, with a sly grin.

With confused looks on all of the staff members faces, Alex asked.

"What are you talking about, dad? You're not going to change your writing style, are you?"

"No son, my writing style will remain the same. What I was referring to however, was the notes that I'll be making for my next book." I said.

"Your next book, dad? Why are you going to start writing another book? You haven't finished this one yet." Justin said.

"I know I haven't son, but I will. I only have three or four more chapters to go, and then this one will be finished. In this story, I will skip the portion of our trip from the time we leave here this morning, to the time we arrive at the ferry. Then once we've arrived there, I'll continue with this story." I said.

"That sounds great, dad. What will the title of your next book be?" Alex asked.

"I'm not sure yet son, but it'll be something about our vacation adventures." I said, with a smile.

"Tom, I don't mean to interrupt you, but it's almost time to board the buses." Mr. Avery said.

"That's okay, Mr. Avery. We have to keep on schedule, so we can make our connections on time." I said.

"Boys, before I dismiss you I'd like to remind you of how important it is that you remain on your best behavior, during this trip. If you ever expect to go on another trip while you are here at 'We Care', it is vitally important that you obey your group leaders, and the staff on this one. Remember, it is possible to remain on your best behavior, and have fun at the same time."

"Once I have dismissed the group leaders, and they have exited the cafeteria, you're dismissed. With that said, group leaders are now dismissed." Mr. Avery said.

Chapter 16

The plane, which had carried the group from General Smith's air force base to Irvine California, had landed successfully. Then, while the plane was being taxied into its parking position, the boys looked anxiously out the windows.

The sight of the many styles and shapes of military aircraft sitting nearby was amazing to the boys. They thought it was funny though, when they saw a single solitary helicopter sitting all by itself. Unbeknown to the boys however, General Smith had arranged for the helicopter to be standing by when he arrived. The helicopter's mission was to transport the General to a location near the ferry, where a special military project was taking place.

When the plane was completely stopped, and the engines had been shut down, General Smith spoke to the group.

"Boys, I have to fly on up to the ferry crossing, and take care of some business there before your arrival. Before I go though, I'd like to say it has been a pleasure flying with you."

"Also during our flight, several of you asked me questions about the mechanics of the aircraft. Andy's question however, was the one that intrigued me the most. His question was; 'Sir, how does a jet engine work?'"

"Since his question requires the use of charts and diagrams to fully explain it, I wasn't able to answer it at the time. We will however, have a class on that topic once we return home.

"I'm on a tight schedule boys, so I have to leave now. I'll see all of you tomorrow evening at dinner. Until then, enjoy your day of sight seeing and entertainment." The General said, before he turned and exited the plane.

With Branden and his parents as their hosts, the boys had really enjoyed their day of sight seeing and entertainment. Unfortunately though, the days fun filled activities were soon over with, and once again it was time for dinner. Joining the boys for dinner as previously promised, were George's family and General Smith. After enjoying their delicious and elegant dinner at the local five star restaurant, Mr. Avery stood up and said.

"George, I know Tom said that this story wouldn't be continued until we reached the ferry, but I feel compelled to say this."

"On behalf of all the boys and the staff at 'We Care', I'd like to thank you and your family for this wonderful day. When you told us that you would have a special surprise for us when we arrived, I could not have guessed what it would be. Taking us to visit your home and then later to the 'Anya Foundation's' home office, are two surprises that we will never forget. Thank you very much, for those surprises." Mr. Avery said.

"You're welcome, Mr. Avery. The visits to our home and the foundation's home office were Branden's idea. He wanted to include those visits too, so the boys would have a better understanding of why the 'Anya Foundation' was formed." George said.

"Thank you Branden. As I said before, we will never forget those surprises. Boys, if you would like to show your appreciation to Branden and his parent's, you may do so at this time. After that however, it's bedtime." Mr. Avery said.

The following morning came far too early, for most of the boys. Even though they had a good night's sleep, they were still tired from the previous day's activities. Once they had taken their showers however, they were once again revived and ready for breakfast.

During breakfast while everyone was eating, Mr. Avery stood up to make the morning announcements. In addition to his praise for their excellent behavior, Mr. Avery also told the boys about the day's activities, and their time schedule.

When the announcements were over with, Steven stood up to say a few words, and then dismissed the boys. Being anxious to get the day started, the boys wasted no time in boarding the buses. When roll call had been taken, and everyone was on board, Mr. Avery informed the General.

"Sir, everyone is present and accounted for. We can leave whenever you're ready." Mr. Avery said.

"Thank you Mr. Avery, I'll inform my drivers that we're ready for departure. Before we leave though, they have to give their passengers some last minute instructions. Then, when each of the drivers is ready to go, they'll honk their horns to indicate their readiness." General Smith said.

After each of the drivers had honked their horns, General Smith gave the command to 'pull out'.

Upon hearing the General's command, the escort drivers immediately turned on their sirens, and red flashing lights. With their sirens screaming, and red lights flashing, the escort vehicles led the convoy out of town. Then, when they were out of town and on the open highway, the sirens were turned off.

Two hours of an enjoyable bus ride had passed, when the boys heard the general speaking into his radio.

"Colonel Collins, this is General Smith; do you have a copy?"

"Yes sir, I have a copy on you. What is your present location?" Colonel Collins asked.

"We're approximately ten miles away from your location; and should be there in about fifteen minutes. Will you be ready for us, when we arrive?"

"Yes we will, sir. In fact, we already have your access lane closed to the public, and are awaiting your arrival."

"Thank you, Colonel. That's all I needed to know for right now, so I'll see you when we arrive."

Branden's family had visited Catalina Island many times over the past several years. He knew how large the public ferry was, and how many cars it could safely hold. He also knew that each of the buses, were much larger then the ferry. Confused about how the General was getting the group to the island, he asked.

"How are the boys getting to the island, sir? The ferry isn't large enough to hold the buses."

"You're right about the public ferry Branden, it isn't big enough. That is why I have called in our special forces, so they could take care of that problem. Their solution will enable us to travel to the island as a group." The General said.

When the ferry came into sight, the boys were awestruck at its massive size. Along with its ability to carry all four buses, the ferry also had an observation deck. While they were waiting to board the ferry, General Smith picked up the intercom, and said.

146

"Good morning, boys. On behalf of myself and the 282nd Combat engineers, welcome to the 'Operation We Care' ferry."

"Once we're aboard the ferry and have secured the buses, you are invited to the observation deck for lunch."

"Also during the crossing, most of you will see a sight that you've never seen before. This small stretch of water that we will be crossing is surprisingly full of dolphins. Many of those dolphins will be swimming along the side of the ferry as we cross. So if you've never seen dolphins in real life before, I'm sure you'll be amazed by their beautiful and graceful motions."

"I had a couple of other things I wanted to say to all of you, but we've just received our green light to board. So at this time I'll end my announcements, and will join you shortly for lunch." The General said.

When everyone from 'We Care' was on the observation deck, the ferry's captain powered it up and pulled away from the dock.

Not realizing the dangers of the larger ferry's wake, an angered civilian passenger went stomping to the civilian ferry's captain.

"Captain, what are we waiting for? We were supposed to have left the dock ten minutes ago."

"We were ordered by the military to stand by, sir. If we would've left on time, their vessel would've overtaken, and capsized us." The captain said.

After noticing the five-foot wake of the military ferry, the angry passenger quickly apologized to the captain.

Back on the military ferry, Steven was enjoying his lunch and watching the dolphins, when he turned toward Branden, and asked.

"Branden, how long does it take to get to the island?"

"It usually takes about an hour, on the public ferry. At this speed though, I'd say about forty minutes."

"Do you think we'll get to the golf course on time?"

"Yes I do, Steven. It's only a ten minute drive, once we've disembarked the ferry."

"I'm glad to hear that, Branden. I was afraid that we were going to be late for your tee time."

"It's not only my tee time Steven, it's yours too." Branden said, with a smile.

"You'll have to play your hardest then; because I'm not going to let you win, if I can prevent it." Steven said, with a grin.

While the boys were exchanging challenges with each other, the voice of the captain came over the intercom.

"Ladies and gentlemen, may I have your attention please? Due to the ideal surface conditions of the water, we will be docking sooner then we had expected. In preparation for disembarking, General Smith would like you to re-board your buses at this time. Also, on behalf of myself and the crew, I would like to wish Branden the best of luck in the tournament."

"Wow! That is fantastic, Branden. That means the size of your fan club just increased, by twenty-five people." Steven said, as they walked toward their bus.

While Mr. Avery was taking roll call, the captain began slowing the ferry down in preparation for docking. Then, with smooth and precise movements, he eased the vessel on into the dock.

Once they were off the ferry and back on the road again, the group continued with their exciting journey to the golf course. The buses had only gone a few miles however, when George turned toward Branden, and said.

"Son, we're going to be arriving at the course at twelve-fifteen. Since we're going to be there early, you'll be able to go to the practice range to loosen up." George said, with a smile.

"That's great dad; and it's what Steven and I were hoping for. We're going to compete against each other today, as if we're actually in a tournament." Branden said.

"That's a good idea, son. If anyone can help you get ready for the tournament, it'll be Steven." George said.

"OH NO! I just thought of something Branden, and it isn't good news. I forgot to bring my golf clubs." Steven said, with exasperation.

"Don't worry about your clubs, Steven. They're in the bus's storage area with Branden's." Mr. Avery said.

"Thanks a lot dad, but who remembered to bring them?" Steven asked.

"George remembered them, son. He told me that you would need them, after you had gotten on the bus. That's when I ran back into the building and got them." Mr. Avery said.

Once the buses had stopped in front of the pro-shop, the boys wasted no time in unloading their clubs. Then, with a minimal amount of delay, they hurried off to the practice range.

With every drive being almost perfect, the boys continued practicing until it was close to their tee time. Then, when it was time to leave the range, Anya said.

"Son, it's time for you and Steven to check in with the starter. Your fan club is already at the tee box, and waiting for you."

"Thanks, mom. Come on Steven, I'll race you to the tee box." Branden said, with excitement.

"We better conserve our energy for the game, Branden. If you still feel like racing after we're finished though, then I'll race you." Steven said.

While the boys were approaching the tee box, they could hear George telling the group about spectator etiquette. Then, when George was finished, they stepped in to the tee box and teed off.

Shortly after the boys had teed off, Branden discovered that Steven was playing his most serious game ever. Matching him almost stroke for stroke, Steven was proving to Branden that it was not going to be easy to win the playoffs.

When the game was all but over, Branden stepped up to his ball and made his final putt. Traveling across the green along the upper edge of a downhill slope, the ball successfully made its way to the cup. The applause and jubilation, which followed, was so loud that it echoed throughout the nearby valley.

Even though the score had been 'nick and tuck' for most of the game; Branden did however, emerge victorious over Steven. With the final score of 66 to 67, Branden had successfully won his toughest game ever.

"That was a good game, Steven. In fact, I think it was the toughest one yet, we've ever played against each other." Branden said, as he shook Steven's hand.

"You're right Branden, it was the toughest one. If you play that good in the tournament, I have a feeling you're going to win it." Steven said.

"Boys, I don't know about you, but I'm hungry. I've worked up an appetite, just watching you play." Justin said with a smile.

"We're hungry too, Uncle Justin. We'll race you to the snack bar, if our dads will carry our clubs for us." Steven said.

"Yes son, we'll carry your clubs for you. You boys have played a wonderful game this afternoon, so you deserve to be first in line." Mr. Avery said.

The race to the snack bar had a surprising finish, when Justin came in first. Totally surprised that Justin was able to run that fast, Steven asked.

"WOW! Where did you learn to run like that, Uncle Justin?"

"I learned how to do it in high school, Steven. Our track and field coach insisted that his sprint runners strive for perfection. I wasn't the fastest runner on our team, but I was close to it." Justin said.

"Well Justin, I've been wondering who we could get for a track and field coach at 'We Care', now I know." Mr. Avery said, with a smile.

"Now that we've decided on who's the fastest between you three; let's go get something to eat." George said.

During the meal, George discussed some of the important facts about the game, with all of the boys. Among the topics that he discussed, was the ability to make a good chip shot while using the proper club. In order to find out if the boys correctly understood what he was referring to, George asked.

"Branden and Steven both made some excellent chip shots during the game. Can any of you give me an example, of one of those shots?"

"Yes sir, I can give you an example. It was when Branden was on the ninth hole, and about ninety yards from the green. I'm not sure what club he was using though, but the shot was beautiful."

"After he had hit the ball, it traveled high into the air and landed about two feet behind the pin. That's when it surprised me, and back spun into the hole." Jeff said.

"I remember that shot too, Jeff. Branden, what club was you using to give it that much backspin?" Alex asked.

"I was using my nib-lick iron, Alex." Branden said, with a grin.

"Did you say a nib-lick iron, Branden? What is a nib-lick iron?"

"I won't tell you what club it was exactly, Alex. I will tell you however, it is one of the clubs that is often used for chip shots such as that one."

"Oh by the way Alex; you can find out what the definition of a nib-lick is, by looking it up in the dictionary." Branden said, with a smile.

"That's sneaky son; but it's a good way to encourage the boys to use the dictionary." Anya said, with a smile.

Even though Branden would not disclose what a nib-lick was, the boys still enjoyed their meal. Then, when everyone had finished eating, they boarded the buses for their trip to the motel and a good night sleep.

Alex tried his best to get to sleep that night, but because of the word nib-lick, he couldn't. Knowing that sleep would not come until he knew the definition, Alex got up out of bed and opened his dictionary. Then, once he had learned the definition, Alex returned to bed and went right to sleep.

The following morning after consuming a delicious breakfast, and boarding the buses, the group returned to the golf course.

When they arrived at the course, Mr. Avery picked up the intercom, and said.

"Boys, this tournament is the most important tournament, any of these players have ever played in. That is why I must insist that any communications among you today, be done in a low whisper. It is permissible however, to applaud your favorite player, whenever he makes a good shot."

"In a few moments, Mr. Fairway will be making his opening comments to the audience. So at this time I would like for you to put on your blazers, and meet me in front of the podium." Mr. Avery said.

After the group had gathered in front of the podium, Mr. Fairway walked on to the stage, and up to the microphone.

"Good morning, everyone. I'm Mr. Fairway, and on behalf of the entire staff here at the course, welcome to the thirty-ninth annual junior golf tournament, here on Catalina Island."

"This year's tournament is the host to one hundred and twenty eight participants, and over one thousand spectators. One of those participants alone will have over three hundred people in his gallery."

"Since this is the first game of the national playoffs, I have a special surprise for the participants. This year's tournament is going to be broadcast live to the nation on the national sports network. That means millions of people will be watching you play, from the comfort of their own living rooms."

"As some of you already know, I could talk for hours about the game of golf. Since it's almost tee time though, I'm not going to be able to. I will however, dismiss all of you at this time, so the players can prepare for their game. Once again, thank you for coming." Mr. Fairway said.

Upon the completion of Mr. Fairway's speech, the crowd responded with a joyous applause. Was the applause because he did not talk for hours, or because tee time was close at hand? Regardless of the reason, the players still had to get to their starting tees on time. As they scurried away, the spectators were close behind them.

Once they had arrived at the tee, and with Steven as his caddy, Branden stepped up to his ball and teed off.

With a tee off that was less then perfect, Branden's ball had only gone an embarrassing, fifty yards. Realizing that Branden had immediately become frustrated at himself, Steven said.

"Relax, Branden. You can win this game, but you're going to have to concentrate."

Even with his poor tee shot, Branden was still able to make par. The expertise of the returning champion was evident though, when he successfully birdied the same hole. Now trailing by one stroke, Branden knew he would have to play some serious golf in order to win.

During the next sixteen holes, Branden's professional playing abilities were unquestionable, to everyone watching the game. Proving himself to be a worthy competitor, Branden was now receiving applauses from the leader's fans, as well as his own.

Realizing that he had lost the loyalty of his own fans, the leader became angry and even more determined to win. That anger, along with the wrong type of determination would prove to be disastrous, before the tournament was over.

Before the current game was over with however, the leader had managed to increase his lead over Branden, by an additional stroke. With a disappointed expression on his face, Branden now began his long walk to the clubhouse.

Even though all of the players had played their best, there was still a wide margin between second and third place. The difference between first and second however, was a mere two strokes.

Trailing the leader for the entire game, Branden had become slightly disappointed in his own game performance; so while walking to the clubhouse with his dad next to him, Branden said.

"Dad, I feel terrible about the way I played today. I should've been able to take the lead several different times, but I just couldn't. I feel like I've disappointed my entire fan club." Branden said, with a frown.

"Don't be too hard on yourself, son. Remember, today was only the first day of the tournament. You still have tomorrow to turn the score around." George said.

"I know that dad, but I'm still worried about not winning. Don't forget, the leader was last year's champion." Branden said, with a worried expression.

Unaware of what Steven's intentions were behind him, Branden continued his conversation with his dad. Then suddenly, and without any warning, Steven grabbed Branden from behind, and quickly hoisted him to his shoulder.

"WH...WH...what are you doing, Steven?" Branden gasped.

Branden had no sooner gotten the words out of his mouth, when his entire fan club began singing, 'For He's a Jolly Good Player'. Looking up at Branden and smiling, George said.

"It doesn't look like your fan club is too disappointed, son. They're giving you a hero's carry off."

"That's fantastic dad, but I'm starving. I sure hope they're taking me to the clubhouse, so I can get something to eat." Branden said.

"Yes son, that's exactly where they're taking you. In fact, your favorite meal is already on the table." George said.

While Branden and his parents were enjoying their meal, Jason walked in and joined them. Then, while they were all eating, Jason intentionally asked George the following question.

"George, did you notice anything unusual about the leader today?"

"No, I didn't Jason; I was too busy watching Branden. Why do you ask?"

"Before I answer that George, did anyone else notice anything?"

"I noticed something, Jason." Anya said.

"What did you notice, Mam?" Jason asked.

"That he was making a lot of mistakes, between the second and seventeenth holes."

"That's exactly right, Mam. Branden, do you know why he was making those mistakes?" Jason asked.

"I'm not sure Jason; was it because he was careless?" Branden asked.

"That's one possibility, but it isn't the real reason. The reason he was making them, was because of your playing abilities." Jason said.

"How could my playing abilities, have any affect on his game?"

"Because you know how to play like a professional Branden, and that's something he doesn't know how to cope with." Jason said.

"Could you be more specific about what you mean?"

"Yes I can, but I'd prefer to do it in private. Mr. Avery, could you close the door to this room, please?" Jason said.

After Mr. Avery had closed the door, Jason began explaining to Branden what he was referring to. His detailed explanation brought Branden to the understanding of how playing his best had put a form of mental stress on the leader. He also explained how that mental stress, had affected the leader's playing abilities.

"Sir, is that sometimes referred to as 'putting the pressure on your opponent'?" Steven asked.

"Yes it is, Steven. Have you ever experienced that sort of pressure?"

"Yes I have, sir. Just about every time that I've played Branden, I've experienced it. I guess that's why I've made so many mistakes, when we've played against each other." Steven said, with a smile.

Eventually, after about an hour's worth of discussion, the group finally called it a day and returned to their hotel. Before retiring for the night however, Branden gave each of his parents a good night hug, and said.

"Tomorrow is going to be different mom, because now I know what I have to do in order to win." Branden said with confidence, before heading off to bed.

Chapter 17

"Welcome back everyone, for the second and final day, of this year's play-offs."

"If yesterday was any indication of how today is going to be, then it's going to be a very exciting day for all of us."

"For those of you that weren't here yesterday, all of our participants played an excellent game. Our top two contenders going into today's game are Branden and last year's returning champion. Even though the returning champion is currently leading Branden by two strokes, it is still anyone's game. So I'm sure you'll agree that those two competitors will be the ones to watch today."

"Before I dismiss everyone so we can get today's game underway, I'd like to wish each of the participants the very best of luck."

"That's all for now, so once again thank you for coming, and I hope that you enjoy today's game. I shall see all of you later at the trophy presentation ceremonies. You're now dismissed." Mr. Fairway said.

Starting the game with a record breaking tee shot, Branden made it completely obvious that he intended on playing, a very serious game. Not only had Branden's tee shot broken a record, but it also brought immediate pressure on the leader.

Being unable to cope with that pressure, the leader soon began making some serious mistakes in his game. Since Branden had anticipated those mistakes, he immediately took full advantage of them and began closing in on the leadership position.

Even though the score had fluctuated slightly during the first nine holes, Branden's consistent pressure was now taking a severe toll on his competitor's playing ability. By the time that they had finished playing their fifteenth hole, Branden and his competitor were tied.

The previous leader's stress level began to increase even more by this time, when he realized that his entire gallery had deserted him, and were now cheering for Branden. He was not the only person with an increased stress level though, Andy's had increased also.

By the time the players had finished playing their seventeenth hole, Andy was so nervous that he had begun biting his fingernails.

"Andy, stop biting your fingernails, or you're going to make them bleed." Billy said.

"I can't help it Billy, this game is making me extremely nervous. Besides that, if I knew it would help Branden win, I wouldn't care if they did bleed." Andy said.

"Making them bleed Andy isn't going to help Branden win. You need to do something else, and get your mind off of biting your nails." Billy said sternly.

Andy took his brother's advice, and began thinking of a way that he could help Branden. It didn't take him very long however, to decide on what he wanted to do. Moving quickly amongst the group, and sharing his idea with everyone; Andy soon gained the support that he so desperately needed.

Then, while walking to the eighteenth tee and following Andy's cheerful lead, Branden's entire gallery began chanting.

"Remember last week! Remember last week!"

"Steven, why is everyone chanting, remember last week?" Branden asked confused.

Speaking to Branden in a low tone of voice, Steven asked.

"Do you remember what happened on the ninth hole last week, Branden? That's what they're referring to."

"That would be one way I could win Steven, but I'm not sure if I can do it again." Branden said, as they arrived at the tee box.

"All of us have faith in you Branden, and we even have our fingers crossed. Just be sure to take a deep breath, and concentrate on your swing."

"Since that's what everyone wants me to try for Steven, maybe you better hand me my niblick." Branden said

While stepping in to the tee box, Branden had a look of worry and concern on his face. That look however, gave the defending champion a false sense of success, and that was exactly what Branden wanted. In reality though, Branden was preparing to show his competition exactly how professionals play, when they are under extreme pressure.

Before addressing the ball however, Branden took a few moments to study the layout of the green, and its surrounding area.

He could see that there was a medium size sand trap on both sides of the green. In addition to the sand traps, there was also a fair size pond located in front of the green. Knowing that he absolutely had to land on the green, Branden then began studying the layout of the green itself.

The first two things that he noticed were that it was elevated, and had a slope. Once he realized that it had a slope, he then began studying the direction of that slope. He could see that the green was higher at both the top rear and upper right side then it was at the bottom left.

With this knowledge, Branden now knew that a properly placed ball would roll downwards and slightly to the left. Then, with a deep breath and a profound determination, Branden stepped up and prepared to address his ball.

Andy knew that this tee off was going to be the most important one of the game for Branden; and would also make the difference between his winning or losing. As he watched anxiously, it seemed as if everything around him had suddenly gone in to slow motion. The few voices that he could hear were now sounding extremely slow and obnoxiously slurred, while all movements had virtually stopped.

As Branden began his back swing, Billy stepped up along side of Andy and placed a hand on his shoulder. Then together as they watched the flight of Branden's ball, they were astonished at how high it had gone. Fearful that the ball would land extremely short of the green, the boys in unison, said.

"YIKES!"

As they continued to watch the ball, the boys soon realized that their first thought was wrong. What they had failed to notice previously, was that the ball also had a perfect arch during its travel. That arch had allowed the ball to travel the required distance to the green; and land exactly where Branden had wanted it. What happened next, can only be classified as a 'Branden's Special'.

Branden had hit the ball in such a way that it had just the right amount of backspin on it. The rolling 'kick start' that the backspin had provided, allowed the ball to start its downhill roll, instantly upon hitting the green.

Rolling in the direction of the slope, the ball had now curved and was heading in the general direction of the hole. Slowing down slightly, and following yet another but smaller ridge, the ball continued to get closer, and closer to its target.

With its forward motion now nearly depleted, the ball gently rolled over the edge of the hole, and made an awesome sound. That sound, which is music to all golfers ear's, was the fabulous sound, of 'KA-Plunk'.

Awestruck at what they had just witnessed, the entire gallery of spectators began applauding with intense exuberance. Branden had just made, a 'hole in one'. Then, with 'legs of Jell-O' and shattered dreams, the defending champion stepped in to the tee box.

Attempting to concentrate on his shot, the defending champion knew that he had to match Branden's shot, in order to keep the game alive. He also knew, anything more then a 'hole in one' would mean instant defeat for him. Then, and with a false sense of confidence that he could match Branden's shot, the defending champion stepped up and addressed his ball. Being polite and giving him their undivided attention, the spectators watched as the defending champion teed off.

At first, the ball looked as if it was following the same trajectory as Branden's had followed. Unfortunately though, the defending champion had used a sand wedge, instead of a nib- lick. The sand wedge had caused the ball to have a steeper arch, thus causing it to land short of the green with a dreadful sound, of 'Ka-Splash'.

Realizing that the game would normally be over at this point, the defending champion approached the referee for an official ruling.

"Sir, I know in a regular game that with my ball landing in the water, the game would be over at this point. Since this is a tournament though, I'm not sure what the official rules say. Could you give me an official ruling, please?"

"You're right about a regular game, and that it would be over with at this point; which would make Branden the victor. He is unquestionably the victor in this game already; but the official rules state that all players must complete the entire game. The rules further state that there will be no exceptions, to the above rule."

"I understand what the rules are saying sir, but what happens if I decide not to finish the game?"

"I wouldn't do that if I was you son, because if you do, then you'll be disqualified. That means you will give up all rights to second, or any other position among the finishers. Now, what would you like to do?"

"I'll finish humiliating myself sir, and finish the game."

"You've made a wise decision, son. Now, if you'll please take you're penalty drop, we'll get this game finished up."

Doing as he was requested to do, the defending champion took his penalty drop at the spot where his ball had gone out of bounds. In order to make the drop properly though, he first had to have his toes slightly behind the out of bounds line. He then had to extend his arm forward and over the line, while still holding on to the ball. Then, once those two requirements were met, he was permitted to drop his ball back in to play.

Since the penalty had cost him a stroke, the defending champion was now ready for his third. After he had taken his third stroke and had successfully landed on the green, he still had to get the ball in to the hole.

Even though he had lined his putt up perfectly, he had failed to notice the small ridge near the hole. That ridge, which had previously helped Branden to make his 'hole in one', was about to create a problem for the defending champion.

As his ball approached the hole, it began to precariously travel along the crest of the small ridge, which eventually caused it to change directions. That change, not only caused the ball to miss the hole by several inches, but it also upset the player. Frustrated that he had missed a simple putt caused the defending champion to begin talking to himself.

"How did I miss a simple putt like that? Well there's only one thing I can do now, and that's to try again. This time however, I'll take a little longer and study the green more thoroughly, before I make my putt."

Then, with a putt that was straight and true, the defending champion successfully completed the game. As the spectators applauded Branden's victory, the defending champion walked up to Branden and congratulated him.

During the course of their conversation however, Branden realized that he didn't know the boy's name, so he asked what it was.

"I know you have a name other then 'the defending champion', but what is it?"

"I thought everyone knew that; it's Michael."

"Son, I don't know about you and Michael, but I'm beginning to get hungry. Let's go and grab a bite to eat, before the ceremonies begin." George said.

"That's a great idea, dad. Steven said earlier, he was getting hungry too."

"Now Steven, while he isn't expecting it!" Jeff shouted.

Hearing the shout and knowing exactly what it meant, Branden instantly and playfully tightened every muscle in his body. He did so with hopes that it would make it more difficult for Steven to lift him. He found out differently though, as his feet suddenly left the ground. Then, in what seemed to be a blink of an eye, Branden found himself sitting on top of Steven's shoulder once again. This time however, there were over five hundred people cheering for him.

As Branden and his cheering fans approached the clubhouse, Mr. Fairway and his associate, Jason, greeted them. Looking up at Branden, Jason said.

"Congratulations Branden, you played a fantastic game today. It looks like you've grown a lot though, since the last time I saw you." Jason said, with a smile.

"Thank you sir, but I haven't really grown this much. Steven, you can put me down now, so I can talk to these gentlemen."

After Steven had put him down, Branden shook hands with Mr. Fairway first, and then with his new friend Jason.

While shaking hands with Mr. Fairway however, Mr. Fairway had also congratulated him on his excellent and victorious game. Branden along with his parents were caught off guard though, when Mr. Fairway also said.

161

"Branden, your victory here today has not only won you the western division championship, but an added surprise as well."

"What sort of surprise, sir?" Branden asked.

"We can't tell you right now Branden, but you'll find out at the ceremonies." Jason said.

"Okay sir, but when do the ceremonies start?"

"They'll start in about two hours. We have to let the rest of the participants finish their game first, and then get something to eat. After that, we'll have the ceremonies." Mr. Fairway said.

"That's fantastic, sir. That will give me plenty of time to talk to my fans, before I eat." Branden said.

"Branden, what Mr. Fairway was also referring to, is that in a few minutes there's going to be several hundred more people showing up to get something to eat. In the mean time however, I suggest that you and your fans get something to eat now, before they get here." Jason said.

"That's a good idea, sir. Come on Steven; let's go get something to eat, so your stomach will stop growling." Branden said with a smile.

"We want to avoid the rush too Branden, so we'll join you." Jason said, with a smile.

"You're right about avoiding the rush Jason, but I'll still need to mingle with the crowd. I'll do that though after I finish eating. All I have to do now is decide on where I'm going to sit, while I'm doing that." Mr. Fairway said.

"You're welcome to join us at our table Mr. Fairway, if you'd like to." Anya said.

"Thank you Mam; I'd like that very much. It will also give me the opportunity, to chat with our new champion a little longer." Mr. Fairway said, with a smile.

After he had finished eating, and was still chatting with Branden, Mr. Fairway said.

I've enjoyed chatting with you Branden, but I have to start mingling with the crowd now. Before I go though, could you do me a favor before the ceremonies begin?"

"I'd be happy to, sir. What sort of favor do you need?"

"I'd like for you and your parents to stand directly in front of the podium during the ceremonies. By standing there, it will eliminate your need of coming through the crowd to get your trophy; and will also shorten the length of the ceremonies."

"Does that mean we'll have to be there early, sir?" Branden asked.

"Yes it does Branden, but I'll take care of that later. What I am going to do is make an announcement in about forty-five minutes, and let the people know when the ceremonies will begin. When I make that announcement, is when I would like for you to come to the podium." Mr. Fairway said.

"Okay sir, I'll be there shortly after you make the announcement. By the way sir, can Steven join us in front of the podium?" Branden asked.

"Yes he can Branden, because we have a surprise for him too." Mr. Fairway said with a smile, as he turned and walked away.

Overwhelmed that he was going to receive something at the ceremonies too, Steven's bubbling excitement soon became extremely evident to those around him. As he impatiently paced back and forth, Branden said.

"Steven, could you please sit down and relax? You're beginning to make me nervous too." Branden said.

"I can't help it, Branden. I've never received anything at a ceremony before."

"Why don't you sit down Steven, and we'll talk about the game. That should help take your mind off of the waiting." Anya suggested.

"That's a good idea, Mam." Steven said, as he sat down.

The forty-five minutes that the boys had waited, had seemed like an eternity to Steven. Eventually however, Mr. Fairway was seen approaching the microphone with the forthcoming announcement.

"Ladies and gentlemen, may I have your attention, please?"

"In approximately fifteen minutes, we'll be having our award presentation ceremonies, in front of the podium. If you plan on attending them and getting a good spot however, may I suggest that you arrive a few minutes early? Since I'd like for our participants to be in front of the crowd during the ceremonies, I'd like for them to come to the podium at this time."

"I would race you to the podium Branden, but right now I better not. Because right now, my legs feel rubbery." Steven said.

"We shouldn't be racing anyway Steven; because there's too many people present."

"That's using good judgment Branden, but it's also a violation of the tournament rules."

"The rules specifically state that there will be absolutely no foot races between anyone, during any major junior golfing event. Then, the rules further state that any participant who willfully violates the above rule, shall without question, be disqualified from the event." Jason said.

"Wow Jason; I wasn't aware of that, so I'm glad you told us. I definitely wouldn't want to do something, and get Branden disqualified." Steven said.

"I already knew that Steven, but I wanted to let you know about the rule." Jason said, with a smile.

As the group arrived at the podium, Mr. Fairway greeted them and said.

"Branden, I've really enjoyed watching you compete during this tournament. In my opinion, the expertise and professional playing abilities that you have shown us this weekend, is only the beginning of your golfing career."

"In addition to your abilities, I would also like to commend you on your selection of such an excellent caddy."

"Thank you for the compliment, sir." Steven said, with a smile.

"You're welcome, Steven. Well boys, it's almost time for me to present the trophies, so I better get back up on stage." Mr. Fairway said.

"Okay sir, but I'm still anxious to find out what my surprise is going to be." Steven said.

Knowing that Steven was expecting a response to his comment, Mr. Fairway turned briefly to smile at him, and then continued on his way.

After he had completed his final preparations on stage, Mr. Fairway stepped up to the microphone, and said.

"Ladies and gentlemen, the award ceremonies are about to begin; so may I have your undivided attention, please?"

"Since I'm aware of how tired the participants are, and that they are ready to go home; I'm going to make these ceremonies, as short as possible."

"Before I begin though, I'd like to congratulate each of the participants on their superb game performances, and sportsmanship. Now, with that said, lets move on to the award presentations."

"For those of you who were following the leaders, you know exactly how difficult this tournament has been for both of them. Even though Branden finished two strokes behind the leader in yesterday's game; it was due to his persistent concentration and playing abilities, which eventually won him the championship."

"Branden, would you please come to the stage at this time, and receive your championship trophy?" Mr. Fairway asked, with a smile.

Instantly upon hearing Mr. Fairway's request, the crowd began vigorously applauding, and cheering for their new Champion. Overwhelmed by the crowd's support, and his own successful victory; Branden's eyes quickly filled with 'happy tears'. That didn't stop him though, because with a sense of pride and the desire to show his gratitude, Branden took a moment of his time, and waved to his fans.

Then, as he arrived on stage, Mr. Fairway greeted Branden with a warm handshake, and a congratulatory welcome. Wasting no time in presenting the trophy however, Mr. Fairway went on to say.

"Branden, it's with great honor that I present to you, this championship trophy." Mr. Fairway said, as he handed Branden the trophy.

"Thank you, sir." Branden said, with a smile.

"Hold it up Branden, so all of us can see it!" Andy shouted.

"That was a good idea, Branden. If you'll hold it up, then I'll try to describe it." Mr. Fairway said.

"Okay sir; but please hurry, because it isn't very light." Branden said, as he raised the trophy above his head.

Before Mr. Fairway had begun describing the trophy, hundreds of pictures had already been taken of Branden with his trophy.

"Ladies and gentlemen, this trophy is so prestigious, it even 'shouts' the word victory."
"Boasting a ten inch crystal golf ball, atop of a seven inch solid silver stem; this trophy has been mounted on a twelve inch square black walnut base."
"The inscription on the trophy's twenty-four karat gold plate, reads; National Champion, Western Division. Then under that, is Branden's name."
"Okay Branden, now you can sit the trophy on the table; but don't leave yet, because I have something else for you."

After Branden had placed his trophy on the table, Mr. Fairway continued.

"Branden, we feel that a trophy presentation isn't complete, without a certificate to accompany it. So it's with great honor that I present you with these prestigious certificates also, which will accompany your championship trophy."

"Thank you sir, but why am I getting two certificates?" Branden asked, confused.

"Because one of them is so you can display it with your trophy. The other one however, is for the 'Wall of Fame', at 'We Care'." Mr. Fairway said.

"Thank you sir, but how did you know about the 'Wall of Fame'?" Branden asked.

"I can't tell you exactly who told me Branden, so lets just say, 'a little birdie told me'." Mr. Fairway said, with a smile.

"I understand what you mean sir; but then again, I know that birdies can't talk." Branden said with chuckle, as he picked up his trophy, and prepared to leave.

"Hold on a minute Branden, because you're not finished yet. We still have a couple more things to give you."

"This certificate is your official invitation to compete in the semi national playoff game; which will be held two weeks from today, in Champaign, Illinois."

"That's all I have for you Branden, so I'll see you in two weeks."

"At this time ladies and gentlemen, I'd like to turn the ceremonies over to the Director of Golf, here on Catalina Island; who will also be presenting Branden with a trophy." Mr. Fairway said.

"Thank you Mr. Fairway, for that fine introduction."

"Branden, as the Director of Golf here on Catalina Island, I've seen hundreds of participants come and go, over the past several years. Even though many of those participants had outstanding playing abilities; none of them could ever compete with the ones that you've displayed here this weekend.'

"As most of you know, it is our policy here on Catalina Island to present only one championship trophy per tournament. That single trophy however, is always awarded to the overall winner of that tournament."

"Branden, it's for that reason it gives me great honor in presenting you with this year's Catalina Island's 39th Annual, Junior Championship trophy; Congratulations."

"Thank you sir, but could you describe it to the crowd for me, please? I'm sure that my friend Andy would like to hear how you would describe it." Branden said, as he accepted the trophy.

"It would be my pleasure Branden, but you'll have to hold it up so they can see it."

After Branden had raised the trophy above his head, the director tried his best to think of a way to describe it. Unable to think of a way to 'spice up' the description, the director finally went on to say.

"This magnificent trophy has an eight sided crystal diamond, which has a height of twelve inches. The base, which the crystal sits atop of, is twelve inches square, and is made of solid black walnut. The base by the way was made from a tree, which came from a location, which is now called 'The Havencrest Estates'."

Shocked that the director had mentioned the words 'Havencrest Estates', Branden said.

"Sir, 'Havencrest Estates' is what we call our new home. I wonder if it's the same place."

"Yes it is Branden; it's exactly the same place. We purchased the tree from the previous owners, in April of last year."

"This is fantastic, sir. Not only have I won the trophy, but part of it even came from our own timber." Branden said, with pride.

"Now you can display it with twice the amount of pride, Branden."

Suddenly remembering that the ceremonies were not over yet, the director continued by saying.

"Branden, I still have to turn the stage back over to Mr. Fairway. Before I do though, do you have someone who could help you carry your awards?"

"Yes I do, sir. In fact, here comes my dad now."

"Ladies and gentlemen, while Branden's dad is helping him with his awards; I'd like to turn the stage back over to Mr. Fairway, at this time."

After Branden and his dad had left the stage, Mr. Fairway once again congratulated Branden on his victory. Then, knowing that he had one more trophy to present, Mr. Fairway went on to say.

"Ladies and gentlemen, the next trophy that I'd like to present is the prestigious caddy award. Before I present it though, I'd like to describe it for those of you who are to far away to see it."

"Since it's a prestigious award, we commissioned one of the largest trophy manufactures in the nation, to design and craft it for this special occasion. This means, there isn't another one like it, anywhere."

"Standing on a three inch solid black walnut base, this eighteen inch trophy is a magnificent twenty-one inches tall."

"The highly glossed and brass figurines depict a teenage caddy congratulating his player, while shaking hands with him."

"Ladies and gentlemen, the details on this trophy are so minute; you can even see the dimples on the boy's faces."

168

"Now, and without further ado, lets hear a round of applause for the recipient of this prestigious award; Mr. Steven Avery. Steven, would you come to the stage, please?" Mr. Fairway asked with a smile, as he too began applauding.

After arriving on stage, and accepting his trophy from Mr. Fairway, Steven said.

"Thank you for the trophy sir, but I was only doing what any good caddy should do." Steven said.

"That's true Steven, but you did more then even a professional caddy would have done. Just do Branden a favor, and keep doing what you've already been doing."

"Okay sir, and thanks again for the trophy." Steven said, with a smile.

"Ladies and gentlemen, at this time I'd like to bring the tournament to a close. I sincerely look forward to seeing all of you here again next year. Once again, thank you for coming to this year's tournament. You're now dismissed." Mr. Fairway said.

With Mr. Fairway's closure, came a thunderous celebration among the people in the crowd. This celebration, which lasted for close to ten minutes, could be heard for several miles around. Finally, when the celebration had subsided to a comfortable hearing level, Anya said.

"George, now that the tournament is over with, it might be a good idea to turn your cell phone back on."

"You're right Anya; it would be a good idea. Who knows, I may have missed a dozen important phone calls, while I've had it turned off." George said with a smile, and in a jokingly manner.

His smile suddenly turned to a frown however, when he discovered that he had actually missed the dozen calls, he had previously joked about.
Seeing his dad's facial expressions change so rapidly, caused Branden to become concerned about what was happening.

"Is there something wrong, dad?" Just a minute ago you were smiling, but now you're not."

"I'm not sure if there's anything wrong or not, son. All I know is that your piano teacher has called twelve times, in the last hour." George said.

"George, there must be something seriously wrong at the school, or otherwise he wouldn't have called. Maybe you should call him back, and find out what is going on." Anya said, in a concerned voice.

"That's what I was thinking too Anya, and that's why I'm going to make the call, right now." George said, as he began dialing the number. . . . .

Chapter 18

After George had failed to reach Ethan after five attempts, he turned toward Anya with a desperate look, and said.

"I still don't know what's going on at the school Anya; because for some reason, I can't get a hold of Ethan. Now I'm starting to get scared."

"That's not like Ethan not to answer his phone calls George, so something is desperately wrong. We better get there, as soon as we possibly can." Anya said.

Overhearing George's conversation with Anya, Steven responded by rushing to the microphone, and saying.

"'We Care', may I have your attention, please? Due to the possibility that we may have an emergency in progress, I want all of you to form up, on the double. Group leaders, as soon as your group is formed, I want you to get them on the buses immediately."

While the groups were hustling to get into position, George took a moment of his time, and apologized to Mr. Fairway.

"Mr. Fairway, I'm truly sorry for this rapid departure; but we're afraid that our friend Ethan is in some sort of serious trouble."

"I fully understand the situation George, so don't worry about it. In fact, if I was in your shoes, I'd be doing the same thing that you're doing now."

"The General is helping too, George. He already has his personnel holding back the traffic, so your buses can get out of the area, without any delays." Jason said.

"Dad, if the General is working with traffic control; does that mean he won't be going with us?" Branden asked.

"I'm not sure son, but I sure hope he goes with us."

While George and his family were still talking to Mr. Fairway, General Smith walked up behind them, and placed his hand on Branden's shoulder. After looking to see who was behind him, Branden said.

"Hello General Smith; it's nice to see you again, sir."

"It's nice to see you again too Branden; and by the way, congratulations on your victory." The General said, while shaking Branden's hand.

"Thank you very much sir; but I've been wondering about something. Since we have to leave in such a big hurry; will you be going with us?" Branden asked.

"Yes I will be Branden; in fact, we're ready to leave now."

"George, if you and your family will board the lead bus, I'd greatly appreciate it."

"Okay sir; we'll be there shortly. Mr. Fairway, I'd like to thank you again for your hospitality and understanding." George said.

"You're welcome George; but you better hurry though, because your bus is waiting for you."

"Branden, I'll see you and your parents in two weeks, in Champaign."

"Okay sir; and thank you again, for everything." Branden said, before him and his parents turned, and jogged to the bus.

Even before he had reached the bus, George had noticed how well the traffic was being contained. Noticing that General Smith's personnel had successfully stopped all movement of other traffic in the area, George said.

"That's the best traffic controlling, I've ever seen sir. We shouldn't have any trouble at all, at least not until we reach the open highway."

"We won't even have trouble then George; because the military is making sure of that." The General said with a smile.

"Are you saying that the military has the traffic stopped, all the way to the ferry, sir?" George asked.

"We're not going to the ferry George; we're going to the naval base here on the island, instead." The General said.

"I realize you're in charge of our transportation sir, and I appreciate that; but we need to get to 'Ethan's school of music', as soon as possible."

"I'm aware of that George, and that's why we're going to the base. Once we get there, we will be boarding helicopters for our trip to Ethan's school, and Branden's. . ... Oops, I almost divulged some classified information." The General said, with a grimaced look.

George had heard the General's comment about the classified information; but since it was classified however, he never pursued the topic.

"That's fantastic sir; but where will we land?" George asked.

"We'll be landing at the Marine base near Irvine, George. Then from there, we'll receive a military escort to the school."

"That's fantastic news sir, but I have a question. Since this is supposed to be an emergency trip; how did the military find out about it?" Anya asked.

"I'm a General Mam; which means I'm in constant contact with the pentagon, at all times."
"When Ethan couldn't get in touch with George on the phone, he called the 'Red Cross' and told them about his situation. They in turn, contacted the pentagon with Ethan's information."
"Then, after the pentagon had placed a 'priority one' classification on our travel plans; they commissioned the 'Dept. of the Navy', and the 'Marine Corps', to assist us."
"Does that explain why we're not going to the ferry, George?"

"Yes it does sir; and thank you for sharing that information." George said.
"That explains our new travel plans sir; but you didn't say anything about how my piano teacher is doing. Is he okay?" Branden asked, with a sincere concern.

Branden was expecting a reply from the General; but due to the unexpected screaming sirens of the escort vehicles, it never came.

As the buses approached their final stop sign, before leaving the golf course, General Smith received a radio call.

"General Smith, this is Colonel Collins, sir. You have a clear passage, to enter the roadway. Will we be using two, or four escort vehicles, sir?"

"Let's use four vehicles, Colonel. Put two of them in front of us, and the other two behind us."
"Oh, by the way Colonel; please inform your escort drivers that we'll be rolling no less then ten miles an hour, over the speed limit."

"Okay sir, but they've already heard you; because they're on the same radio frequency that we are."

"I'm sorry Colonel; I should've already realized that." The General said, as the buses rounded the corner, and sped off down the road.

Factoring in their use of the escort vehicles, along with the ideal traffic controlling along the way, the buses were able to arrive at the naval base, in record-breaking time. As they were approaching the helicopters, Branden asked.

"Dad, are you going to try calling Mr. Ethan again, before we get there?"

"Yes I am son, but I'll wait until we're airborne to do it."

The buses had no more then stopped, when Steven and the group leaders jumped off of them, and assumed their leadership positions.
As the other boys were disembarking the buses in a disorientated state of mind, Steven shouted.
"Over here 'We Care'; and fall in behind your group leader, on the double!"

While the boys were quickly responding to Steven's request, General Smith and the base's Admiral were discussing the group's movement.
Then, once all of the boys were present and accounted for, Steven approached the General, and said.

"Sir, all of the boys are present and accounted for. What would you like for us to do now?"

To Steven's surprise, the Admiral answered him, instead of the General.

"I need for you to tell the boys that as soon as they're on the helicopters and sitting down, they have to fasten their seat belts. Also tell them; the helicopters are forbidden to take off, unless all seat belts are properly fastened."

"Steven, once you've made that perfectly clear to the boys; I want one group, on each of the helicopters as quickly as possible."

When Steven hesitated at the Admiral's request, he looked questionably at the General for a response. Then, when the General smiled, and nodded his head in approval, Steven turned, and ran back to the groups.

After quickly informing the boys about what was expected of them, and making sure that they had fully understood; Steven then hustled each of the groups, to an awaiting helicopter.

With the 'click' of the final seat belt, on each of the helicopters came the deafening sound of the engine, as it began its rotation.

When the engine's required warm up period had elapsed, the pilots then began advancing their throttles; while at the same time, the crew chiefs closed the doors.

All of the boys were anxiously looking forward to their flight; but they became a little nervous when the helicopter that they were in 'began hopping' prior to take off. They relaxed though, when they heard the air traffic controller say.

"Pilots of 'Operation We Care', may I have your attention, please? Gentlemen, you are now clear for take off; have a safe trip."

Instantly, after receiving the tower's clearance, the pilots throttled up to full power, tilted their blades and took off.

Unbeknown to the group however, the military helicopters were also equipped with jet engines. These jet engines, would allow the helicopters to fly at twice the speed, of normal helicopters.

When they had reached their cruising altitude, George took his cell phone out of his pocket, and prepared to call Ethan. He was interrupted though, when the pilot made the following announcement.

"Ladies and gentlemen, this is your pilot speaking. I forgot to tell you this before we took off; but the use of cell phones while we're in flight, is strictly forbidden."

"The reason for this restriction is because the cell phone's signal will seriously interfere with our navigational equipment."

"Since we will be flying near restricted air space; any interference of that nature could result in our being shot down by a military fighter. So I must emphasize to you, please do not use your cell phone, while we are in flight. Thank you for obeying this restriction; and enjoy your flight."

"Dad, what are we going to do now, since we can't use our cell phones?" Branden asked.

"There's only one thing that we can do son; and that's to wait until we land."

"George, if we fly in a direct line from here to the Marine base; we should be able to see Ethan's school, as we fly over Irvine." Anya said.

"That's right mom; and if we can at least see the school from the air, then we'll know if there's anything wrong, outside of it." Branden said.

"You're right about that son; but since you're the one sitting by the window, then you'll have to be our observer. Just let us know when we start flying over the suburbs' of Irvine." George said.

"Okay dad; but at this speed, it shouldn't take us very long to get there." Branden said, as he turned and began looking out the window.

Approximately ten minutes had passed when Branden turned toward his dad, and said.

"Dad, we're over the mainland now, so we should reach Irvine in a few minutes."

While Branden was talking to his dad, he began hearing a strange buzzing sound behind him. When he turned to investigate it, he was appalled at the sight of a stiff window shade, which was being mechanically lowered over the window.

Frustrated at the fact that he could no longer look out the window; Branden turned back toward his parents, and said.

"I wonder what's going on now, dad. It's as if they don't want us to look out the windows."

"I'm thinking the same thing, son. If you'll excuse me for a minute; I need to have a chat with the General."

"Okay dad; I sure hope you can find out what's going on." Branden said, as his dad left to find the General.

While George was walking toward the front of the helicopter, he met the General in the isle way.

"Excuse me sir; but may I have a word with you?"

"Yes, by all means George; but let's step in to the cockpit where it's a little quieter.

After they had stepped in to the cockpit, the General asked.

"George, are you wondering why we closed the shades, so Branden can't see out?"

"Yes I am sir; because Branden is really upset about it. He's still worrying about his piano instructor, and if there's something wrong at the school."

"I fully understand Branden's concern for his piano instructor George; but we've been operating under direct orders from the pentagon, on this mission."
They actually didn't want you or Anya to know what was going on; but they said that we could tell you, if a problem like this came up. That's why I'm going to ask you for a couple of favors, George."

"What sort of favors do you need, sir?"

First, I want you to go back and reassure Branden that there is nothing wrong at the school; and that his instructor is perfectly fine. You might want to tell him that Ethan has been outside, working on a 'VERY BIG' project."
"Then, once you have reassured him; I want you and Anya to come back to the cockpit, so I can show you something."

"Okay sir; we'll be back in a couple of minutes." George said, before leaving the cockpit.

Being a man that was always on time, and true to his word; George and Anya walked into the cockpit, in less then the two minutes previously mentioned. Being surprised by their early arrival, the General said.

"Wow George; that was sure fast. Were you able to get Branden calmed down though, before you came back?"

"Yes I was, sir. He was okay after I told him what you had said about Ethan's well-being. He also wanted me to thank you, for that information."

"George, I've really hated the way that we've kept you and your family in suspense during this trip. However, I feel that in the end, you'll understand why we've done it."

"What are you talking about, sir?" Anya asked.

"I'll tell you in a moment Mam; but let's close the door first, so Branden can't hear us."

After the door had been closed, Anya asked.

"Okay sir; now that the door is closed, what were you going to tell us?"

"I was going to tell you about it Mam; but I've decided to show you instead. Remember though, what you are about to see is only a small portion, of what lays ahead for Branden. Before I let you see it though, lets give it a name; and call it, 'Ethan's Ultimate Surprise'."
"Captain, I believe we're ready now; so bring it around, and lets begin Branden's 'Honorary fly by'."

As the pilot turned the helicopter toward the school, George and Anya instantly became aware of the military's secret mission. With a look of awe upon her face, Anya said.

"George, now I can understand why we couldn't reach Ethan on the phone. Branden is going to be thrilled, when we finally get to the school."

"He sure is Anya; and the best part about it, is that he won't even be expecting it."

After the helicopters had made their 'Honorary fly by', the General said.

"George, we'll be landing in a couple of minutes, so I need for you and Anya to rejoin Branden now. Then, once we've landed, I'd like for you and your family, to board the lead bus."

After George and Anya had sat down, and had fastened their seat belts, Branden asked.

"Dad, while you and mom were in the cockpit; did you happen to see the school, as we flew by?"

"Yes we did son; and we could see it very clearly. We don't know what's going on though; but it looked like Ethan is having a gigantic event, out in front of the school."

"Could you tell if there were very many people there?"

"Yes we could, son. In fact, there must have been close to three thousand people there. The funny part about it was; is when we flew over, all of them waved 'hello' at us." Anya said.

"I'm confused, mom. Ethan has never had a major event at the school, which we didn't know about in advance. What sort of event, do you think he's having today?"

"I'm not sure son; but we'll find out in a little while. In fact, it feels like we're beginning to descend now."

Anya had no sooner said the word 'descend', when Branden once again heard the strange buzzing sound behind him.

After turning quickly, and looking out the window, Branden said.

"Mom, I can't see the school from here, but the Marines already have our buses lined up, and ready for us. They even have several escort vehicles lined up, and the traffic on the street stopped."

"Speaking about buses son; General Smith would like for us to get on the front one, after we disembark the helicopter."

In less then ten minutes, the pilots had landed their helicopters, allowed

179

them to cool down, and shut down the engines.

Then, after hearing some loud commotion outside of the helicopter, Branden asked.

"General, what's all that noise I'm hearing outside?"

"I'm not sure, Branden. Why don't you open the door, and find out for yourself?" The General said, with a sly grin.

Branden wasn't aware of what was about to happen; so he grabbed the door handle, and slid the door completely open. Immediately, after the door had been opened, Branden was greeted by a very loud, and demanding...

"Detail; ATTEN-HUT!"

Shocked, and confused by the reception; Branden looked questionably at General Smith, and said.

"I'm not sure sir; but I think they were expecting you to open the door, instead of someone else."

"No they weren't Branden; they knew exactly who was going to open it. Go ahead and step down on the top step, and see what happens next."

"Okay sir; but shouldn't you be the first person to walk down the red carpet?"

"Not today Branden; because today you're the Guest of Honor."

Taking a moment to view the sights before him, Branden could see the following.

There were two rows of marines, with one row being on each side of the red carpet.

Each of the marines was proudly wearing their official dress blue uniform, which included the one-inch red stripe along the length of each of the trouser legs.

On their uniform blouses, Branden could see the large clusters of medals, which each of them had received, during their long military careers. In addition to their medals, Branden could also see that all of them were officers.

What he couldn't see however, was what each of them was holding at their sides.

Branden had been viewing the sights longer then he thought; when he suddenly discovered that, the other helicopter's passengers were standing behind the marines.

Realizing that he was delaying their travel plans, Branden then stepped down to the top step, where he suddenly heard.

"DETAIL, PRESENT ARMS!"

As quickly, and as smoothly as a well-oiled machine, each of the marines then snapped their precisely replicated weapons, in to the 'present arms' position.

Startled by the sight of their weapons; Branden quickly stepped back in to the helicopter.

"What's going on out there, mom? Those guys are holding real guns!" Branden gasped.

"They're not real guns Branden; but they have been precisely replicated. That means they are fake guns, which were made to look exactly like real ones." The General said.

"Okay sir; but I didn't know that. I'm sorry that they scared me." Branden said, as he stepped down on to the red carpet.

After joining their son on the red carpet, George and his family walked to their awaiting bus.
Within minutes, Branden and the entire 'We Care' group had completed boarding the buses; and were now awaiting their departure. Then, shortly after the buses were loaded, and ready to go; General Smith stepped on to the lead bus, and said.

"Okay Sergeant; lets get this bus rolling, so we can get Branden and his parents to the school."

"Okay sir; we're on our way." The driver said, as he pulled the bus in to gear, and began moving.

Taking the lead while exiting the Marine base, the escort vehicles led the convoy to their first prearranged stopping point. Confused about why they had stopped, Branden asked.

"Sir, why have we stopped? We only have about fifty more yards to go, before we turn left; and then an additional two blocks to the school."

"Relax Branden; we've only stopped long enough, to let you and your parents off of the bus." The General said.

"What are we suppose to do General; walk the rest of the way to the school?" Branden asked.

"No Branden; you and your parents will be riding in the stretch limousine, which is in front of us."

After reaching up and grabbing the radio's microphone, General Smith transmitted a message.

"Colonel Collins; we're ready for now, sir."

"George, if you and your family will follow me now, I'll walk you to the car."

After seeing just how long the limousine actually was, Branden said.

Dad, I have no idea about what's going on; but I would've never dreamed that we would ever be riding in a limousine, to go visit Mr. Ethan."

"I know it all seems strange to you now son; but you'll understand what's going on, in a few minutes." George said.

"Son, you'll want to see what's happening outside of the car, once we've turned the corner. That's why we're going to let you sit in the middle; or should I say, stand in the middle." Anya said.

"How would I be able to stand up mom; the roof isn't high enough." Branden said.

"Normally that would be correct son; but this limousine has a sun roof, which opens up completely. Once it's opened, you'll be able to stand up, and place your hands on top of the car." George said, as he began opening the sunroof.

"Son, there's a lot of things you'll want to see after we turn; so go ahead and stand up now, so you don't miss anything." Anya said.

"Okay mom; I'll go ahead and stand up, but I still don't know what's going on."
"The only thing I do know, is that this trip has been packed full of suspense, and confusion." Branden said, before standing up.

Even before the limousine turned the corner, Branden could see the thousands of people, who were waiting for his arrival. In fact, he was so intrigued by the size of the crowd; that he had failed to see the escort vehicles make a right turn, instead of a left one.

Then, as the limousine began its turn, Branden's attention was drawn to the sound of the Air Force's marching band, and the sight of their prestigious Honor Guard.

Even though he was enjoying listening to the music, and watching the honor guard; something else that was even more amazing, suddenly caught Branden's eye.

Above the street, and directly in front of him, was a very large banner, which stretched from one side of the street to the other. Written on the banner, were the words.

"CONGRATULATIONS; BRANDEN!"

"I can't believe this, mom. This is a celebration; and it's for me." Branden gasped, with excitement.

"Yes it is son; but you've only seen the beginning of it. We still have a block and a half to go, before we get to the school." Anya said.

Branden's excitement continued to increase, as he began waving back at the cheering crowd, and the sight of hundreds of congratulatory posters.

His excitement was temporarily interrupted however, when all he could hear from the marching band; was the rhythmical click of the drums.

After looking forward at the band, Branden could see that it was now making a right hand turn at the upcoming intersection.

Branden was disappointed by the loss of the Air Force's marching band; but became 'happier then a lark' however, when the honor guard went straight through the intersection, instead of turning.

Then, as the limousine passed through the intersection, Branden began hearing some very familiar, and beautiful piano music. Taking only a moment to speak to his parents, Branden said.

"Dad, I'm hearing piano music; but I don't know where it's coming from. Could you and mom stand up please, and help me find them?"

"We would be happy to, son." Anya said, as her and George stood up.

"What's confusing me mom, is when I turn my head to the left, I hear a piano; but when I turn it to the right, I hear a different one. It's like I'm hearing two separate pianos, but I'm not seeing any." Branden said.

Branden's curiosity was quenched, when the honor guard reached a designated point, in front of the pianos.

It was then that everyone who was standing near the street stepped behind the sidewalks and revealed the whereabouts, of the mysterious pianos.

To Branden's surprise however, there were more then just the pianos that he was presently hearing; because further down the street, he could see two more pianos, and then two more beyond those.

"This is fantastic, mom. There are a total of six pianos along the street; but I wonder if they're all playing together."

"No they're not son; but you'll see why in a couple of minutes." Anya said.

Even though the pianos were approximately fifty yards apart, Branden was still confused when the first pair stopped playing. That however, was only the beginning of 'Ethan's Ultimate Surprise'.

As additional banners began to be unfurled along the street, the first pair of pianos once again began playing. This time however, the song was very familiar to both Branden, and his parent's.

Excited that they were playing that specific song, Branden said.

"I know that song mom; and it's my favorite. It has been my favorite ever since my cousin wrote it, composed it, and had it copyrighted a few months ago. He even set a new world's record with it; when he played it at his first concert." Branden said proudly.

"That's true son, but I have a couple of questions for you. What was the date of that concert; and where was it held?" George asked.

"Those are easy questions, dad. It was held on March 25th, at the 'Barclay theatre'." Branden said.

As Branden's motorcade slowly approached the second pair of pianos, they too began playing the song. They however, began with the first stanza, while the first pair was starting the second stanza.

Then, while Branden continued to wave to the crowd, and move closer to the last pair of pianos, he noticed something unique.

"Mom, I just noticed something. The pianos are playing the song in roundelay. Why are they doing that, I wonder?"

"I'm not sure son; but I'm sure that Ethan has a good reason for it though." Anya said.

"Son, now that we're approaching the third pair of pianos; have you noticed anything new?" George asked.

"Yes I have dad; I've noticed a couple of new things."
"I've noticed that the third pair have started playing, and the first pair is now on the last stanza."
"If I'm right; then by the time we reach the stage, only the third pair will still be playing."

After completing their journey along Celebration Boulevard, Branden and his parents, finally arrived in front of the stage. Mr. Ethan however, was already standing at center stage, and awaiting their arrival.

"Look mom; Mr. Ethan is already up on stage, and waiting for us. Can I run up and talk to him, please?"

"No son, you may not. The reason that you can't, is because we're going to be ushered on to the stage, after we get out of the car." Anya said.

Even though he was slightly disappointed, Branden still complied with his mom's request, and waited to be ushered to the stage.

Then, with his arrival at center stage, came an overwhelming silence among the crowd. This silence however, was the direct result of their prior knowledge, of Ethan's forthcoming and ultimate surprise.

After personally congratulating Branden on his win, and welcoming his family to the stage, Mr. Ethan said.

"Ladies and gentlemen; let's hear a round of applause for our new champion."

With Ethan's request came a thunderous roar of applause, and some exuberant heart felt cheering that lasted for more then five minutes. When the crowd was silent once again, Branden responded by saying.

"Thank you Mr. Ethan and thank you too Ladies and gentlemen, for that fabulous welcome."

"I would also like to thank those responsible who diligently organized, and made this celebration possible."

"In addition; I would especially like to thank whoever is responsible, for including the song that the pianos were playing, as I was coming down Celebration Boulevard."

"Branden, I understand that particular song is your favorite, and that you enjoy playing it on the piano; is that correct?" Mr. Ethan asked.

"Yes, that's correct sir."

"Ladies and gentlemen, Branden is an excellent pianist; so would you like to hear him play the song for us?" Mr. Ethan asked, with a smile.

After receiving a thunderous 'YES!' from the crowd, which echoed off the nearby buildings, Branden began walking toward the only visible piano on stage. When he was only half way to it, Mr. Ethan suddenly said.

"Wait a minute Branden; I have something else to say."

"Ladies and gentlemen, Branden's parents not only informed me that he enjoys playing the piano; but that he prefers to have someone accompanying him when he does. Is that correct, Branden?"

"Yes it is sir; and that's why I enjoy playing along with my cousin's C.D."

"I'm sorry Branden, but we don't have your cousin's C.D. here today, so you won't be able to do that."

"We do however, have something even better then that. Today, your friends here at the school, along with me, have the ultimate surprise for you." Mr. Ethan said, before he paused.

With Mr. Ethan's pause, came the rising of the stage curtains; and the sound of a mysterious piano, which was being played behind them.

"Ladies and gentlemen, let's hear a BIG round of applause for our very special guest, and Branden's cousin; Mr. Lyon and his friends." Mr. Ethan said, as he held his arm outstretched toward the rising curtain.

"Awestruck by Mr. Ethan's ultimate surprise, Branden was unable to contain his excitement, when he said.

"Thank you Mr. Ethan; thank you very much!" Branden said, before turning, and hurrying off to the piano.

After Branden had sat down at the piano; Mr. Ethan stepped up to the microphone, and made the following announcement.

"Ladies and gentlemen, get ready to listen to some wonderful music, by these very talented young pianists."
"The first song that Branden and Lyon will be playing was written and composed by Lyon himself."
"Lyon debuted this beautiful song at his first public concert; which took place on March 25th of this year. I am proud to announce that during the concert, and while this song was being played; 'Lyon and his Friends', successfully set a new world's record."
"Lyon, on behalf of everyone here, which includes the writer of this story; I'd like to congratulate you on that new world's record."
"Now ladies and gentlemen, without further ado, I'm proud to present; Branden, and 'Lyon and his Friends, in the playing of, *'_513 Days_'."

After a short burst of applause from the crowd, the music began to softly fill the air with a melody that was both stimulating, and soothing to the soul. In fact, it was so soothing that when it concluded, the crowd enthusiastically cheered for more.
After both of the boys had taken their bows, Lyon walked over to Branden, and said.

"That was fantastic Branden; you play as good as I do. So since the crowd wants us to play some more songs together, I'd be honored, if you would accompany me." Lyon said, with a smile.

"I would be delighted to Lyon, but what songs will we play?"

"We'll stay with the songs on my C.D., if that's okay with you. In fact, here's a list of songs that we'll play, and the order that we'll play them in." Lyon said, as he handed Branden the list.

After looking at the list, Branden and Lyon returned to their pianos, and once again began playing for the crowd.

As one song followed another for the next thirty minutes, Branden and Lyon's music had held the crowd in a total state of awe.
Then, as the final note of the final song sounded, Mr. Ethan stepped up to the microphone, and said.

"Ladies and gentlemen, if you have enjoyed listening to these talented young pianists, as much as I have; let's hear a round of applause for their excellent performance."

As the roar of applause echoed off the nearby buildings, Branden and Lyon took their first of three bows. As the crowd's cheering and applauding continued; Lyon motioned for his accompanying friends to join him and Branden, at front stage.
Even though the entire group had taken a bow together, it still took another one, before the crowd became silent.
While the performers were busy waving their appreciation to the crowd, Mr. Ethan noticed that General Smith was trying to get his attention. After being acknowledged by Mr. Ethan, the general said.

"I have a gentleman and his wife standing here Ethan, who would like to ask you something."

"What would you like to know, sir?"

"Sir, does Lyon have any CDs that can be purchased by the general public?"

"Yes he does sir; but I'll let his spokesperson explain how they can be obtained. George, would you come to the microphone, please?"

"Thank you Mr. Ethan; and thank you too sir, for your inquiry.
"It's really quite easy to obtain one, or even more of Lyon's CDs. All you have to do is go online to http://anyafoundation.com; and click on the

products link. Then, once you've connected to the products link, you just follow the simple instructions on how to purchase his CD." George said.

"Thank you sir; I'll do that just as soon as I get home. In fact, I'm going to buy a copy not only for myself, but for each of my friends, and family members as well." The man said.

"Thank you, sir. I'm sure that Lyon and his family will appreciate that very much."

"If there are no further questions, then I'll turn the microphone back over to Mr. Ethan."

With no further questions to be heard, George said.

"Ladies and gentlemen, let's hear a round of applause for our Master of Ceremonies, Mr. Ethan."

"Thank you George, for that introduction."

"Ladies and gentlemen that concludes our victory celebration.

On behalf of Branden, his parents, Lyon, and all of us here at the school of music; I'd like to thank all of you for coming today, and showing your support for Branden; Good night." Mr. Ethan said, as the curtains began to be lowered.

When the curtains were all the way down, Mr. Ethan turned toward everyone on stage, and said.

"As all of you know, a victory celebration isn't complete without a feast. That's why you're now invited to the auditorium, and the partaking of Branden's victory celebration feast, and festivities."

"Lyon would you and Branden do us the honor, of leading us to the auditorium, please?"

"It would be our pleasure too, sir" Lyon said with a smile, as him and Branden took the lead....

Chapter 19

As the boys entered the auditorium, they were amazed at the amount of food that was on display, and available for the festivities.

There was food for all ages and tastes, which ranged from nutritional, to the not so nutritional sweets.

In addition to the abundant food choices, there were also two pianos on the auditorium's stage. Those pianos would become part of the festivities, as Branden and Lyon would come to discover, during the course of the festivities.

After a short announcement was made by Mr. Ethan, and George, everyone joyously filled their plates, and began socializing with those around them.

As the festivities continued, everyone was enjoying the celebration, which even included me. That is, until I received one of the saddest phone calls, I had ever received in my entire life.

As my friend on the phone, told me about the sad news; I haphazardly staggered toward a nearby chair to sit down.

Seeing my unusual movements, and fearing for my well-being, Alex and Justin came running from across the room, to be by my side.

"What's the matter, dad?" Alex asked, with concern.

With tears running down my cheeks, I looked up at my sons, and said.

"That was my friend from North Carolina, son. He called to let me know that our dear friend from Ohio has passed away."

"I'm sorry to hear that, dad. Was he very old?" Alex asked.

"No he wasn't, son. He just turned twenty-one, a few months ago."

"I know how good of a friend he was to you dad; so I can understand your grief. The main thing right now is; are you going to be okay?" Justin asked.

"I think so son; but what I really need right now, is to hear some nice soothing piano music." I said.

"I'm sure that can be arranged, dad. Alex, I want you to take dad, over to one of the tables near the pianos; while I go and tell George and Mr. Ethan, about what's going on."

Alex and I had just sat down, when Lyon and Branden approached our table with a cup of hot chocolate for each of us.

Then, after each of them had expressed their condolences, they stepped on to the stage, and walked to their pianos. Before they sat down however, Branden stepped up to the microphone, and said.

"Ladies and gentlemen, our dear friend 'Uncle Tom', and a friend of his from North Carolina; have lost a true friend to poor health, at the very young age of twenty-one."

"In respect, and homage to their departed friend, Lyon and I will be playing some of his favorite songs, for the rest of the evening."

"Uncle Tom however, doesn't want this sad occasion to interfere with our celebration festivities. That's why we'll begin with soft soothing music; and then gradually taper up to more joyous music, which will reflect the care-free, and good natured friend that he was."

During the next hour, the boys had played some wonderful consoling music, which had helped to reduce the pain of my loss, at least for the time being.

By 8:30, George had noticed that many of the boys had stretched out on the floor, and had gone to sleep. After discussing the matter with the other 'We Care' staff members, George decided that they should call it a day, and head for the hotel.

Disappointed that they had to leave; Branden asked his dad if he could talk to Lyon for a few minutes, before they said their good-byes.

"Yes son, you can talk to Lyon. After all, he is your cousin." George said, with a smile.

After walking up to Lyon, Branden said.

"Lyon, dad said we have to get ready and leave shortly; but that I could talk to you for a couple of minutes, before we do though."

"I wanted to let you know that I've really enjoyed accompanying you on the piano, during the festivities; and also to ask you this question."

"Would it be possible for you to attend my next tournament?" Branden asked, hopefully.

"I'd be honored to attend Branden; but I'll have to ask my parents first. If you can wait a minute; I'll give them a call right now." Lyon said, as he began dialing the number...

After his father had answered the phone, and Lyon had explained why he had called; his father said.

"Yes son, you can go to the tournament, but not without us. Tell Branden that all of us will be there, and cheering for him. In fact, tell him that we'll be there a couple of days in advance, so our families can spend some time together visiting."

"Thank you father; I'm sure Branden and his parents, will be looking forward to that."

"I better let you go for now, so I can tell Branden the good news before they leave," Lyon said, before ending the call.

As the conclusion of the festivities drew nigh; Mr. Ethan, along with the entire 'We Care' staff, came walking up to my table. With Mr. Avery as their spokesperson, he asked.

"Tom, we realize this isn't the most appropriate time to ask this; but would you like to say anything to the people, before we leave for the hotel?"

"Yes I would Mr. Avery; thank you."

After walking up to the microphone, I said.

"Ladies and gentlemen, and readers alike; I would like to take this opportunity to thank each and every one of you for your support, and understanding this evening."

"I'd like for everyone to know that I had just finished writing the previous chapter of this story, when I received the phone call today about my friend."

"The devastating news about my friend has played havoc with my thought patterns for this chapter. That is, until Branden and Lyon, so graciously played their wonderful music this evening, in memory of my friend Mark. Boys, on behalf of myself, and my friends from Ohio, and North Carolina, I want to thank you from the bottom of my heart."

"I would also like to thank each of my story's characters, along with my story line for helping me to some what cope, with the loss of my dear friend."

"Please, don't misinterpret my last comment; because I do, and always will, grieve over the loss of my friend."

"For those of you who are wondering why I have even included this sad portion in my story; I've done it for two reasons. First, it is because Mark had followed my story from the very beginning of my first book. Second, and most importunately; it's so his name and his memory will last forever; even if it's only in my story."

"Thank you again ladies and gentlemen, for listening to the heart felt appreciation of this writer."

"Okay Mr. Avery; lets see if I can get back into the story now."

"Tom, on behalf of everyone at 'We Care', and its associates, we join with you in your remembrance of your friend Mark."

"Now ladies and gentlemen, without further ado, here's our Master of Ceremonies, Mr. Ethan." Mr. Avery said.

"Thank you, Mr. Avery."

"First, I would like to thank everyone for coming to the festivities this evening, and showing your support to Branden. His next playoff game for the National Championship title will be held in two weeks, in Champaign, Illinois. I hope that all of you will be able to attend the game."

"Now ladies and gentlemen, since all of you will be leaving shortly; I would like to once again thank you for coming, and bid you a safe and joyful, good night."

Before everyone had left the auditorium, Branden thanked Mr. Ethan for the fantastic surprises that he had received since his arrival; and then bid him farewell.

After all of the goodbyes had been exchanged; Branden, his parents, and the entire 'We Care' group, boarded the buses for their trip back to the hotel, and a good nights sleep.

The following morning, as the sun began to peek over the mountaintops;

Steven had already awoken to a new day. Afraid that he had overslept, Steven hurried to his dad's room, to awaken him too. After Steven had knocked on his dad's door for several minutes, Mr. Avery finally opened it, and said.

"Good morning, son. Why are you up so early this morning?"

"What do mean by early, dad? I thought I had already overslept." Steven said.

"No son; you didn't oversleep. In fact, you could've slept for another hour."

"I didn't know that dad; but what time does our plane leave?"

"It isn't scheduled to leave for another four hours. Since you are awake though, why don't you go ahead and take your morning shower, and have it out of the way. Then after you've finished, you can go ahead and wake up the other boys."

"That's a good idea, dad. That will give all of us more time to enjoy our breakfast, and still get to the plane on time." Steven said, with a smile.

"That's what I was thinking too, son. By the way; when everyone is ready for breakfast, let's meet in the hallway outside of the dinning room. Then, when everyone is there, we'll enter as a group."

"Okay dad; I'll see you in a little while." Steven said, before he turned and walked back to his room.

After everyone had gathered, and entered the dinning room; they were amazed at how closely it resembled the one at 'We Care'.
The layout of the room consisted of two long buffet tables, which held any sort of breakfast food imaginable.
In front of the room where the head tables set, was an extra special surprise for Branden and his family. Lyon and his family had come to have breakfast with them; before the group had to leave for the airport, and their flight back home to 'We Care'.
After their enjoyable breakfast, and their time together, everyone boarded the buses for the trip to the airport.

Their arrival at the aircraft was earlier then had been expected however; which allowed Steven to see the pilot underneath the airplane. Curious about what he was dong; Steven turned to General Smith, and asked.

"Sir, what's that man doing underneath the airplane?"

"That's our pilot doing his pre-trip inspection, Steven. That's something he has to do, before we're allowed to take off."

"Are we allowed to board, while he's doing that, sir?"

"Yes Steven, we can go ahead and board; because that's only a routine inspection. The main one, along with any required maintenance, was done after we landed."

"I'm glad to hear that, sir. I'll go ahead and take roll call, and then get the boys on to the plane; while we're waiting for them to finish with the inspection." Steven said, before he hurried off.

While the group was busy boarding the plane, the pilot walked up to General Smith, and said.

"We're finished with the pre-trip inspection sir; so we can take off, whenever you're ready."

"That should be in about fifteen minutes, sir. We still have a few more people, which have to board yet."

"Okay sir; just let me know when you're ready. I'll be in the cockpit, taking care of some last minute flight log entries."

With the last of the departing farewells completed, and everyone now on board; General Smith walked to the cockpit, and informed the pilot that they were now ready for takeoff.

Following the sequenced flipping of several switches, came the loud high-pitched scream of rushing air, as the engines began their rotation.

When the engines' required warm up period had elapsed; the pilot released the brakes, and taxied to the end of the runway. Then, after only a couple of minutes, the pilot received his clearance for take off, from the control tower.

After gradually advancing the throttles to their maximum position and achieving lift off speed, the pilot began to gradually pull back on the yoke.

As the landing gear left the surface of the runway, Steven turned to Branden, and said.

"Well Branden, we're finally heading for home. What's the first thing that you're going to do when we get there?"

"I'm thinking about raiding the refrigerator, for a piece of grandma's delicious cheesecake, Steven. That is, if there's any made when we get there." Branden said, with a smile.

"I'm sure there will be Branden; because the cooks know it's your favorite desert."

For the next couple of hours the boys were enjoying their conversation amongst themselves, when Branden noticed a fighter jet, flying along side of them. After mentioning it to his dad, George said.

"That's one of our escort planes, son. The general has told me that we're less then one-hundred miles from home; and should be landing within the hour."

"Dad, will I have to start practicing for my next tournament, as soon as we get home?" Branden asked.

"Not necessarily son; but don't forget, two weeks will pass quickly. If I may ask, what did you have in mind?"

"I was thinking about taking a couple of days off, to rest up and relax some. Then I'll practice several hours each day, until Lyon and his parents come to visit."

"That sounds like a good idea, son. Don't forget though, Lyon has challenged you to a game when he gets here."

"Oh, I haven't forgotten his challenge, dad. Since he has won the 'Best in the West championship, and I have won the 'Western Division championship'; I have a strong feeling that our game will be very interesting." Branden said with a smile.

After their landing, which was as smooth as silk; the group was escorted on to 'We Care', by several military vehicles. Upon their arrival and disembarkation of the buses, Mr. Avery said.

"May I have everyone's attention, please?"

"The acting head cook has called, to inform me that we are to come to the cafeteria, for some sort of special event. Since Branden will be the guest of honor however; we'll let him, and his parents enter first."

Not knowing what to expect when he entered, Branden was very surprised, when he walked into the cafeteria, and heard over one hundred people shout.

"CONGRATULATIONS, BRANDEN!"

Branden's surprise consisted of a celebration feast, and was being attended by Judge Riley, the principal, and many of her students. The students however, were members of the school's recently formed golf team, who had come to help celebrate Branden's victory.

During the festivities, Branden had shaken hands with many of his fans; while at the same time receiving their personal congratulations, and well wishes.

With all of the feasting, and socializing that was taking place however, something else that was very important had been neglected. Stepping up to Branden, Steven asked.

"Branden, was you planning on presenting your extra certificate, to the 'Wall of Fame' this evening?"

"Yes I was Steven, but I had forgotten all about it; until you just mentioned it. I'll go talk to my dad, so we can get that taken care of before the festivities end."

Within the next fifteen minutes, Branden had presented the certificate to Mr. Avery, so it could be placed on the 'Wall of Fame'. After accepting it on behalf of the school, Mr. Avery said.

"Thank you Branden; you can be sure that it will be displayed, with the utmost honor."

"Now ladies and gentlemen; it's time to bring our festivities to an end for this evening. Before we do however, I'd like to make a final toast to our new champion."

After the final toast was made, and the festivities had ended; Branden began his two days of rest and relaxation. Those two days passed quickly however, and it was now time for him to start his strenuous practicing.

His parents knew that two hours on the driving range, one hour on the putting green, and a full game of golf each day; would be extremely strenuous on him, but Branden still insisted on completing his strenuous routine.

Finally, a couple of evenings before they were scheduled to arrive, George received a phone call from Lyon's father.

"Good evening George; how are you and your family this evening?"

"For the most part sir, we're doing great; that is with the exception of Branden."

"What's the matter George; has Branden been ill?"

"No, he hasn't been ill, sir. It's just that he has been practicing so much that he's keeping himself exhausted."

"He shouldn't be doing that, George. I'm afraid he'll suffer the consequences in the tournament."

"His mother and I have tried to explain that to him sir; but he still insists on doing it his way."

"Sometimes boys are like that George; they just won't listen to their parents, but they will listen to their peers."

"That's true sir; because I remember doing that when I was a boy. Do you think Lyon would talk to him, and convince him to ease up on his practicing?"

"I'm sure he'd be happy to, George. He's in his studio right now, composing a new song. If you'll hold on for a couple of minutes though, I'll go get him."

"Okay sir; while you're doing that, I'll call Branden to the phone."

After both of the boys were on the phone, and had exchanged greetings with each other, Lyon asked.

"Branden, I was told that you've been practicing so much this week, you're keeping yourself exhausted. Why may I ask, have you been practicing so much?"

"I haven't been satisfied with the distance of my tee shots Lyon; so I've been working hard to remedy that problem."

"I'll help you with that when we get there Branden; but in the mean while, I want you to do me a favor."
"I want you to completely stop practicing until we arrive; so you can rest up, and regain your strength."
"I'd be happy to rest up for a couple of days; but do you think that will interfere with my game performance?"

"No I don't Branden; in fact, I believe it will actually improve it."

"Okay, I'll take your advice and rest up until you get here; but only because you've told me to." Branden said, with a chuckle.

"I'm glad to hear that Branden; and believe me, you won't regret it."

The boys had talked to each other for about fifteen minutes, before they finally decided to say their good-byes.
As Branden walked slowly back in to the family room, Anya noticed how depressed he looked.

"What's the matter, son? Did Lyon say something, you didn't want to hear?"

"Not really mom; but he doesn't want me to practice anymore, until they arrive."

"He's concerned about your health son, the same as we are. However, the final decision is yours to make; so what are you going to do?" George asked.

"I'm going to take his advice dad; but in the mean while, I'll clean up my clubs, and restock my golf bag."

"That's a good idea, son. Just remember though, they'll be here before we know it." Anya said, with a smile.

Anya was correct about the rapid passage of time; and before they knew it, Lyon and his parents were coming up their driveway.

"Mom, it's only seven o'clock in the morning; and someone is already coming up the driveway in a limousine. I wonder who it is."

"I'm not sure son; but I bet it's someone you'll want to meet at the car." Anya said, with a smile.

After a joyous reunion, and a delicious breakfast, Lyon and Branden excused themselves, to go to the driving range. Before they left the house however, George said.

"Son, we'll join you boys on the driving range, in about thirty minutes. So do us a favor, and don't leave until we get there."

"Okay dad; we'll see you when you get there."

After arriving at the practice range, Branden told Lyon about the problem that he had been having during practice.
Reassuring him that the problem could be resolved with just a minor swing adjustment, Lyon decided to watch, as Branden teed off several times.

"I can see what you're doing wrong, Branden. You are not following all the way through with your swing. That by itself will reduce your distance by several yards."

After taking Lyon's advice, and correcting his swing, Branden said.

"Wow! I didn't think a small adjustment like that, would make such a big difference, but it did. Thanks a million for the help, Lyon."

"You're welcome, Branden. I'm just happy that I was able to help you with your problem."

Unbeknown to the boys, their parents had been watching them from the nearby cart path. As they walked up behind the boys, George said.

"Son, it looks like Lyon has given you some excellent pointers, on how to improve your game. I know you have challenged each other to a game; but with your permission, we'd like to join you, if we may."

"Sure dad you can join us; and it'll be more fun since we'll be playing as a family. Before we tee off though, do any of you want to loosen up a little?"

"Since we're going to be playing against you boys, we better loosen up. At my age, I need all the help I can get." George said, with a smile.

"Oh dad, you're not that old; so who do you think you're kidding?" Branden said, smiling back at his dad.

After everyone had finished loosening up, Branden turned to Lyon, and asked.

"Well now that you've shown me how to reduce my score Lyon, are you ready for our game?"

"Yes I am Branden, but you better play your best today though; because I won't be giving you any breaks." Lyon said, with a smile.

"That's okay with me, Lyon. Since both of us have won championships of equal difficulty; I want to find out which one of us is the better player."
"George, since both of the boys have the capabilities of playing like a professional; who do you think will win?" Anya asked.

"Considering that they have both won major championships Anya; I really can't answer that. All I know is; it's going to be a very interesting game." George said with a smile.

After walking to the first tee, and with the entire 'We Care' staff as spectators, Lyon and Branden began their extraordinary and challenging game.
With every tee shot, chip shot, and putt made with precise accuracy; the boys soon discovered that their talents were both of equal professionalism.
By the time, the game was over with however; both Lyon and Branden were mentally and physically exhausted.

"Lyon, I have a confession to make to you. That was the toughest game that I have ever played. It was even tougher then the combined games of the tournament, and when I played Steven, before the tournament."

"I agree with you, Branden. It was a tough one for me too."
"I believe if anyone else had been watching us play, and didn't know the difference; they would've thought we were twins, with the same exact playing abilities."

"I can understand why someone would think that, Lyon. It's because you and Branden, do look exactly alike." Steven said, with a smile.

"Son, I don't mean to interrupt; but have you boys tallied up your scores yet?" Anya asked.

"Yes we have mom, and you're not going to believe this; but we came up with the same score." Branden said.

"I can believe that, son. After all, both of you did take lessons, at the nation's best golfing institute."

"That's true mom; and we learned a lot from David."
"I realize it cost a lot of money, for me to take those lessons; but I want you to know, I really do appreciate it."

"We've known that all along, son. Your dad and I have always wanted you to have the best; and that's why we chose 'Ethan's school of music', as well as 'David's institute of better golf'."

"Anya, I don't mean to interrupt; but the head cook just called, and informed me that dinner will be served in about thirty minutes." Mr. Avery said.

"Okay Mr. Avery; thank you for that information." Anya said.

"Get your things together boys, and we'll go... Boys, where did you go?" George asked confused.

"We're over here, dad. As soon as we heard Mr. Avery mention food; we raced back to our cart." Branden said.

"Well George, we should've known the boys would be the first ones ready to eat."
"Even though they're totally exhausted; a boy always seems to have that magical burst of energy, to be the first one to the table." Anya said, with a chuckle.

"That's true Anya; because I use to be the same way, when I was a boy." George said.

"What do mean by that, George? You still do it on occasions. I've seen you and Branden race each other many times, trying to be the first one to the table." Anya said, with a grin.

"That may be true Anya; but have you ever noticed, I've never won?" George said, in self-defense.

"Hey dad, are you and mom going to stand there and talk, or go get something to eat? Lyon and I are famished." Branden said.

"We better go George, so the boys can eat. If you want to, we can continue this conversation over dinner." Anya said.

After enjoying their delicious meal, Lyon and Branden's families left for the new 'Havencrest Estates', and their long awaited family reunion.
Finally, when their time together had slipped away, George said.

"Son, I want you to get a good night's sleep tonight; because tomorrow is your tournament."

"I know it is dad; so that's why I'm going to say good night now."
"I know my bedtime isn't for another hour yet; but I can use that extra hour of sleep."

"Okay son; good night, and sweet dreams." Anya said.

"Good night, mom. Good night, everyone. I'll see all of you in the morning."

"Good night, Branden." Everyone said, as Branden headed off to bed...

Chapter 20

The following morning while Branden was still asleep, the sun began peeking through the window, and directly on to his face.

Even though he had rolled over to avoid the bright light, Branden's sense of smell was suddenly, and fully wide-awake.

Realizing where the delicious aroma was coming from, and what it was Branden opened his eyes, and saw an unusual sight. There, standing at the foot of his bed, was his dad holding a plate full of fresh cooked bacon.

That by itself would have been enough to wake Branden up; but this time his dad was using his hand, to fan the aroma directly toward him.

In a sleepy tone of voice, Branden asked.

"Is it time to get up already, dad?"

"Yes it is son; unless you don't want any of this delicious bacon." George said, with a sly grin.

"You better not, eat all of it dad. Tell mom I'll be there, in less then ten minutes."

"Okay son; we'll see you at the breakfast table." George said, as he exited the room.

After finishing their delicious breakfast; George and his family rendezvoused with the group from 'We Care', at their new 'Havencrest Country Club'.

Unaware that a special event had been planned, for their morning gathering; Branden and his family were very surprised, when Steven stood up, and said.

"Branden, we know it isn't customary to do, what we're about to do; but it's something the boys wanted to have for you this morning."

It's a known fact that many, if not all, high schools have these events before they play their football, or basketball games."

"The purpose of this sort of event, is so the students can show their school spirit; and hopefully to get the players hyped-up, and motivated to win their game."

"Now without further ado; here's Jeff, and the rest of the 'We Care' cheerleaders, in their first ever and unprecedented, pep rally."

Following the pep rally, which had lasted for approximately thirty minutes, Mr. Avery stood up to make the morning announcements.

Included with the announcements; were his special instructions to the boys, and their behavior requirements during the tournament.

As he was finishing up with the announcements, Mr. Avery saw General Smith enter the room. After being acknowledged, and receiving a 'good morning, sir' from Mr. Avery; the general responded by saying.

"Good morning to you too, Mr. Avery."

"Good morning Branden; are you ready to win that championship trophy today?"

"Well sir, I'm not sure if I'll win the trophy or not, but I am ready for the game."

"Just think positive, and play your best today Branden; and I'm sure you'll do fine."

"Here's something that you might be interested in knowing, Branden."

"On my way here this morning, I passed the golf course where the tournament is being held today. You wouldn't believe the number of cars, trucks, and vans that I saw; where the people had written their support for you on their windows."

"In fact, the closest that some of the people could park, was nearly a mile from the golf course." The principal said.

"Wow! Thank you for that information, Mam."

"General Smith, with the information that the principal has just given us; do you think we should get the boys loaded on to the buses?" Mr. Avery asked.

"That may not be a bad idea, Mr. Avery. After all, we may end up walking more then a mile too."

"Boys, you heard the general. Unless we want to walk a long ways when we get there, we better get going now."

"Steven, see if you can have the boys on the buses, and ready to leave within the next fifteen minutes." Mr. Avery said.

"Okay dad; but we'll be ready to leave, sooner then that."

"Boys, I want you to exit the building in an orderly fashion, so you don't disturb anyone. Once you're outside however, I want you to form up in to your groups, immediately."

"Remember boys, the clock is ticking so we have to hurry. You are now dismissed.

It took Steven less then ten minutes to have roll call taken and almost everyone on the buses. He became alarmed however, when he realized that someone very important was missing. After running to his dad, Steven said.

"Dad, I have everyone on the buses except for a few people. I don't have a clue where Branden or his entire family could be though."

"You don't have to worry about them son; because General Smith furnished a limousine for them."

"Now that you have the boys on the buses though; I'll go tell the general that we're ready."

The group's travel time from the 'Havencrest Country Club', to the front door of the tournament's clubhouse, had only taken forty-five minutes to complete.

After getting out of their limousine, and walking to the clubhouse, George said.

"Son, there's the sign that points toward the registration table. While you're taking care of that, I'm going over there in the corner, and wait for you."

"Okay dad; I'll be over there in a few minutes."

While Branden was completing his registration, he was asked a question by the official, which totally stumped him.

"Who's going to be your caddy, Branden?"

Unsure of his chose; Branden said.

"I forgot to make arrangements to have a caddy, sir. There are two boys I'd like to choose from, but I haven't had a chance to talk to either one of them yet."

"Are those boys here with you today?"

"Yes they are, sir. They're standing over there in the corner; talking to my dad, and that other gentleman."

"Do you know who that gentleman is, Branden?"

"He's to far away sir, so I'm not sure who he is."

"I think you'll know who he is, once you're over there talking to the boys, Branden. In the mean while however; I'll hold off from writing down the name of your caddy, until you come back and tell me."

"That sounds fair to me, sir. I'll be back in a few minutes with the name." Branden said, before he left to talk to the boys.

As Branden approached the group, Steven asked.

"Branden, did you tell the official who your caddy was going to be?"

"I haven't told him yet, Steven. I told him that I had forgotten to make arrangements for one; so that's what I'm here to find out. Which one of you, is going to be my caddy?"

"I was going to caddy for you Branden, but something else has come up. I'll let Mr. Fairway explain the situation to you though." Steven said.

"What's going on, sir? Is there going to be a problem, with me getting a caddy?" Branden asked, with concern.

"No Branden; there's not going to be a problem with you having a caddy. What Steven was referring to, involves the eligibility of this young man standing here with us."
"He has been selected as a 'wild card player' in next week's National Championship game; but has to meet his eligibility requirements first. That's where you come in to the equation." Mr. Fairway said.

"That's fantastic sir, but what can I do to help?"

"In order for him to meet his eligibility requirements Branden; he must first take part in this tournament, in some regard. Acting as your caddy, will meet those requirements."

"What do you think, son? Would you like to help this young man meet those requirements?" George asked.

"I'd be delighted to help him, dad. I've seen him play golf many times, and he's a fantastic player; so I'm sure he'd make a great caddy."

"I have a question though; what happens if I lose today? Will he still be eligible to play in the National Championship game?"

"I'm sorry I have to say this Branden; but that's the other part of his eligibility requirement. The player that he's caddying for today must win the tournament for him to be eligible."

"Your welcome to be my caddy, but are you willing to take the chance of me losing?" Branden asked, the young man.

"Yes Branden, I'm willing to take that chance; but I don't think you'll lose. In fact, I believe we'll both be playing for the National Championship next week." The young man said, with a smile.

"This is a tough decision, Steven. What do you think I should do?"

"I want to help him qualify, but I don't want you to get mad at me either."

"I understand your desire to help him Branden; but you should know better, then to think that I'd ever get mad at you."

"Just remember that if you win today, then I'll be your caddy next week." Steven said, with a smile.

"Since it won't make you mad Steven; then I'll choose him to be my caddy."

"Well Branden, now that you've decided who your caddy will be; why don't you boys get acquainted, while I go tell the official." Mr. Fairway said.

"Okay Mr. Fairway; and thank you for this opportunity." Branden said.

After informing the official of the young man's name, Mr. Fairway also said.

"It's customary not to mention a caddy's name during a tournament; so I want to put a strong emphasis on that policy, on behalf of this caddy."

"Under no condition, do I want this young man's name revealed during the game. If Branden should happen to win the tournament however; then I'll disclose his name to the audience, when I present the trophies."

"Do you have any questions, in regards to what I expect?"

"I only have one question sir; but other then that; you've made yourself perfectly clear."

"Are we allowed to mention that he has been selected as a 'wild card player'?"

"I'll make that known, when I do the opening ceremonies." Mr. Fairway said, before ending their conversation, and rejoining Branden and his caddy.

After talking to Branden and his caddy for only a short time, Mr. Fairway excused himself, and went to the podium to begin this extraordinary event.

Within minutes after his arrival, Mr. Fairway had made the announcement that brought everyone scurrying to the stage, for the opening ceremonies.

Amazed at the size of the trophies sitting on the table, Andy said.

"Wow Steven; have you noticed the size of those trophies? That championship trophy alone must be a foot taller then the one Branden won last time."

"You're right Andy, it is taller. The caddy award looks taller, and even more prestigious, too."

Since Steven and Andy had been talking to each other, instead of listening, they had missed most of what Mr. Fairway had said. They did however, hear him say the following.

"Again ladies and gentlemen; before I dismiss the participants, I'd like to emphasize something that I said earlier."

"Since this is only a one day tournament; I strongly encourage the players to play their best, from the very beginning of the game."

"Now with that said; I'd like to wish the players the best of luck, and I'll see each of you after the game. You're now dismissed."

With Mr. Fairway's dismissal came the hustling and bustling of the many players and spectators alike, as they scurried off to begin the game.

After arriving at the first tee, and with their excitement at an all time high; Branden's fans watched, as he stepped up to the ball, and teed off.

With a tee shot that had been perfectly executed; Branden's entire gallery then became ecstatic, as they watched the ball land within fifty feet of the green.

"That shot was fantastic, Branden. If you could do that on every hole, and then follow it up with a good chip shot; you wouldn't have any trouble at all winning this game." His caddy said.

"I wish I could, but I won't be able to. Don't forget, some of the fairways are par fives." Branden said, with a smile.

"That's true; but I'm sure you'll do fine, even on those."

"It's your turn again Branden, so what club will you need to make your chip shot?"

"I'm usually fairly accurate when I use my niblick from this distance, so I'll use it."

Branden's comment about being 'fairly accurate' was an understatement; when in actuality; he was quite accurate with it.

Recognizing the club as it was being removed from the bag, Andy said.

"Look Steven; Branden is getting ready to use his favorite club. Since he's using that one, I have no doubt that he'll make it."

"I have the same feeling, Andy. If he does make it, then that will be two under par for him; and that's also known as an eagle."

As the deafening sound of silence fell over the crowd, Branden stepped up to the ball, and prepared to make his swing.

Then, with their breath held, and fingers crossed; Branden's entire gallery watched, as he made his swing with precision and acute accuracy.

The flight of the ball had been awesome to watch, but the results were even more spectacular.

After landing within a foot of the hole, the ball had then begun rolling toward the pin. That roll ended, with the awesome sound of, 'KA-PLUNK'.

Branden continued to amaze the audience and announcers alike; as he played with precision, and top notched professionalism, during the entire tournament.

Then, while Branden and his caddy, were walking to the clubhouse from the eighteenth green; the rest of their family members joined them.

"Son, what came over you today? I've never seen you play that good, until now." George said, with a smile.

"I don't know dad; I guess it's because I wanted . . .

Branden's response to his dad had ended abruptly however, when Steven suddenly lifted him onto his shoulder.

After gathering his thoughts once again, Branden looked down at his parents, and said.

"Well dad, even though he caught me off guard again; at least I know what he's doing this time."

"I'm glad I did Branden; but this time I'm going to carry you all the way to the snack bar. That is, unless we meet Mr. Fairway along the way again." Steven said, with a smile.

Steven's plans were interrupted though, because as they approached the building, Mr. Fairway and his associate Jason, came out the door to greet them. After cheerfully congratulating Branden on his victory, Jason said.

"Well Branden, at least this time I know you haven't grown that much; but I do know of a couple things that have happened."

"Other then winning this tournament, and qualifying for the national game sir; what else has happened?"

"You're right Branden, you have qualified for the national game; but that isn't one of the two things I was referring to."

"Put me down Steven, so I can be closer to eye level with Jason."
"Now that I'm standing on the ground sir; what were you referring to?"

"I wish I could tell you Branden; but unfortunately, I can't. That information must come directly, from 'The National Director of Jr. Golf', himself."

Turning to Mr. Fairway with hopeful eyes, Branden said.

"Sir, what is...?"

"I'm sorry Branden, but I can't tell you that in private. The official rules specifically state that this information can only be disclosed during a public gathering, and while a trophy presentation ceremony is taking place."

Don't worry Branden, you'll find out what Mr. Fairway is referring to during the ceremonies today"
"In the mean while; I suggest you go get something to eat, before they begin." Jason said, with a smile.

"That sounds like a great idea, sir. My caddy and I have been extremely hungry, ever since I played the sixteenth hole."

"Okay Branden; enjoy your meal, and we'll see you at the ceremonies." Mr. Fairway said.

After filling their plates with some delicious food, Branden and his entire family, was escorted to a table in front of the podium.
Prior to sitting down however, Branden noticed a small sign on the table, which read.

"This table is reserved, for our VIP's."

"Sir, I think you've made a mistake. Isn't this table reserved, for the tournament's VIP's?"

"Yes it is Branden; but you and your family, are those VIP's. In fact, it was Mr. Fairway's wishes that you sit here, during the ceremonies."
"Now, if you'll please excuse me; I must be getting back to work."

Even though Branden was enjoying his meal, and the conversation that went with it, his curiosity was still getting the best of him.
Then, while he was still trying to analyze, what Mr. Fairway was referring to earlier; Branden noticed his caddy had a big smile on his face. Looking across the table at his caddy, Branden said.

"You're sure doing a lot of smiling over there. I have a feeling that you know what's going on; don't you."

"Yes I do Branden; but I'm bound by the same official rules that Mr. Fairway, and Jason are. So I can't tell you either."

"I know how you must be feeling though; because I've been in the same position before."

Branden was about to respond to his caddy's comment, when Mr. Fairway stepped up to the microphone, and said.

"Ladies and gentlemen, may I have your attention, please? Since we have several things to take care of during these ceremonies; we better get started."

"Our first order of business is the presentation of the Championship trophy. Branden, would you come to the stage at this time please, and receive this magnificent trophy?"

Following the declaration of his Championship victory, Branden received a standing ovation, from the entire crowd of several thousand. Unbeknown to him however, he was about to receive more then just a Championship trophy.

When Branden was on stage, and the applause had subsided; Mr. Fairway continued.

"Branden, I believe you're going to need help carrying your trophies today. So at this time, I'd like to call your caddy to the stage as well."

With Branden's caddy now on stage, Mr. Fairway continued with his presentation.

"Branden, on behalf of all of your fans, and the entire Jr. golfing association; I'd like to congratulate you, on your amazing victory today." Mr. Fairway said, as he presented Branden with the trophy.

After Branden had thanked Mr. Fairway for the trophy, he turned, as if to return to his table.

"Just a minute Branden; we're not finished yet."

"I'm sorry sir; but I thought you were."

"No; there's a few more things I still need to say, before you leave the stage; and a couple of those items pertain to both you, and your caddy."

Turning back to the microphone, Mr. Fairway continued with the ceremonies.

"Ladies and gentlemen, I have some additional surprises for Branden; but before I award those, I'd like to present the caddy award first."

"This magnificent trophy, is only slightly smaller then the championship trophy; but is equally as eloquent."

"As you already know, the caddy award is only presented to the caddy of the tournament's Champion. Therefore, it gives me great honor, to present this year's trophy, to Branden's caddy."

"Thank you, Mr. Fairway; it was a pleasure being Branden's caddy today."

"I've played against him in the past; but I've never seen him play as well, as he did today. I have a feeling that he's going to be very difficult to defeat, even for me."

After the thunderous round of applause for Branden's caddy had subsided, the registration official stood up, and asked.

"Mr. Fairway, you have kept us in suspense all day today, and haven't told us what Branden's caddy's name is. Could you tell us now, sir?"

"I'm not ready to disclose that yet sir; but I will in a few minutes. Right now though, I have an announcement to make; which will be followed, by the presentation of a trophy."

"Branden, could you step up here next to me, please?"

After placing his hand on Branden's shoulder, Mr. Fairway smiled and said.

"Ladies and gentlemen, this young man standing next to me never ceases to amaze me. His game performance here today, was an example of that."

"Speaking about your game performance Branden; do you have any idea, what your score was today?"

"No I don't sir; because I was to busy eating, and forgot to check the scoreboard."

"Well Branden, what would you say if I told you that your closest competitor, had made even par for the game; but was still thirty-six strokes behind you?"

"Sir, if that was the case, then I scored a thirty-six under par; which also means, my score was a minus thirty-six."

"That's true Branden, but that isn't all you've done. You have also set a new tournament record, and earned this trophy for doing it. Congratulations." Mr. Fairway said, as he presented Branden the trophy.

After Branden had thanked Mr. Fairway for the trophy, and the applause had subsided, Mr. Fairway continued.

"Now, while I still have you on the stage Branden; I have a couple more surprises for you."

"It's true that your victory here today, has won you a couple of new trophies; but that's not all it has done."

"In addition to qualifying for next week's final playoff game; you have also sky rocketed, in the national point standings."

"Branden, it gives me great honor to inform you, and your fans that you are now tied for first place in the nation; congratulations."

Overwhelmed by the news, Branden said.

"That's fantastic sir; but who am I tied with?"

"I'm surprised you don't already know that, Branden. After all, you've just finished playing an entire game, with him as your caddy."

"Boys, shake hands with your toughest competitor, for next week's tournament." Mr. Fairway said, with a smile.

"I know we're family; but I didn't know you were ranked number one in the nation." Branden said, with a surprise look on his face.

"I'm sorry that I didn't tell you sooner Branden; but I didn't want to distract you during your game."

"I'm glad you're going to be my toughest competitor next week, though."

"Boys, you can return to your table now, because you're finished here on the stage. I just have a few more things to say, before I bring the ceremonies to a close."

After the boys had left the stage, and returned to their table, Mr. Fairway continued.

"Ladies and gentlemen, for those of you who are planning to attend next week's tournament, and watching these boys compete; I strongly suggest you purchase your tickets today. Those tickets will be available in the clubhouse, after these ceremonies are completed."

"Next week's tournament by the way will be held in Augusta, Georgia; at the course which was designed by 'Bobby Jones'."

"Now, to answer the baffling question, of who Branden's caddy was. Ladies and gentlemen, I'm proud to announce the name of Branden's caddy, is Lyon."

"That concludes this year's tournament ladies and gentlemen. Thank you for coming, and please drive safely going home."

The post ceremony activities were very hectic, as people scrambled toward the clubhouse for their tickets.

Watching the crowd with sincere concern, Steven said.

"Dad, I wish we could go to the game next week; but it doesn't look like the tickets will last very long."

"Relax Steven; I've already bought tickets for everyone at 'We Care'."

"Mr. Fairway knew the tickets would sell out fast; so he allowed me to purchase ours, before the ceremonies were over." The general said.

"Thank you for doing that for us sir; I really appreciate it." Steven said.

"You don't have to thank me Steven; because I enjoyed doing it for you."

"Son, if you want to help Lyon, and Branden carry their trophies to their car; the general and I, will get the boys on to the buses."

"Okay dad; I'll be there as soon as I can."

Since everyone was exhausted from the day's events, it didn't take very long at all to get them on the buses, and heading toward home.

Within an hour however, the buses were once again pulling in to the driveway at 'We Care'.

The last words that were spoken, before anyone was allowed to exit the buses, were by Mr. Avery.

"Boys, I want everyone to report to the cafeteria immediately, after you get off of the buses. If you have to wash your hands first that is okay, but make it quick. I'll see you in a few minutes, in the cafeteria...."

Chapter 21

Mr. Avery's announcement brought a flurry of activity as the boys scrambled from the buses, in their attempt to be the first in line to wash their hands.

After nearly being knocked down by the stampede of boys, the adults decided to wait for a few minutes, before entering the building.

Unsure of what the adults were doing, Alex walked up to them, and asked.

"Dad, why are you and the other adults just standing here? Aren't you going to wash your hands, before you eat?" Alex asked.

"We're going to wait for a few minutes son, before we wash ours. That will give the boys time to wash theirs, and out of the way; before we go in." I said.

"Can I wait out here with you? I don't like congested areas either."

"You sure can son; and we'd be happy to have you."

During the next ten minutes, and while they were waiting to go in to the building, Alex noticed an unusual sight.

"Dad, I wonder why there are so many military vehicles parked along that street? They are parked on both sides of it, all the way down to the corner. There's even a police car sitting at the corner, with its red lights flashing."

Before I could respond to Alex's question, Steven had come bursting out of the cafeteria's door.

"DAD; we've been robbed, and they've taken everything in the cafeteria. They took the tables, chairs, and even the buffet tables."
"I'm scared dad; because I couldn't even find the cooks." Steven said, with tears rolling down his cheeks.

After sprinting in to the building to see for themselves, the adults discovered that Steven was right. The cafeteria was in deed, completely empty.

"Mr. Avery, you better calls the police, and report the robbery." I said, in a disgusted voice.

Unbeknown to myself, and the rest of the adults; Branden had walked up behind us, and was listening to our conversation. With a river of tears flowing down his cheeks, Branden said.

"I'm sorry Uncle Tom, but this is entirely my fault."

"Why do you think it was your fault, Branden?" I asked.

"Because if everyone here at 'We Care', hadn't been watching me play in the tournament; this would've never happened."

"Branden, I know you may think it's your fault, but it isn't. In fact, I want you to calm down, and relax for us. Will you do that for me?" The general asked.

"I'll try to sir; but I'm not sure if I can."

"Well, try your best for me; but in the mean time however, I need to talk to the adults, out in the hallway."
"Alex, would you and Johnny stay here with Branden, please? Steven, you come with us, because I need to talk to you too."
As the adults were entering the hallway, Mr. Avery, and Colonel Collins met them.

"Mr. Avery, did you call the police?" I asked.

"I was going to Tom, but this gentleman wouldn't let me. He said I would have to talk to General Smith first."

"That's right Mr. Avery, but he was just following my orders. So if you'll follow us please, I have something to show all of you."

Prior to opening the doors to their destination, Steven asked.

"Why are we going in to the gymnasium, sir? Couldn't you just tell us, what you want us to know?"

"I could Steven, but I've always thought that seeing is actually better then believing."

As they entered the total darkness of the room, General Smith asked.

"What do you think, George? Do you think Branden will be surprised, when he sees this?"

"I don't have a clue to what you're talking about, sir. I can't see a single, solitary thing in here."

"Well, I guess it would help to have the lights on, wouldn't it."
"Major Fitzgerald, could you gradually bring up the lights for us, please?"

Major Fitzgerald's compliance revealed an awesome sight for George and Anya, as they began seeing the previously invisible sights.
The first item, which was dimly lighted; was the immaculate red-carpeted walkway, which led to the head tables. Positioned on both sides of the red carpet, was a theatrical style red rope.
Just inside of the door, and waiting for Branden's arrival, were four fully adorned, military honor guards. These four honor guards represented each of the four branches of military service.
Then, as the lights continued to achieve their fullest extent of brightness, the adults were awestruck at the gymnasium's décor.
In addition to the many banners, posters, and various other signs of support to him; was the neon scoreboard which was flashing, 'Congratulations Branden'.

"This is absolutely amazing, general. Who is responsible for getting all of this accomplished, in such a short time?" Anya asked.
"The two main people were Colonel Collins, and Major Fitzgerald, Mam; but they had a lot of help."
"In addition to the one hundred and fifty air force personnel, from my base; they also received assistance from the V.F.W. post in Tuscola."

"Now I understand, why there are so many cars sitting along the street." I said.

"Since it's so dark outside Tom; I didn't think anyone would see the cars." Major Fitzgerald said.

"Alex saw them first sir, and that's when he asked me about them." I said.

"Oh my; I almost forgot about the boys. Sir, how are we going to get the boys in here, without letting Branden know what's going on?" Colonel Collins asked.

"My dad and I can take care of that, sir.
"Dad, I can take Branden with me to the office; while you wait in the hallway, out of sight. Then, when we are out of sight, you can get the boys in here. How does that idea sound?" Steven asked.

"It sounds like a great idea to me son; but what are we waiting for? Let's get this celebration started." Mr. Avery said, with a big smile.

As Mr. Avery and Steven were leaving the gymnasium, they overheard General Smith say.

"Colonel Collins, have your personnel prepare themselves for a stampede, of some very hungry boys."

Within minutes, Mr. Avery had relocated the boys from the cafeteria, in to the gymnasium. Then, after Mr. Avery had given the boys some final instructions, George and Anya stepped out of the room, as it was returned to the state of total darkness.
Approximately ten minutes had passed, when Steven returned to the gymnasium's entrance with Branden. When George and Anya saw their son approaching, they greeted him, and asked.

"Are you feeling any better now, son?" Anya asked.

"Yes I am mom; but I can't figure out why the police haven't arrived yet."

"They have arrived son; but they're in the gymnasium waiting for you. In fact, everyone on the police force is in there." George said.

"Why are they waiting on me, dad? I haven't done anything wrong."

"We know you haven't son; but they just want to ask you a few questions."

"Okay dad, even though I'm so scared that I'm trembling; let's go get this over with."

"We're going to walk in to the gymnasium behind you son; but Steven and Jeff will open the doors for us."
"Steven, I believe we're ready now." Anya said.

As the doors swung open, Branden was completely surprised, when he saw that the room was devoid of any lighting what so ever.
Before he had a chance to say anything though, the lighting along side of the red carpet began to glow its immaculate glow.
Then, with a little bit of coaxing from his parents, Branden took that first scary step through the open doorway.
Suddenly, and to Branden's surprise, the sounds of whistles and bells began to be emitted from the scoreboard, which was also flashing its congratulatory welcome. Hesitating for only a moment to look at, and listen to the scoreboard, Branden was startled when he heard.

"Honor Guards, fall in." Colonel Collins commanded.

As the Honor Guard began their prestigious escort of Branden, and his parents toward the head table; the band from the nearby high school, began playing the 'We Care' victory song.
When they had arrived at the head table, Branden said.

"Mom, I'd like to thank the band members for their reception, but I can't see them. I wonder if someone could turn the lights on for us."

"I'm sure that can be arranged, son. Colonel Collins, could you turn the lights on for us, please?" Anya asked.

Anya had no sooner made her request; when the sound of heavy duty light switches, which was being turned on, was heard throughout the entire room.
Then, because of the system's unique capabilities, every light in the room instantly reached its peak operational potential. After quickly covering his eyes with his hands, Branden said.

"Ouch! That hurt my eyes, mom."

"It hurt my eyes too, son. But look at what we missed, when we covered them up." Anya said.

Branden was expecting to see just a small band, before he uncovered his eyes; but was astonished at the sight before him, when he did.

There before him, was a gymnasium full of now cheering fans; that were there to help him celebrate, his amazing record setting victory.

Awestruck at what he was hearing, and seeing; Branden turned to his dad, and said.

"Dad, this is absolutely fantastic; but how did anyone have the time, to get all of this accomplished before we arrived?"

"I'll explain that to you later son; but for right now though, lets just enjoy the celebration." George said, with a smile.

"Good evening everyone; and welcome to this evening's celebration festivities."

Since we know all of you are extremely tired, and hungry this evening; we are not going to bore you with any long drawn out speeches. We will however, have a few short ones."

"Now, without further ado; here are our very own, victory cheerleaders." General Smith said, as he began applauding.

The general's announcement immediately brought the hundreds of fans to their feet, with a deafening applause of their very own.

Then, while the applause was at its highest, the first cheerleader made her entrance, followed closely by the second, then the third, and so forth until there were ten.

The entrance of the cheerleaders had been amazing to watch, as each of them used a different tumbling technique, to make their entrance. Among those were the cartwheel, front-flip, and the amazingly dangerous back flip.

Then, after performing several of their victory cheers, a few of the cheerleaders ran to a nearby table, to get something for their next performance.

Up until now, Branden had really enjoyed the cheerleader's performance; but now he was extremely curious, about what they were going to do next. As he watched six of the girls take their positions along the center court line, he asked.

"Dad, I wonder what they're going to do with those golf clubs?"

"I don't know yet son, but we're about to find out." George said.

Unnoticed by Branden or his parents, the principal from the nearby school had stood up to make the following announcement.

"Ladies and gentlemen, as most of you already know; the school at which I'm the principal of, along with 'We Care', have joined together and formed a golf team."
"When we first started the team, it was only for the boys; but we soon discovered that the girls wanted a team too. That's why we now have a team for both, the boys and the girls."
"Branden, you don't know this yet; but you've really been an inspiration, for all the girls on our team."
"Since you have the ability to make chip shots, almost every time you use your favorite club; the girls have made it their goal, to master the use of that same club. Their next performance, will demonstrate how well that goal has been accomplished."
"Once again ladies and gentlemen, here are the 'Victory Cheerleaders."

With a five-gallon bucket as their target and a dozen golf balls in front of each of them, the girls proceeded to demonstrate their unique chipping abilities, to the fans.
By the time the demonstration was over with however, Andy was awe-struck.

"WOW! Those girls are fantastic, Steven. They never missed a single shot that they hit."

"You're definitely right about that, Andy. I know one thing for sure; I'm glad I don't have to worry about competing against them." Steven said, with a smile.

After the applause for the cheerleader's demonstration had subsided, a young boy in the crowd impolitely yelled.

"I loved your demonstration girls, but when do we eat; I'm starving."

"Colonel Collins, I'm sure that boy isn't the only one getting hungry; so let's bring in the food." General Smith said.

The rest of the evening's celebration had lasted for over three hours; and had consisted of several speakers, and an abundance of delicious food.

Amongst the speakers were the chief of police, Judge Riley, the principal, and several guest speakers, from the National Jr. Golfing Association.

As each of the speakers talked about Branden's professionalism, and his superb golfing etiquette, he soon realized that his popularity was no longer on a local level, but on a national one instead.

Then, by the time the last speaker had finished; Branden had reached a state of awe. Turning in his chair to look at his dad, Branden said.

"Dad, I had no idea that I was this popular. I wonder what I've done to deserve it."

"By just being yourself son; and by playing the only way you know how to." George said, with a smile.

"Well dad, since the ceremonies are about over with; can I say a few things to the people?"

"Sure you can say something to them, son. In fact, Mr. Avery isn't going to close the ceremonies, until you do."

After standing up, Branden began to thank everyone who had been responsible for the evening's festivities; as well as the support, he was receiving from his fans. In addition to expressing his gratitude, Branden also said.

"Mr. Avery, I'd like to put my trophy on display, so everyone can see it; but is there enough room in the trophy case, to do that?"

"There wouldn't have been, in our old one Branden; but there is now. While we were at the tournament, General Smith had a new one installed for us. In fact, the new one is two times larger, than the old one was."

"Why is the new one so much larger, sir?"

"Because we wanted to be sure, it would be large enough to hold your future trophies too, Branden."

"Can Steven and I, go put my trophy in it now, sir?"

"You sure can Branden; and while you and Steven are doing that, I'll close the ceremonies.

With Mr. Avery's closure, also came his request for an orderly departure from the gymnasium. While back in the foyer, Branden had just finished putting his trophy in to the trophy case, when his entire family walked up behind him.

"It's a good thing the general had a new trophy case built for you son. That trophy by itself makes the other trophies look like miniatures." Anya said, with a smile.

"That's what we were thinking too, mom." Branden said.

"Son, Mr. Avery suggested that we form a reception line, here at the doorway; and give you the opportunity, to thank your fans personally for their support." George said.

"That's a great idea dad, but where would I be standing in it?"
"I'd like to be standing next to the trophy case, when I greet everybody; but if I'm the first person in line, I wouldn't be able to."

"I know how we could solve that problem Branden; and it's really quite simple."
"All we have to do is let you stand by the trophy case, and we'll line up next to you. That way we'll be between you, and the foyers outside entrance door." Lyon said.

Following Lyon's suggestion, Branden and his family stepped in to their positions, and began greeting the many fans.
Then, after Branden's last fan had shaken his hand, and had congratulated him, he turned toward his parents, and said.

"Mom, this celebration has been fantastic; but can we go home now, so I can go to bed? It's been a long day, and I'm extremely tired." Branden said, after he had yawned.

"You're right son; it has been a long day. Good night everyone; we'll see you in the morning for breakfast." Anya said.

After arriving at the 'Havencrest Estates', and before going to bed, Lyon said.

"Branden, I'd like to start practicing for next week's tournament, as soon as we possible can. What do you think of the idea, of getting started right after we finish breakfast in the morning?"

"That sounds like a great idea to me, Lyon; but for right now though, I'm in desperate need of some sleep." Branden said, as he stumbled off to his bedroom.

The following morning, began with Lyon and Branden enjoying a delicious, and nutritional breakfast together. This however, was only the first morning, of an entire week, which would eventually be written down, in to the history books of 'We Care'.

While everyone was still eating, Steven decided to bring up, an interesting question.

"Lyon, I know that I'm going to be Branden's caddy during the tournament; but who are you going to have as yours?"

"Actually Steven, I haven't given that much thought yet, but I guess I should. After all, I am going to need one."

"Well, if you don't mind me making a suggestion; I'd like to recommend you let Alex caddy for you."

"Does he know very much about the game, and how to play it, Steven?"

"Yes he does Lyon; in fact, he knows a lot about it."

"Steven is right Lyon; Alex would make a good caddy for you. In fact, here at 'We Care' Steven and I are tied for first place; whereas, Alex is ranked a very close second." Branden said.

"If he's ranked a close second Branden; then how many points separate him, from you and Steven?"

"You're not going to believe this, but it's only a minute one one-hundredths of a point."

Sitting within hearing distance, and listening to every word that was being said about him, Alex was now grinning, from ear to ear.

227

When the other boys had finished their discussion, Lyon turned toward Alex, and said.

"Alex, I'm going to need a caddy for the tournament that knows what he's doing. I was wondering if you...

"Yes Lyon; I'd be honored to be your caddy." Alex said with excitement.

"Now that we have that taken care of Lyon; there's one more thing that you, and I have to discuss." Branden said, with a smile.

"What would that be about, Branden?"

"I'd like to challenge you to a private tournament; which I'd like to refer to, as the ultimate challenge."

Overhearing, and the thought of an ultimate challenge, between the two greatest players in the nation, had instantly taken the room's two hundred occupants, in to a state of total silence.

After stepping up to the microphone, so everyone could hear his challenge without any difficulty, Branden said.

"Lyon, my ultimate challenge to you, is as follows.

"We'll play a game on each of the next three days, as if we're actually competing, in the national tournament."

"There will be no mulligans allowed, nor will there be any special breaks given to either one of us."

"In short, the entire official tournament rules will apply; which will also include, the use of unbiased scores keepers."

"What do you think, Lyon? Will you accept my challenge?"

After walking up to the microphone, Lyon simply responded, by saying.

"Yes Branden; I'll accept your challenge."

Then, after Lyon had accepted the challenge, which had included a gentlemen's handshake; I turned to Mr. Avery, and said.

"Get out the history books Mr. Avery; because there's a new chapter, about to be written.

The period following Mr. Avery's group dismissal; was just the beginning, of not only the three exciting days of practice, but for the entire week as well.

With the tension of excitement, running amuck amongst the boys of 'We Care', they began, with great difficulty, to choose their favorite player to cheer for. Confused however, about why he had to make a choice, Andy asked.

"Steven, I can't decide on who I want to cheer for. Why do I have to choose one friend, over the other one, anyway?"

"You really don't have to Andy, if you don't want to. The other boys just thought it would be more fun, if they chose a favorite player."

"I'm not going to choose one then Steven; because they're both my favorite player."

"What about when we go to the tournament Andy? Who are you going to cheer for then?"

"Both of them will still be my friends, even at the tournament, Steven; so I'm going to cheer for both of them." Andy said, with determination.

"That's one thing that truly amazes me about you Andy; you are unquestionably, a loyal friend."

While Steven and Andy were still talking, they saw Alex running toward them, as fast as his legs would carry him. When he got close enough to them, Steven asked.

"Why are you running, Alex? Is there something wrong?"

"No, there's nothing wrong Steven; but I have a message for you from Branden."
"He wanted me to tell you that he's over at the driving range loosening up; and that he wants you to come over there too."

"I should've already been there Alex, but I've been talking to Andy. Let's hurry up, and get over there as fast as we can."

To each of the boys, the words 'as fast as we can', meant that a foot race was inevitable. Therefore, without a moments worth of hesitation from any of them, Steven, Alex, and Andy took off running, as fast as they could.

After racing past the cart path, and up to where Branden was standing, Steven said.

"I'm sorry I'm late Branden; but I was talking to Andy, about a problem that he was having."

"That's okay Steven; I'm not worried about your being late. I am however, concerned about Andy's problem, and how serious it was."

"It was really serious at first Branden, but he has it figured out now."

"The problem that he was having was that he couldn't decide on which one of you to cheer for."

"That had to be a difficult decision for you Andy; but if I may ask, which one of us did you finally decide on?" Lyon asked.

"I really didn't want to choose one of you, over the other one Lyon; so I didn't choose either one of you." Andy said, with a grin.

"I really find that hard to believe, Andy; so why didn't you make a choice?" Lyon asked, as he noticed Andy's big smile.

"Andy, you're being mischievous again; but only this time, you're also being a tease. Behave yourself, and tell Lyon the rest of the story." Steven said, sternly.

"Okay Steven, I'll go ahead and tell him."

"Lyon, it's like Steven said earlier; I couldn't make up my mind, which one of you to cheer for, but now I know."

"If, there was ever a good thing that my biological parents taught me, before they abandoned me; it was to remain loyal, to all of my friends."

"That's why I couldn't make up my mind Lyon; because you're both my friends." Andy said, and then hesitated.

"That explains your loyalty to us Andy; but what about your decision?" Branden asked.

"That's the easy part Branden; I'm going to cheer for both of you." Andy said, with a big smile.

"Boys, I don't mean to interrupt your conversation; but it's almost time for you to tee off." George said.

Each of the next three days, were identical for the boys in regards to their scores, and playing abilities.

However, even though they had made some minor mistakes during the games, both of the boys were still able, to make successful comebacks.

Then, on the third day, and while enjoying their after game snack, Lyon and Branden received a special surprise.

"Well, good afternoon Mr. Fairway. This is quite a pleasant surprise, sir. What brings you out to the golf course today?" George asked.

"I have a special surprise for Lyon and Branden, George; which also includes, the entire 'We Care' family."

"Everyone is busy, grabbing a bite to eat, sir. You're welcome to join us, if you'd like to."

"Thank you George, I don't mind if I do. After all, I am getting hungry." Mr. Fairway said, with a smile.

After sitting down with his food; Mr. Fairway joined in, with the conversation at the head table. Then, after everyone had finished eating, Mr. Fairway stood up to make his surprise announcement.

"Lyon, I have a special surprise for you and Branden; but I need to know something first. Have either one of you, ever been to Orlando, Florida?"

"No we haven't sir; but we'd like to go, someday."

"How about tomorrow, Lyon; would that be soon enough?"

"That would be great sir, but unfortunately, we can't go. We still have to get ready for the tournament." Branden said.

"According to my friend Jason, you and Lyon have already accomplished that, Branden."

"How would he know, sir? He hasn't been here, for at least three months."

"Yes he has been Branden, but you just haven't recognized him. In fact, he's in this room, at this very moment." Mr. Fairway said, with a smile.

Looking around the room, Branden still couldn't see his friend Jason, so he asked.

"Mr. Fairway, I believed you when you said that he's in the room, but where is he?"

"He's standing right over there, Branden. Jason, take your disguise off, so Branden can recognize you; and then join us here at the head table."

After Jason had joined them at the head table; and had given his progress report about the boys, Mr. Fairway said.

"Now boys, I'm going to tell you what your surprise is; and then hopefully, your parents will let you go."
"Starting at seven o'clock tomorrow morning; both of you, your parents, and everyone at 'We Care' and the 'Havencrest Country Club', will depart for Orlando's International airport."
"Once we have landed, we will be staying the night in one of Orlando's luxurious hotels."
"Then, Friday morning after breakfast, we'll begin a full day of amusement and entertainment, at one of the world's largest resorts."
"Lyon, you and Branden should know what resort I'm referring to; because there's a smaller version of it located near your California homes."
"We're scheduled to leave there at four-thirty in the afternoon, and begin the next leg of our journey. That portion of our trip, will take us to a hotel, which is located just a couple of miles from Cape Canaveral."

"That's fantastic sir; because there's suppose to be a shuttle launching Saturday morning. I sure hope we can stay long enough at the hotel, to watch it take off." Andy said.

"I'm sorry Andy, but that won't be possible; because we'll be leaving right after breakfast."

"Sir, since that might be the only chance the boys will ever get to watch the shuttle take off; couldn't we change the trip plans a little?" Mr. Avery asked.

"That isn't possible either Mr. Avery; but if you'll give me a moment, I'll explain why."

"Boys, the reason that we'll be leaving the hotel right after breakfast, is because we'll have to be at the V.I.P. welcoming center at Cape Canaveral by eight o'clock."

"Once we're there, and after Lyon and Branden have received their V.I.P. welcome; we'll be escorted by an honor guard to the V.I.P. observatory, where we'll watch the nine o'clock launching. Then, once the shuttle has been launched, and it's out of sight; we'll depart the facilities for our trip to Augusta."

"Just remember everyone; the tournament will start at exactly ten o'clock sharp on Sunday morning, so be sure you get a good night's sleep Saturday night."

"Now that I've disclosed the surprise; are there any objections, questions, or comments from any of the adults?" Mr. Fairway asked.

After everyone had recovered from his or her state of awe, Mr. Avery said.

"I don't have any objections, sir. In fact, I think this is a wonderful opportunity, for all of us. I do however, have a question."

"Who will be providing the transportation, and the hotel accommodations?"

"General Smith has already taken care of the arrangements, Mr. Avery. In fact, he'll be at 'We Care' this evening during dinner, to give you the details."

"Now I have a question for Lyon and Branden's parents. George, do any of you object to the boys going on this trip?"

"No sir; in fact, we're in full agreement that it would be both educational, as well as a relaxing adventure for the boys."

After the approval session was over, Jason said.

"Mr. Fairway, you forgot to mention what the resort's theme would be for the day."

"You're right Jason, I did forget; but I didn't mean to."

"Boys, the resorts' theme for the day while we're there, is going to be, 'Lyon and Branden's Day'." Mr. Fairway said.

"Now, since that's all I had to say; I'll turn the floor back over to Mr. Avery."

With the conclusion of Mr. Fairway's surprise, came an overwhelming standing ovation, from everyone present. In fact, the group's enthusiastic applause was so loud; that Mr. Avery finally had to intercede. After everyone was finally quiet, Mr. Avery said.

"Mr. Fairway, on behalf of everyone here, and especially for Lyon and Branden; I'd like to say thank you."
"Steven, at this time I'll turn the floor over to you, so you can dismiss the boys."

With Steven's final instructions, came an orderly, but rapid departure of all the boys. Then, after the staff had said good night to Mr. Fairway, everyone went home to prepare for the following day.

Three days later, and while on their way to Augusta, Branden said.

"I don't know about you Lyon, but I've had a lot of fun the last couple of days."

"I have too Branden; but they've been exhausting days too. I sure hope that we can get enough sleep tonight, so we'll be ready for the tournament tomorrow."

"I'm sure we'll get enough rest Lyon; but we'll have to go to bed, right after dinner." Branden said.

"Son, you and Lyon won't be the only ones going to bed early; because the rest of us will be too." Anya said, with a smile.

"Dad, it's going to be after dinner time, by the time we get to the hotel. Do you think they'll still let us eat?" Branden asked, as his belly was growling.

"Yes son, we'll still be able to eat. In fact, we'll be eating in the V.I.P. room when we get there."

"Uncle George, Branden and I sure have been getting some royal treatment, for the last couple of days; but why?" Lyon asked.

"Because there's a lot of people who wanted it that way Lyon; but more specifically however, the author of this story wanted both of you to have the best."

"I wish there was someway I could thank the author for his hospitality Uncle George; but I don't think that's possible."

"He's already aware of your gratitude Lyon; after all, he is the author." George said, with a smile.

"George, I don't mean to interrupt your conversation with the boys, but we'll be arriving at the hotel in a few minutes."
"When we get there; Steven will organize the boys, so they can enter the building in an orderly fashion. However, I'd like for Lyon and Branden to be the first ones in line; followed by you, and the rest of your family." General Smith said.

"What about our luggage, sir? Should we unload it before, or after we eat?" George asked.

"You won't have to worry about unloading the luggage, George. I'm going to have my men do that, while everyone else is busy eating."
"When it's unloaded, they'll put it in the lobby and stand guard over it, until everyone is ready to take it to their rooms."

When the buses finally arrived at the hotel, Steven's organization of the boys went as smoothly as a well-oiled machine.
Even though their dinner had been tremendously delicious, the boys had soon finished eating, and were now ready for a good night's sleep.

"Good night everyone; we'll see all of you in the morning for breakfast." Branden said.

"Good night boys; we'll see you in the morning." Anya said.

Chapter 22

The following morning, Lyon and Branden awoke to the new day; fully rested, and ready for an energizing breakfast.

As Branden was opening his eyes however, he could hear the soft and soothing sound of a cooing morning dove nearby. So in a soft-spoken voice, he said.

"I don't know about you Lyon; but I really enjoy hearing that sound, when I first wake up. Because when I do, it seems like I always have a great game of golf that day."

"I know this may sound silly; but I actually think it's a good omen."

"I feel the same way Branden, but let me ask you something. What does it mean, when there are two of them sitting on the window sill cooing, and looking in at us at the same time?"

After looking at the window and smiling, Branden said.

"There are only two possible reasons for that, Lyon. Either I'm going to have twice the amount of luck today; or we're both going to have a great day."

"Well, I guess we'll find out about that, later today. Fore right now though, we better hurry up and get to breakfast."

As the boys were departing their room for breakfast, they could hear the fluttering of wings, as the doves took flight.

Assuming that they would not see the doves anymore that day, Lyon and Branden were both surprised however, when they entered the cafeteria.

There, outside of the patio doors, and sitting on the door handles; were the two doves, which were awaiting Lyon and Branden's arrival.

After the boys were sitting down, and enjoying their meal, George suddenly heard a commotion, near the patio doors.

"Jeff, what's all the commotion about over there?" George asked.

"You're not going to believe this sir, but there are two doves pecking on the window. They're acting like they want in, sir."

"Doves don't normally act like that, Jeff. Maybe you and the other boys should move away from the window, so they'll leave."

"Okay sir, but there's something else you should know about too."

"What would that be, Jeff?"

"You're not going to believe this either sir; but each of them has a letter on their chest."

"Are you sure they're actually letters Jeff; and not just part of the bird's plumage?"

"Yes sir, they're definitely letters and very plain ones too."

"Jeff, just out of curiosity; what letters are they?" Branden asked.

"Well Branden, one of them has an 'L', and the other one has a 'B'."

"George, I've never known Jeff to say anything, which wasn't true; but this, I have to see for myself." Mr. Avery said, as he began walking toward the door.

"Wait for us Mr. Avery; because we want to see it too." Anya said.

After walking up to the door, Branden said.

"This is amazing, dad. They're not even afraid of us."

"Son, I want you to try something for us. Put your finger on the glass next to the bird that has the 'B', so we can see what it does."

Branden complied with hid dad's request, and was pleasingly surprised at the results.

"Ah, look at that, mom. The dove is rubbing its head against the glass, as if it was actually rubbing my finger." Branden said, with a smile.

Unbeknown to the group; the hotel's manager had walked up behind them, and was watching the strange phenomenon.

"George, those birds showed up here a couple of days ago, and have refused to leave; but now I know why they've stayed. It's because they've been waiting for Lyon and Branden to arrive." The manager said, with a smile.

"Sir, I wonder what they would do if we opened the door." Branden asked.

"That's a good question Branden; so why don't we find out. George, is that okay with the rest of you?"
"Yes that's fine with us sir, but let us sit down first."
When everyone was sitting down, the manager slowly slid the door open, and allowed the doves to enter the room.
Then, after circling the room twice to get their bearings, the doves landed gracefully in front of Lyon and Branden.
Several minutes had passed, and the boys had become acquainted with their newfound friends, when George stood up and said.

"Well everyone, I must admit that this has been quite an unusual morning for all of us.
However, regardless of how unusual it has been for us; we still have to get Lyon and Branden to their tournament.

For the next hour, the group's activities involved getting ready for the tournament, as well as their short trip to the golf course.
Before getting off the bus however, Branden turned to his dad, and said.

"Dad, after Lyon and I get signed in, we'll be going to the driving range to loosen up."

"That's a good idea, son. Since this is the last and most important game of the season; you definitely don't want to injure yourselves." George said.

After following the boys in to the clubhouse, George and Anya were greeted by Mr. Fairway.

"Good morning, George. Are the boys ready for their game?"

"Yes, I believe they are sir. They've been anxious to get started with it, ever since breakfast this morning."

"They won't have to wait much longer George; because the opening ceremonies will start, in about forty-five minutes."

"Should I go tell the boys about the opening ceremonies, George?" Anya asked.

"That won't be necessary Anya; because here they come now." Mr. Fairway said.

"Good morning, Mr. Fairway. How are you this morning, sir?" Branden asked.

"I'm doing real well this morning Branden; and I understand, you and Lyon are too."

"Yes we are sir; we're feeling great this morning. Oh, by the way sir; thank you for signing us in."

"You're welcome Lyon; but that isn't the only thing, we've done for you boys this morning."
"We've also reserved the two center practice boxes for you, out on the practice range. So you better get on out there, and start loosening up." Mr. Fairway said, with a smile.

"How much time will we have sir, before the opening ceremonies start?" Branden asked.
"They'll start in about forty-five minutes Branden; but I want both of you to be there, in about thirty minutes."

"Okay sir; we'll be there on time." Lyon said, before they took off for the driving range.

The boys practice session, had passed quickly however, when Mr. Fairway made the following announcement.

"Ladies and gentlemen, may I have your attention please?"
"Since the opening ceremonies will commence shortly; I'd like for the contestants, to come to the stage at this time."

The arrival of the contestants at stage front was followed with the traditional greetings, along with any final instructions, required by the national golfing association.

In addition to the above, Mr. Fairway also took a few moments to make a special introduction.

"Branden, would you and Lyon come up on the stage please?"

Even though the boys were not sure of Mr. Fairway's intentions, they still felt compelled to comply with his request.

Then, once they were on stage, Mr. Fairway continued.

"I'm sure very few of you; know these young men standing here next to me. Therefore, I'd like to introduce them to you."

Standing to my left, and looking like a professional, is Lyon. On my right, and looking equally as professional, is Branden."

"I'm not sure if any of you are aware of this; but both of these young men are ranked number one, in the national standings. Therefore, they are the ones that you'll have to defeat today; if you have any hopes of winning this tournament."

"Now, with that said; let's get the opening ceremonies under way."

"Good morning everyone; and welcome to this year's national championship game."

"As most of you already know, this year's competition will only consist of the top fifteen players in the nation. These players have not only won their divisional championships, but their regional ones as well. Therefore, I believe that during the next several hours, we will be witnessing some extraordinary competition."

"For those of you, who don't already know; the winner of today's game, will also be awarded the prestigious 'Grand Slam Award for juniors. That's another reason, why I believe that today's competition will be very competitive."

"Now, since I gave the players their final instructions, prior to these ceremonies; I'm going to dismiss all of you, at this time."

"Good luck everyone; and may the best player prevail."

While the hundreds of the spectators were scurrying off, to begin watching this exciting game, Branden turned to Lyon, and said.

"Lyon, I'm anxious to get this game started, but I'm extremely nervous too."

"I'm feeling the same way, Branden. We're going to have to relax though, if we expect to win today."

Lyon had no sooner said 'relax', when the two doves once again came into their lives.

After landing on the boys' golf clubs, the doves' presence brought an instantaneous sense of peace and serenity, to each of the boys.

"Lyon, I can't believe how relaxed I feel now. Do you think the doves had anything to do with it?"

"I'm sure they had everything to do with it, Branden. After all, they came to us this morning; we didn't go to them." Lyon said, with a smile.

By the time the boys had reached the tee box; they had ended their conversation, and were preparing themselves mentally for the game. Prior to entering the tee box however, Lyon turned to shake Branden's hand, and said.

"Good luck with your game, Branden. Just remember one thing though; I'll be trying my best to win today."

"I wouldn't want it any other way Lyon; besides, I'll be doing the same thing." Branden said, with a smile.

After the boys had wished each other the best of luck, Lyon stepped in to the tee box, and teed off.

Then, after only four holes of play, came the official announcement from Mr. Fairway.

"Ladies and gentlemen, you may find this hard to believe; but Lyon and Branden, have already set a new course record this morning. Their closest competitor however, is each other."

After Mr. Fairway had completed his announcement, Jason turned to him, and said.

"You were right about their closest competition sir, but you didn't say how close."

"I didn't want their competition to know that Jason; so that's why I said it that way."

"Besides, I think it'll encourage everyone else to play better." Mr. Fairway said, with a smile.

Mr. Fairway's announcement had caused the boys to realize that they were either tied, or very close to it. Therefore, with even more determination to win then before, they began playing more aggressively, with the hopes of defeating each other.

Unbeknown to them however, they were actually matching each other, stroke for stroke on every hole.

Finally, after two and a half hours of play, and the completion of the ninth hole, it was now time for their mid game break.

"May I have everyone's attention, please? I'd like to inform the contestants that their current scores, are now available for viewing." Mr. Fairway announced, before turning off the microphone.

"Jason, I knew this tournament would bring out the best, in both Lyon and Branden; and their scores have proven that.

"In your honest opinion; do you think they'll still be tied, at the end of the game?" Mr. Fairway asked.

"Yes I do sir; in fact, I'm almost positive of it." Jason said, with a smile.

"That's what I was thinking too, Jason; and that brings me to my next question."

"Did you take care of that special project for me?"

"Yes, I've taken care of it for you, sir. In fact, I put all four of them into a heavy duty box, and then put it on the stage for you."

"Thank you for doing that for me Jason, but isn't that a security risk? After all, those trophies are very expensive." Mr. Fairway said, with concern.

"That's not going to be a problem sir; because General Smith has four of his police officers guarding them."

"That sounds fantastic Jason, but could you do me a favor? Could you thank the general for me, while I'm getting the second half of the game started?"

"Then, after I get it started, I'm going to look up something in the rules book."

"If you don't mind me asking sir; what are you going to look up?"

"The rules which pertain to any required play off holes, Jason. Because I have absolutely no doubt, they will be applied here today."

With the game's advancement, came the continuation of Lyon and Branden's quest, for the national championship title. Only a few holes had been played however, when Anya said.

"George, this is absolutely incredible. Never in my entire life; have I ever seen a junior contestant play as well, as Lyon and Branden have today."

"That's what I was thinking too, Anya. Actually, I believe the boys know they have everyone defeated already, except for each other. That's why this game is going to get interesting, before it's over with." George said, with a smile.

"Sir, is there a possibility of the other players catching up with Lyon and Branden?" Johnny asked.

"They won't be able to now Johnny, because the game is almost over."

"If that's the case sir; then all we have to do now, is wait and see who wins." Johnny said, with a smile.

"That's true, and we'll know the answer to that question, in about thirty minutes."

The boys had been playing a flawless game, until their arrival at the eighteenth tee. Before stepping in to the tee box however, Branden said.

"Lyon, we've been tied for the entire game, so do you think this hole will make a difference?"

"No I don't Branden; but we still have to play it. Just remember one thing though; if you're planning on winning the tournament in regulation play, then you'll have to defeat me on this one."

"I just might be able to do that, Lyon. Because this is a small green and those are my specialty." Branden said, with a smile.

243

"Don't forget Branden, we had the same golf instructor, so they're my specialty too. Now, hurry up and tee off, so we can get this game over with." Lyon said, with a return smile.

In their haste to tee off however, both boys had made a crucial mistake, in their judgment of the wind. Then, after walking up to the green, Branden said.

"Wow! This is going to be a tough shot for both of us."
"If I would've paid more attention to the wind, before I teed off; then I wouldn't be in the sand trap now, or up against that steep edge." Branden said, with a frown.

"Don't worry about it Branden; because I ended up in the one on the other side of the green. I'm even up against a steep edge like you are."

Even though the boys had landed in the sand traps, their professionalism still prevailed however, as they ended regulation play. Then, as their cheering fans followed them to the clubhouse, Branden asked.

"What do we have to do now, Lyon?"

"I don't know about you, but I'm going to get something to eat, while I'm waiting."

The boys had just finished eating, when Mr. Fairway stepped up to the microphone with the official results.

"Ladies and gentlemen, may I have your attention, please?"
"All of our contestants have now finished their game; and their final scores have been tallied. Our Champion however, has not yet been decided upon."
"Our two leading finalists both have a score of fifty-six; which requires them to play some additional holes."
"Normally, in situations like this, the winner is decided upon, after only one playoff hole. However, the official rules do state, there may be as many as three. Therefore, if they are stilled tied after the first one; we will then move immediately, to the second one."
"The first fairway which will be played is rated the third hardest on the course; while the second fairway, is rated the second hardest. Now with that said; let's get the final eliminations underway"

"Lyon, you and Branden may now take your places, on the number two tee box."

The boys continued with their expertise playing abilities, and completed the first two holes, with amazing results. Along with the results, came Mr. Fairway's historical announcement.

"Ladies and gentlemen, this has never happened before, in the history of junior golf; but Lyon and Branden, are still tied."
"Therefore, since they are still tied, we must now move to the third and final hole."
"Okay boys, you may now take your positions, in the eighteenth tee box."

While everyone was walking toward the eighteenth tee, Jason turned to Mr. Fairway and asked.

"Sir, why are we going to the eighteenth hole, instead of number six? Isn't six harder then eighteen?"

"Six may be rated the hardest; but the wind caused them problems, on eighteen. That's why I'm having them replay it."

"That's a good reason sir; but isn't the wind blowing harder now, then it was during regulation play?"

"Yes, it's definitely blowing harder, Jason. In fact, it has picked up to twenty M.P.H., but has intermittent gusts of thirty. So therefore, if either one of them, are the least bit careless in their tactics; we'll definitely have a single champion today."

"Sir, just out of curiosity; what happens if the boys are still tied, after this hole? What do the rules say about that?"

"I can't answer that question now Jason; but I will, if they do." Mr. Fairway said, with a smile.

Upon arriving at the tee box, Lyon and Branden quickly began to scrutinize the green's possibilities, as well as the wind's variations. Then, once they were satisfied with their own individual strategy, the boys took their turn, and teed off.

The results of their tee shots were historical however; as the boys ended the game, with a pair of hole in ones.

Amongst the roar, and the cheers of the crowd, Billy turned to his dad, and said.

"Dad, I can't believe how Lyon and Branden have played this entire game tied with each other. It's almost like; they're a mirror image of each other."

"They are son; but that's because they've grown up together."

Before Billy could say another word, Mr. Fairway's voice came over the loud speakers.

"Ladies and gentlemen, I'd like to invite each and every one of you to attend the trophy presentations; which will begin in fifteen minutes."

After arriving at the stage, Jason walked up to Lyon and Branden, and said.

"Boys, I've been in broadcasting for fifteen years, and that was the best game I've ever seen. Congratulations."

"Sir, since Lyon and Branden ended the game with a tie; who will they declare the champion?" Alex asked.

Temporarily forgetting about the special favor, which he had done for Mr. Fairway, Jason said.

"I asked Mr. Fairway that same question Alex, but he wouldn't tell me. I guess we'll just have to wait, and find out for ourselves"

While Jason and the boys were talking, Mr. Fairway stepped up to the microphone, and said.

"Jason, could you come to the stage please, and help me with the trophy presentations?"

After Jason was up on stage, Mr. Fairway continued.

"Ladies and gentlemen, I know I've said this before, but I'm going to say it again."

"I've watched Lyon and Branden play in many of their games this year, but they've never ceased to amaze me. Their dual win here today, is just another example of that."

"Most of you are probably wondering, which one of these boys will be today's champion. The answer to that question is really quite simple, and is found in the official rule book."

"The rules clearly state; that if two players are tied after regulation play, then they must play up to, but not to exceed, three elimination holes. If those players are still tied after the third elimination hole; then they are mandated by these official rules to share the championship title."

"Therefore ladies and gentlemen, I'm proud to announce that this year's 'National Championship' title goes to both Lyon, and Branden."

"Now, for the moment we've all been waiting for; the presentation of the 'National Championship' trophy."

"Lyon would you and Branden come up on the stage, please?"

With Mr. Fairway's request, came the loudest, and most exuberant cheering, the boys had ever heard. Then, after the crowd had finally calmed down, Mr. Fairway picked up the second trophy, and asked.

"Jason, now that we're holding both of the trophies; do you think we can present them at the same time?"

"Yes sir; I'm positive of it."

Satisfied with Jason's answer, Mr. Fairway turned toward Lyon and Branden, and said.

"Boys, both of you have had an extraordinary season this year; and for that, you are to be commended. Therefore, on behalf of the 'National Junior Golfing Association', and all of its members, it gives me great honor to present you with these 'National Championship' trophies. Congratulations." Mr. Fairway said, as both boys received their trophies.

Upon the presentation of the trophies, came yet another overwhelming applause from the crowd. While waiting for the applause to subside, Andy said.

"Dad, those trophies are gigantic. They look like they're as tall as I am."

"They're not quite that tall son, but almost. Remember, you're almost four and a half feet tall now." Justin said, with a smile.

"Ladies and gentlemen, it's now time for the presentation of this year's 'Grand Slam' award.

"In order to win this prestigious award, the player must meet certain criteria; which are mandated, by the official rules of junior golf."

"Amongst those criteria are; the winning of their divisional championship, the semi national championship of their region, and the 'National Championship'. Out of all of our contestants here today; only two, have met those requirements."

"The official rules allow for two players, to win this award in the same year; but they must tie for the National Championship. That ladies and gentlemen, is what happened here today.'

"Therefore, it gives me great honor, to present these highly prestigious awards, to Lyon and Branden. Congratulations boys." Mr. Fairway said, as he shook their hands.

"Thank you for the trophies sir; but how are we going to carry both of them at the same time?" Branden asked.

"You won't have to worry about that Branden, because your parents will help you."

"Ladies and gentlemen, I'd like for Lyon and Branden's parents, to come to the stage at this time. Steven, I need you and Alex up here too, please."

"Why does he need us, Steven? Have we done something wrong?" Alex asked nervously.

"We'll find out in a couple of minutes Alex; but I'm sure it's nothing to worry about." Steven said, with a sly grin.

When Steven and Alex were on stage, Mr. Fairway continued.

"Ladies and gentlemen, as we all know a player's caddy is vitally important during a game, but is seldom rewarded. That is, until today."

"Steven, would you and Alex step forward, please?"

After the boys had stepped forward, Mr. Fairway continued.

"Boys, your performance here today, as Lyon and Branden's caddies, was outstanding. Therefore, in recognition of a job well done, I hereby award each of you, with these prestigious caddy awards. Congratulations." Mr. Fairway said, with a smile.

"Thank you for the trophies, sir." Steven and Alex said, as they shook Mr. Fairway's hand.

"Now ladies and gentlemen, before I bring this year's tournament to a close; General Smith has something, he would like to say."

"Thank you Mr. Fairway, but I'll only take a moment of your time."
"Ladies and gentlemen, this message is for everyone from 'We Care'; to inform them that we'll be leaving for the airport in approximately thirty minutes. Please be on the buses before then though, so roll call can be taken."
"Thank you Mr. Fairway, but that's all I needed to say."

"I don't know about you ladies and gentlemen, but I believe this has been the most exciting tournament, I've ever witnessed. Unfortunately however, I must now bring it to a close."
"So with that said; I now declare this tournament over, and the ceremonies completed. Thank you for coming, and please drive safely going home."

With Mr. Fairway's closure, came a round of applause from the audience, while at the same time, Lyon and Branden said their goodbyes to Mr. Fairway, and their friend Jason.
Within twenty minutes however, everyone from 'We Care' had boarded the buses, and roll call had been taken.

"Everyone is present and accounted for now, sir. We can leave whenever you're ready." Mr. Avery said.

"Okay Mr. Avery, but before I give the command to pull out; did you make sure the boys had their trophies with them?"

"Yes sir; I did that before I came to you."

"Okay; I'll go ahead and give the command then." The general said, as he reached for his radio.

Several hours later, as their airplane was circling to land, Branden said.

"Look down there, Lyon. There's that big round building, we've heard so much about."

"You're right Branden, it is big. In fact, it looks like a big flying saucer." Lyon said, with a grin.

"I did some research on it, after my tournament up here Lyon; and what I found out about it, was amazing."

"What did you find out about it?"

"I found out that it's eleven stories high, has six hundred and fourteen miles of steel wire in it, is three hundred and sixty degrees in shape, has a seating capacity of seventeen thousand, its diameter is four hundred feet, and has four thousand four hundred tons of concrete in its structure." Branden said.

"That's fantastic Branden, but what is it used for?"

"They've used it for a lot of different things since it was built; but they use it primarily, for their college basketball games."

"Do they ever host concerts there, Branden?"

"Yes they do, Lyon. In fact, there have been many concerts held there over the years."

Ladies and gentlemen, this is your captain speaking. We'll be landing shortly; so please return your seats to their up right positions, and make sure your seat belts are securely fastened."

When the aircraft was safely on the ground and parked, General Smith walked up to George, and said.

"George, there are several hundred people inside the terminal, who are waiting for Lyon and Branden's arrival. That won't be a problem though, because there's also an honor guard standing by, to escort you and your family members to your limousine."

"Then, once you're in the limousine, you will be escorted to the largest public assembly building in town."

"Sir, does that assembly building look like a concrete flying saucer?" Branden asked.

With a slight chuckle, General Smith said.

"It's been known to be called that Branden, but how did you know about it?"

"Because of the research I've done on it, sir. The only problem is I never did see a picture of the building's interior."

"Well if you'd like to see its interior, then we better get started. Besides that, we're keeping your fans waiting."

On their way off the airplane, George asked.

"How far is it to the assembly building, sir?"

"It's about three miles from here George, but the parade route will start in two."

"We weren't expecting to be in a parade, sir. Whose idea was that?" Lyon asked.

"I can't remember his name Lyon; but I know he has a school of music, in Irvine, California." The general said, with a grin.

"That would have to be Mr. Ethan, sir. How could that be possible though; because I saw him at the tournament."

"You're right Branden, Mr. Ethan was at the tournament; but his staff was here making arrangements for your arrival." The general said, as the last of the group entered the limousine.

Their journey toward the assembly building, wasn't anything special though; that is, until they approached the beginning of the parade route.
There in front of them, and taking the lead were the Air Force's marching band, and prestigious honor guard. Separating the marching band from the honor guard however, was the high school's baton twirling team.
As their motorcade proceeded down Florida Avenue toward its destination, the boys were amazed at the various sights along the way. Included in those sights; were the hundreds of fans along the street, the baton twirlers who were using golf clubs instead of batons, and the falling confetti.

"Dad, this reception is amazing. I think it's fantastic how the girls are twirling golf clubs, instead of batons; but I'm confused about something else. Why are people throwing confetti out of their windows at us?" Branden asked.

"This isn't just an ordinary parade Branden; it's what is referred to, as a ticker-tape parade." Lyon's father said.

"I've heard that name before sir, but what makes it so unique?" Branden asked.

"People have ticker-tape parades to welcome their returning hero's son; and that's why you and Lyon are receiving it." Anya said with a smile.

Once they had arrived at the assembly building, Lyon and Branden were astonished at the reception they received when they walked in the door. For there, in the main assembly room of the building, were a record number of fans, totaling seventeen thousand. Then, while receiving a standing ovation from everyone in the room, Lyon and Branden were escorted to the 'Head Table of Honor'

Over the next three hours, the boys were treated as if they were of a royal family. In fact, they had been treated so well, even a wealthy king, would have been envious of them.

Then, at the end of the celebrations, Mr. Ethan stepped up to the microphone and said.

"Ladies and gentlemen, on behalf of Lyon and Branden and their families, I would like to thank all of you for coming out on so short of notice, to welcome them home."

"Since the boys have had a long day, and are extremely tired, I'm going to bring the celebrations to a close at this time. Thank you for coming, and good night."

"Mom, Mr. Ethan was right about us being tired; but can we talk to him for a minute, before we leave?" Branden asked.

"Sure son, we can talk to him. That will also give us the opportunity, to invite him for breakfast tomorrow morning." Anya said.

"Sir, Lyon and I would like to thank you, for having this celebration for us. It's been fantastic, but we didn't realize we had this many fans." Branden said.

"You're welcome boys, but this was only a small percentage of your fans. There was twice that many, standing along the parade route."

After several minutes of talking to Mr. Ethan, Lyon's father said.

"Son, we need to be leaving now, so you and Branden can get some sleep. Besides that, I still need to book our flight reservations, for our trip home tomorrow."

"Your father is right, Lyon. Both of you have had an exhausting day, so you need your sleep. I'll see you in the morning."

"Okay sir; we'll see you in the morning." Lyon said.

Upon the completion of their conversation, Lyon and Branden were both escorted to the limousine, and then on to 'We Care'. When they arrived, everyone went straight to bed, with the exception of Lyon's parents. They however, had stayed up just long enough to make their flight reservations; before they too, went to bed.

The following morning during breakfast, Mr. Avery sensed an air of sadness among the boys.

"Steven, what's wrong with everyone this morning?"

"They're all sad sir; because they know what's going to happen after breakfast."

"If that's the case Steven, then we better open the floor for discussion."

After Steven had opened the floor, everyone in the room took their turn, and congratulated Lyon and Branden on their victories. Being the last boy to stand up, Jeff said.

"Branden, I'd like to congratulate you and Lyon on your victories, but I have a question for you."
"We all know your favorite club this season has been your niblick. What exactly, is a niblick?"

"That's really quite simple, Jeff. The dictionary defines it as: an obsolete golf club, which is similar to a modern nine-iron."

With Branden's description, came the closure of the open floor discussions. It was at that time, I said.

"Branden, now that you and Lyon have both won the 'National Championship, and the grand slam award; what are your plans now?"

"Well sir, Lyon will be starting his first European tour in a couple of months, with his piano concerts; and I think I'll go with him." Branden said, with a big smile.

"Well Tom, I really hate to have to say this, but it's about time we should be leaving for the airport."

"Before we leave though, I'd like to thank everyone here at 'We Care' for their hospitality. We've really enjoyed our visit." Lyon's father said.

"It's been an honor having you and your family visit us, sir. On behalf of everyone here at 'We Care', I sincerely hope you'll come back again someday and visit us." I said.

"We will Tom, and that's a promise. Besides, we'll have to bring Branden back home." Lyon's mother said, with a smile.

"Sir could you and your family help us to do something, before you leave?" I asked.

"We'd be delighted to Tom. What is it that you need help with?"

After discussing my request with him, Lyon's father said.

"We would be honored, to do that for you Tom; but we'll let Lyon be our spokesperson."

"Son, would you like to do that for us?"

"I'd be delighted to, but I'd like for everyone here to be waving to the readers, when I do."

With everyone now standing, and waving goodbye to the readers, Lyon continued.

"Ladies and gentlemen, and readers alike; it gives me great honor to have been chosen, to make this announcement."

"Therefore, on behalf of my entire family, Mr. Ethan, and all of our friends here at 'We Care'; I would like to thank you for reading our story. Goodbye, and happy golfing."